Island Nights

Books by P.J. Mellor

Pleasure Beach

Give Me More

Make Me Scream

Drive Me Wild

Between the Sheets

Island Nights

The Cowboy
(with Vonna Harper, Nelissa Donovan, and Nikki Alton)

The Firefighter
(with Susan Lyons and Alyssa Brooks)

Naughty, Naughty
(with Melissa MacNeal and Valerie Martinez)

Only With a Cowboy
(with Melissa MacNeal and Vonna Harper)

Under the Covers
(with Crystal Jordan and Lorie O'Clare)

Published by Kensington Publishing Corporation

Island Nights

P.J. Mellor

APHRODISIA

KENSINGTON BOOKS
http://www.kensingtonbooks.com

APHRODISIA BOOKS are published by

Kensington Publishing Corp.
119 West 40th Street
New York, NY 10018

All Kensington Titles, Imprints, and Distributed Lines are available at special quantity discounts for bulk purchases for sales promotions, premiums, fund-raising, and educational or institutional use.

Special book excerpts or customized printings can also be created to fit specific needs. For details, write or phone the office of Kensington special sales manager: Kensington Publishing Corp., 119 West 40th Street, New York, NY 10018, attn: Special Sales Department, Phone: 1-800-221-2647.

Aphrodisia and the A logo Reg. U.S. Pat & TM Off.

ISBN-13: 978-0-7582-3819-1
ISBN-10: 0-7582-3819-3

First Kensington Trade paperback Printing: March 2011

10 9 8 7 6 5 4 3 2 1

Printed in the United States of America

To Dr. Phyllis Wolfe, former Homecoming Queen at Michigan State, college professor, my cousin, my friend, my biggest fan. May you rest in peace, Phyl. I miss you.

Acknowledgments

Thanks always to my editor, John Scognamiglio, words cannot express my appreciation for your patience.

Thanks, too, to my fabulous agent, the imcomparable Jennifer Schober, at Spencerhill Associates, Ltd. I can't say enough great things about you—all true!

I'd also like to thank Stephanie Finnegan for her attention to the tiniest of details as my copy editor. Great job!

1

"Ow-wee!" Reese Parker hissed at the paper cut and stuck her index finger in her mouth while she continued digging through the pile of papers in her desk drawer. The stupid itinerary and instructions the Dragon Lady had e-mailed her just before quitting time had to be there, somewhere.

A glance at her watch had her cussing under her breath. Paige and Bailey probably thought she'd forgotten about coming back to the bar. Dang the Dragon Lady for ruining what could very well be the last margarita night with her friends, for who knew how long.

Reese doubled her efforts, then paused and listened. Deciding she was hearing things, she resumed her search, only to stop and listen again.

She wasn't alone.

Her shaking hand finally closed around the stupid paperwork. Was that a moan? It sure sounded like a moan.

"Easy," she cautioned, under her breath, "it's probably just your imagination." Slow, silent footsteps brought her to her partially closed door.

A peek into the darkened hallway revealed nothing. Easing the door open, she stepped out.

Sure enough, a light glowed around the half-opened door of her boss's office. It could only mean one thing. Dorinda Laughlin, the Dragon Lady herself, was burning the midnight oil. Of course, she was. The Dragon Lady had no life and expected none of her employees to have one either.

A deep breath calmed Reese somewhat as she forced her feet to take her down the carpeted hall to the Dragon Lady's lair. Since Reese had already sacrificed part of her last night in town to come back to the office, she dang well wanted credit for it.

Hand poised to knock, she stopped when she heard another low moan. Breath held, she eased forward and peeked through the crack.

And promptly fell back against the wall, her hand clamped over her mouth. She wasn't sure if she would scream or giggle, but it was a safe bet neither would be appreciated by her boss. When she was reasonably certain she could contain herself, she snuck another peek.

Bathed in what appeared to be either candlelight or the soft glow of a table lamp on the other side of the office, Dorinda's preteen-like breasts jiggled with her movement. Her tiny nipples were puckered up like raisins.

Reese's first thought was to wonder if Dorinda had done something spontaneous, like shove everything off her desk in a pique of sexual frenzy. Nah, not the Dragon Lady. Everything was probably neatly stacked on the credenza on the far end of her office. She wondered if her boss had stacked while naked. That thought caused her to swallow a nervous giggle.

Despite feeling she may have to gouge out her eyes, she couldn't resist taking another look.

A man was stretched out on the desk, the Dragon Lady astride him. He had an interesting bald patch on the crown of his head. Reese wondered if anyone noticed when he was upright. While she contemplated this, he raised both hands to skim Dorinda's bony ribs. Round and round his hands went, while his partner moaned and rode him harder, before he palmed her minuscule breasts. Probably took him that long to locate the puny things.

That thought had Reese spinning around and clamping her hand over her mouth again.

When she could control herself, she turned to make her way out of the office. What the heck. There was something exciting about watching someone have sex, even her emaciated boss. *Just a few more minutes,* Reese promised her conscience.

Suddenly the man sat up, grabbing Dorinda's legs, arranging her so she lay back along his legs, a stiletto-clad foot on either side of his ears.

Reese watched, shifting to relieve the uncomfortable ache between her legs. When the man reached forward and twisted Dorinda's little nipples, Reese winced and rubbed her own.

Unable to tear her gaze from the raunchy scene, her breathing became shallow, her heart rate hitched up a notch. Or two.

"Oh, yeah, baby!" Dorinda's husky voice drew Reese's attention. "Harder, you whore! Drill me!"

The man slid her forward, then pounded her back against his groin. They groaned, and for a horrifying second, Reese worried she'd done it too.

"You naughty little cunt," the man said in a guttural voice, "you have to be punished."

He slid off the desk, dragging Dorinda with him.

Reese jumped, flattening her back along the wall next to the door.

When neither lover charged the door, she peeked around again.

The man bent her normally stiffly formal boss over the arm of her desk chair, revealing way more of her skinny anatomy than Reese ever wanted to see. He spread Dorinda's legs wide, than slapped her swollen labia with the palm of his hand. The wet, slightly hollow sound echoed in the quiet office.

On his knees, he pinched her together and alternately bit and licked her until she was writhing on the smooth leather.

Turn a little more toward the window, Reese silently urged. She wanted and, for some reason, needed a better view.

As though he'd heard her mental plea, he turned Dorinda toward the moonlight spilling in from the big plate glass window.

One hairy hand grasped his neon green condom–covered member. He thumped her, sort of like he was spanking her with his wanger. Dorinda growled deep in her throat.

Reese swallowed a shriek of laughter that threatened. Enough. She really needed to get back to the bar.

But when he flexed, driving his green penis deeply into the now-screaming Dorinda, Reese's breath caught. Watching the couple go at it should not have been titillating. Yet . . .

How pathetic could she get? She was jealous of her boss. Jealous of raunchy, secret sex.

Lord help her.

She wanted it too.

2

A sheen of perspiration had developed on her forehead by the time Reese hopped out of the elevator and headed for the door of her office building. A glance at her watch told her if she hurried, she could make the end of happy hour.

The big black limo she'd noticed on her way in was still idling at the curb in front of the door.

Jerk, she thought, hurrying toward the corner. Some people thought because they had money they didn't have to obey the law or even show common courtesy.

Good thing the Bullfrog Pub was less than a block from her office, or else she wouldn't have made it. Especially in her current state of sexual frustration.

The comforting smell of fajitas and beer greeted her as she stepped through the door. Her friends Paige and Bailey were still seated in the round booth in the far corner, their usual spot on Thursday nights.

"About damn time," Paige groused as Reese slid into the booth. "We were taking bets as to whether or not you'd remember to come back."

"Cute." Reese shrugged out of her blazer and flopped back on the padded seat. "Y'all are not going to believe what I saw! Wait! First we need to order another pitcher."

"Just did," Bailey said, with a smile, over the salted rim of her glass.

"Don't just sit there and eat!" Paige glared when Reese grabbed a fried crawfish from the appetizer platter and popped it in her mouth. "So . . . what did you see that we won't believe? Swallow your food and tell us!"

Reese glanced over her shoulder, then leaned over the table. Her friends leaned with her.

"I just saw a horrible, shocking sight. . . ." Reese nodded at the waiter when he set a fresh salted margarita glass in front of her.

"Well?" Bailey whispered when he'd walked away. "Are you going to tell us or do we have to guess?"

Reese snickered and took a fortifying sip of her drink. "You'd never guess. Trust me."

"Shit, Reese!" Paige gripped Reese's forearm. "Tell us already."

"Ow. No need for brutality." Smiling, she met the gaze of each of her two best friends. After a pause for effect, she said in a low voice, "I just saw the Dragon Lady getting her brains screwed out."

"Eww!" Bailey set her drink on the table and did a theatrical shudder. "I think I'd have to gouge my eyes out."

Paige snickered. "No shit? Is she as much of a skinny ass naked as she looks fully clothed?"

Reese blinked. "Yeah. But after a few minutes, I didn't notice, I guess."

"After a few minutes?" Bailey looked horrified.

"Damn, Reese, how long did you watch?" Paige laughed

and poured another drink. "And," she added, glaring at Reese, "more importantly, I have to wonder why? Were you turned on?"

Reese swallowed and reached for a fried cheese stick. "I don't know. Maybe a little." She bit into the stick and chewed thoughtfully. "Makes me wonder if I have a latent voyeuristic tendency."

"Honey," Paige said, dipping a crawfish into the hot avocado sauce, "we all have a voyeuristic tendency. That's why they invented porn."

Bailey and Reese groaned.

"I'm just saying." Paige tossed her long, dark hair over her shoulder as she popped the crawfish in her mouth and chewed with gusto. Which was pretty much the way Paige did anything. Reese envied that quality.

After she swallowed, Paige asked, "So, did the Dragon Lady see you?"

"Thankfully, no." Reese snickered. "She was, um, otherwise occupied." At that, she and Bailey broke into hysterical laughter.

Paige did an eye roll. "A better question would be, did you get the stuff you needed? Remember? That was the reason you had to run back to the office. Is any of this ringing a bell?"

In answer, Reese reached down into her satchel and produced the papers. "Right here. At least now I won't have to worry about leaving for the airport tomorrow morning in time to swing by and pick them up."

"Trust me"—Paige licked the rim of her empty glass—"you'll just find something else to obsess over. It's what you do." She shrugged and leaned on the table. "And speaking of what you do, why on earth did you agree to do this? You're not up to it, Reese. You get plane sick, train sick, and carsick. Hell, you practically puke in the elevator."

"I know." Reese shrugged and reached for the last crawfish. "But it wasn't really an option. I want a promotion. When Dorinda told me about her dream to open a bed-and-breakfast, I felt like we'd, well, bonded. Sort of." She chewed and swallowed. "And now, every time I look at her, I know I'll have flashbacks of her sexual romp. I need to get away for a while." She shuddered. "Besides, business has been slow. It's not like I have anything major going on. Maybe, if I do this for her, it will give me a leg up on my competition."

"Sweetie." Paige patted Reese's hand. "Listen to me very carefully. There is no competition. No one wants your job."

"I'm afraid she's right," Bailey said in a meek voice.

"I'm her executive assistant! I handle a lot of important clients—"

"And then the Dragon Lady reels them in and takes all the credit, not to mention the commission. Am I right? You know I am, I can see it in your eyes."

Reese looked at Bailey, who nodded.

"Face it," Paige continued, "you're a glorified gofer. A step-up from a secretary. Maybe."

Reese's shoulders slumped. "You're right." She sighed. "But I've already committed to going. So I will. One last time. Bailey, if you'll look around for a better job, I'll start sending out my résumé when I get home."

"She'll do better than that," Paige assured her. "I'll update your résumé while you're gone. When I'm finished with it, people will be falling all over each other to hire you, at twice your current salary. Maybe more. As soon as I'm done, Bailey can start submitting it. Then, when you get back, you just have to go on interviews and make your selection."

"Thanks. I think."

"Where are you going again?" Bailey scratched the bridge of her nose.

"Sand Dollar. According to the map, it's on the Gulf Coast."

"I thought you said it was an island." Paige signaled for another pitcher.

"No, none for me," Reese told her, "I'll never make it out of bed on time for my flight if I have any more. And you're right. The place I'm bidding on is an island, just off the coast."

"Sand Dollar has an airport?" Bailey threw down a wad of money.

"According to my itinerary, it's a municipal airport."

"Which is small-town speak for a hole-in-the-wall," Paige said, digging in her briefcase, then tossing her platinum card on top of Bailey's cash. "Put your wallet away, Reese. Tonight's on us."

Bailey nodded. "A going-away present."

"Y'all do realize I'm only going to be gone five days, a week tops? Maybe two weeks if I have to stay for the auction."

"Yes, we know." Bailey sighed as they made their way to the door. "But that means we'll miss margarita night next week. Maybe even the following week."

"I'm sure you'll survive." After hugging her friends outside the bar, Reese waited for traffic to clear before crossing the street to her loft.

What little buzz she had going on from the margaritas dissipated by the time she ran up the stairs to the fifth floor. She told herself the stairs helped keep her legs toned and her lungs strong.

Besides, a lot of people disliked elevators.

The thought of the moving sidewalk at the airport and, worse, her upcoming flight made her palms sweat. A glance confirmed her packed bag was ready and waiting by the door. Nothing to do but try to get some sleep.

She didn't even want to contemplate the shuttle flight to Sand Dollar. For that matter, how the heck was she going to get out to the island? She'd promised to check out the property before the auction. What had she gotten herself into?

"You can do this," she told her reflection as she flossed her teeth while preparing for bed. "You have to do this." Paige's words about her less than prestigious job echoed in her head. One more trip and her association with the Dragon Lady would be history.

3

By ten the next morning, Reese knew if she survived the trip, she would never travel again. Ever.

Her distinctly green face stared back at her from the cracked mirror in the ladies' room at the Sand Dollar Municipal Airport as she wiped the wet paper towel across her forehead.

How could she possibly throw up again? Everything had already made a reappearance.

The flight from Houston had been fairly uneventful. It gave her false confidence. The flight from hell in the little plane, which she could have sworn was held together with baling wire, shot said confidence all to heck. She wouldn't have been surprised to see her shoes come up into the paper bag they gave her. That they hadn't done cartwheels down the runway on landing was nothing short of a miracle.

"It's all behind you," she muttered, picking up her bag and heading for the exit. "Just find the limo and get on down to business."

*   *   *

Benjamin Adams fanned the piece of cardboard and watched the passengers ignore his sign as they hurried past.

"Where the hell could she be?" He visually searched both gates again. How in the hell could he have missed her? The airport wasn't that big.

If he wasn't desperate for money, he'd leave.

But he was, so he waved the sign again as he turned, looking for anyone who looked like they might be expecting to be picked up.

That's when he saw her.

Built like a Barbie doll, she wobbled on too-high heels, her gaze darting around. Short, baby-fine–looking blond hair fringed her face in a messy sort of way.

He knew the moment she spotted him. Her small body drew more upright, her little face taking on a look of disdainful horror.

Oh, yeah, he still had a definite effect on women. True, it wasn't the effect he would have preferred, but at least they still noticed him. Just not necessarily in a good way.

"I'm Reese Parker," she said in a hesitant voice as she walked toward him.

Of course, she was. Just his luck.

"Is that all your luggage?"

"Yes. I pack light. Besides," she added in a breathless voice as she trotted along next to him, "I don't plan to stay long."

Good. He had a bad feeling about Miss Reese Parker. From her attire, she obviously wasn't in Sand Dollar for a vacation. That left only one other logical reason: she'd come for the auction of his grandmother's island.

Shit-fire-spit, as his grandmother used to say. Could his day get any worse?

The exit door *whooshed* closed behind them.

"Where is the limo?" his annoying passenger asked, shielding her eyes against the sunshine.

"Don't you have any sunglasses?" Her face was all scrunched up.

"Huh?" Beneath her palm, pale eyes looked dumbfounded.

"Sunglasses. You're on the Gulf Coast. Sunglasses are basic necessities here. Did you bring any?" Was he going to have to lead her around? Wait. Maybe that might not be a bad thing.

"Of course, I brought sunglasses." Her mouth pulled down in a very annoying way. "We have sun in Houston too, you know."

"Good. Put 'em on. You're going to get all wrinkled from squinting. Not to mention getting a headache from the glare."

"I can't. I lost them." When she had her head over the trash can in the restroom, but she wasn't about to tell that to the scruffy, overaged surfer/limo driver.

"We can stop somewhere for you to pick up another pair." Hell, why was he persisting? What did he care? But he just couldn't seem to let go of the sunglasses topic. It was just such a dumb-ass city woman thing to do, losing sunglasses.

Her jaw tight, she said, "Fine. Thanks. Now, where is the limousine?"

"You're standing in front of it."

"No, this is a truck." And not a very nice one, at that. "I was distinctly told there would be a limo waiting for me at the airport."

The man towered over her. If he thought he could intimidate her, he was sadly mistaken. She hadn't worked for the Dragon Lady for the last two years for nothing.

Instead of stepping back or cowering the way she was sure he'd hoped, she straightened to her full five-foot-one-and-a-half-inch height. Her gaze rose from his broad, faded T-shirt–covered chest, over a stubborn jaw, with its stubble glistening in the sunshine, past the hard line of his lips, to blue eyes framed with a thick row of golden lashes. Fine lines radiated from the corners of his eyes, making her wonder if he practiced what he preached when it came to wearing sunglasses.

He pointed to a hand-printed cardboard sign taped to the back window of the pickup with what looked like duct tape. It read: B.A. LIMO AND CAB CO.

She blinked at the sign, then looked back up at him. "What does the B.A. stand for?"

He took her suitcase and tossed it into the bed of the truck, then opened the passenger door.

"Bad Ass." Turning on his heel, he rounded the hood and slid behind the wheel. "Are you coming or not?"

4

_____

Reese clutched her shoulder bag to her chest and breathed through her nose. The knot holding together her seat belt dug into her hip bone.

Across the cracked seat, her *chauffeur* chuckled.

"Don't look so worried, Reese Parker. I'm not going to charge you for the seat belt."

"I did *not* break your seat belt! It fell off when I went to buckle it."

His grin flashed white in his tanned face. "All I know, it was fine before you got in."

Her throat worked convulsively.

"Cat got your tongue? Or don't you have any biting sarcasm to toss at me? Aw, don't be like that. Talk to me."

"Could you pull over? Please?" She clawed at the knotted seat belt. "Pull over! Now!"

Ben winced at the sound of his passenger losing her lunch on the gravel shoulder next to the truck. He tried not to gag. Hell, how much could a skinny chick like that have in her stomach?

The retching stopped. Reese crawled back into the seat of the truck and wiped her mouth with the back of her hand.

He quickly lowered his window to dissipate the vomit smell. "There're some breath mints in the glove box, if you want some." As an afterthought, he added, "And there's bottled water in the cooler behind the seat."

After a curt nod, she dug around in the console, paused, then dug a little faster.

That was when he remembered the old box of condoms. He opened his mouth to explain, to tell her they weren't his, then thought better of it. Let her think he was a player. It might help. The bigger the distance they maintained, the easier it would be to do whatever he had to do to prevent her from bidding on the island. "I said the glove box, not the console."

Heat seared Reese's cheeks. She obviously saw the box of condoms in the console. "Sorry." The old door to the glove box flopped down and smacked her on the knees. "Crap!" She shot a self-conscious look at him. "Sorry. I was just surprised. I didn't mean to blurt that out."

Great. Little Miss Puke Queen thought *crap* was a bad word. He swallowed a chuckle. They might just have some fun this weekend, after all.

Beside him, her crunching told him she'd found the stale mints. He glanced over to see her relaxed against the seat, mopping the sweat from her forehead with a wad of tissues. "Feel better?"

One thin shoulder shrugged. "I guess. I'll be fine, once we stop." She met his gaze. "How much longer until we get to the hotel?"

"A while." Reaching behind the seat, he hoisted the cooler to set between them. "Why don't you drink some water? It might help. Get me one too, will you?"

After a moment of hesitation, she opened the lid and dug around in the ice. "All I see are bottles of beer."

"I'll take one of those, then."

"You can't do that! It's illegal to drink while you're driving."

Promptly pulling over again, he braked as a plume of dust enveloped the truck. "Okay. You drive, then."

She blinked. "You're kidding, right? What do the words *open container* mean to you?"

"If you'd hand me the damn beer, it would soon be an *empty* container." He jerked his hand away just as she slammed the cooler lid. "Watch it, lady! I need that hand."

Instead of replying, she dug around in the big purse she wore like a shield and pulled out a pocket-size spiral notebook and a pen and began furiously scribbling.

"Now what are you doing?"

"Making a note of things to report when I get to the hotel."

"Does this mean I'm going to have to get my own beer?" He didn't want one, but he found he really enjoyed teasing her.

In answer, she slammed her bony hand on top of the cooler and glared at him. "No one is having any beer until we reach our destination and are not in a moving vehicle."

"Oh, so you changed your mind and are going to join me?" Damn, it was fun to watch her get all flustered.

Her blue eyes shot daggers at him. "I don't drink beer. And, even if I did, I wouldn't drink with you."

"Watch it, you're apt to hurt my tender feelings."

Ice rattled against the side of the cooler. A cold, wet bottle of water hit him square in the chest.

"Here. Now drive."

"Yes, ma'am." After taking a long swallow, he dropped the truck into gear and pulled back out onto the road.

"So," he said after a few minutes of silence, "did you come to Sand Dollar for a vacation?"

Her cool gaze shot his way before she returned to watching the asphalt. "Hardly."

"Well, no offense, but you seem like you could use one. Sand Dollar may not be a resort-type place, but it has its amenities."

"Like what?" Never taking her eyes off the road, she tilted the bottle to her lips.

He knew he should watch the road, but he couldn't stop looking at her mouth and the way her elegant neck rippled with each swallow.

It shouldn't have gotten to him. And it sure as hell shouldn't have turned him on.

"W-well, the beach is nice. The marina is pretty well-equipped for just about any sport fishing you'd care to do."

"I don't fish."

Of course, she didn't. The woman would probably be bored to tears if he took her out on his boat. Of course, there was always the cabin belowdecks. Maybe he could help her see the allure of the open water.

"Why are you smiling like that? What's so funny about me not fishing?"

"Nothing. Not a damn thing. In fact, I wasn't even thinking about you," he lied. "I like my boat. I was thinking about going out on it after I drop you off."

"Oh."

"Yeah, oh. Not everything is about you."

"I, well, I—"

"Duck!" Grasping the back of her head, he slammed her forehead into the cooler as he pressed her to bend in half on the seat. "State trooper up ahead," he explained. "He knows the passenger seat belt doesn't work. I don't want another ticket."

"Ah-hah!" She struggled against his hand.

"Stay down! I'll let you up after he's down the road a piece."

Twisted in order to glare at him, she ground out, "I knew that seat belt was broken before I touched it."

"Yeah." He released her. "You're a regular genius."

"What's that supposed to mean?" She sat up and rubbed her forehead.

"Nothing. There's the hotel, up ahead on the right."

Reese didn't know what she'd expected, but the large structure squatting on the far end of the sandy parking lot wasn't it. The Sand Dollar Inn looked, well, almost homey, with its pale blue clapboard siding and the brilliant white of its gingerbread trim. White colums supported a wraparound porch, complete with porch swings and rocking chairs. Between each column hung a fat pot of riotous blooming plants.

As she stepped from the truck, her stiletto heels sank into the sand. In the distance, waves made a distinctive sound as they slapped the shore. Reese took a bracing breath of sea air and felt her tenseness ease.

Her suitcase plopped on her foot. Aging surfer dude grinned down at her.

"C'mon," he said, walking toward the hotel without waiting to see if she followed. "I'll introduce you to Rick and Rita. They run the hotel."

Suitcase wheels were not meant to roll on sand. Half rolling, half dragging her burden, Reese finally made it to the bottom step of the hotel.

"Having fun?" Her driver smirked down at her from his perch on the porch rail.

"Screw you," she muttered as her suitcase bumped its way up the wooden stairs.

"Tsk-tsk, such language." He stood when she approached. "Ow! Why'd you hit me?" He rubbed his shoulder.

"If you have to ask, you're dumber than I thought. Get out of my way."

"Here, let me help you with that." He reached for her suitcase, but she only tightened her grip. "What is your problem?"

"You! You're my problem. You're lazy and rude and condescending and—"

"I resent being called lazy." He jerked on the handle again. "I prefer it as conserving my energy."

"Conserve away! I'm perfectly capable of carrying my own luggage."

"Couldn't prove it by the way you hobbled and stumbled across the parking lot."

"Well, if you'd just—"

"Hey, hey, what's going on out here? We can't hardly hear our TV program for all your hollering." A thin middle-aged man with a receding hairline stood in the doorway, fists propped on lean hips. He looked from her driver to Reese. "You Ms. Parker? We were fixin' to get worried about you. You missed your check-in time."

Chastised, Reese hurried forward, hand outstretched.

"I'm sorry. Yes, I'm Reese Parker."

They shook hands. "Rick Weaver. C'mon in and relax a spell. Ben, you may as well drag your sorry carcass in too."

"Ben?" She frowned.

"Ben Adams, you know, the feller who drove you from the airport?" Rick indicated the overaged surfer leaning against the door frame.

Reese bared her teeth in a smile. "Of course. I just think of him differently." Following Rick into the lobby, she looked at Ben with narrowed eyes and muttered, *"Bad Ass."*

"Since you're preregistered," Rick said, his back to them as he made his way to the front desk, "all I need is for you to sign in and then I'll show you to your room."

She'd scarcely finished signing the charge slip before Ben plucked the card key from Rick's hand and smiled.

"I know your knee's been acting up lately, Rick. I can show her to her room."

"Thanks, Ben, appreciate it." Oblivious to the charged looks, Rick turned to Reese. "Rita's fixin' cube steak for supper.

We eat at six sharp." He leaned closer and lowered his voice. "You don't want to be late. It makes Rita mean."

"Thank you, but I—"

"We'll make sure to be on time, Rick," Ben chimed in.

"Excuse me?" In what universe did Ben Adams speak for her?

Arm around her shoulders, Ben turned her toward the grand staircase. He looked back at Rick with a smile and a wink. "The woman just can't get enough of me."

5

Before Reese could open her mouth to protest, Ben swept her halfway up the wide, curved staircase. Despite stiffening her back, his momentum kept them moving upward.

"Will you stop? Let go of me!" At the top of the stairs, she wrenched away from his grasp. "You heard Rick, Rita gets mad if guests don't get to eat the food she prepared. That means you need to eat elsewhere."

"I'm practically a guest here," he countered, steering her down the floral-print runner on the polished hardwood floor. "I eat here almost every night."

"Are you homeless?" A hop still kept the card key he held aloft out of her grasp. "Give me that!"

"No, I'm not homeless," he said, swiping the key in the door of room seven. "I just eat here because, well, I like Rita's cooking. And Rick's company." He motioned for her to enter the room, then looked pointedly at the suitcase she'd dropped in the hall.

"A gentleman would carry my bag in for me, especially since I brought it up the stairs."

"Never said I was a gentleman."

With a huff, she picked up her suitcase and tossed it into the room, making sure it hit Ben on its way in.

"Ow! Hey, where do you think you're going?" He followed her back down the hall after she'd plucked the key from his fingers and walked away.

At the newel post, she turned and glared. "Not that it's any of your business, but I thought I'd go to the courthouse before dinner."

"You don't have a car. How did you plan to get there?"

"Walk?"

"You don't even know which way to go."

"The ocean is that way." She pointed. "Ergo, it doesn't take much deductive reasoning to figure the town is in the other direction."

"Yeah?" He trotted next to her as she descended the stairs. "Well, smart-ass, there are three other possible directions left. *Ergo,* I still say you have no idea where to head."

"Come on! The town isn't that big. I can probably see the courthouse from the porch."

She probably could, but he wasn't ready to stop arguing. Besides being the most fun he'd had in a while, if he stalled long enough, the courthouse would be closed for the weekend. The way he saw it, the more roadblocks he threw in her way, the better. He refused to feel guilty.

"Fine. You can drive me." She stepped down into the lobby and turned back to him.

"Why would I do that?"

"I dunno . . . money?" She smiled sweetly.

"My seat belt doesn't work properly. I'm not supposed to haul passengers until it's fixed." He bared his teeth to smile back at her.

"And yet, that didn't stop you earlier, did it?"

"Teatime!" A brightly dressed woman in her mid-thirties

came through the swinging door next to the desk, bearing a large tray with a platter of assorted cookies and a pitcher of iced tea.

Ben hurried to her. "Hey, Rita! Let me take that for you."

"Why, thank you, Ben, that's so sweet of you."

Reese made a gagging motion when Ben's gaze met hers.

"I'm going back to get glasses," Rita said, turning toward the door. "If you'll just set the tray out on the table on the front porch, we'll join you and your lady friend directly."

"I'm not his lady friend!" Reese's objection went unheard as her hostess was already gone.

"Give it a rest." Ben nudged her with his elbow. "Open the door for me, will you? Please? This tray is getting heavy."

"Will you drive me to the courthouse?"

He glanced at the grandfather clock by the front door. Four-fifteen. The courthouse was closed until Monday morning. "Of course."

Rita reappeared, tucking tendrils of dark hair back into her ponytail with one hand as she held the tray with four glasses of ice in the other. "Hold the door! Thanks." She set the tray next to the first one and straightened. "Hi." She extended her hand. "You must be Reese Parker. I'm Rita Weaver, Rick's wife. Welcome to Sand Dollar!"

She motioned for them to be seated and began pouring tea. "So, what brings you to town and how long do you plan to stay with us?"

Dorinda's words, begging Reese to keep her desire to change careers a secret, echoed through Reese's mind. How much should she tell without breaking her boss's trust? "Um, I'm actually here to look at some property."

Rita's dark eyes lit up. "Really? Which property? Maybe I can give you some advice."

Ben settled back in the rocker and took a sip of his tea. His lips curved into a smile as he regarded Reese across the rim of his glass. "Yeah, which property?"

Why did she get the impression he knew exactly which property she wanted to scope out?

"Well, I'm not sure I know the exact location. That's why I wanted to go check with the courthouse."

Rita bit into a cookie and chewed. "Oh, that's too bad. The courthouse closed about half an hour ago. Won't be open again until Monday morning." She took a sip of tea. "But I'm sure Ben or I can answer just about any questions you have, since we've lived here most of our lives." She leaned forward and said in a conspiratorial whisper, "Rick tells everyone he's a native, but he really didn't move here until he was in high school. Don't let on I told you, though, it would hurt his feelings."

Nodding, Reese swallowed her last bite of cookie. "Okay. Well, I'm here to bid at a land auction. There's an island with an old hotel on it."

Rita's shout of laughter echoed from the ceiling of the porch. "You're kidding! Ben's—"

"Starving!" Ben jumped up and shoved a cookie in his mouth, then pushed one into Rita's. "I'm sure you are too," he said, crumbs flying. "In fact, you should probably go get started on dinner. You know, before the crowd hits."

Rita swallowed and glared at Ben. "What is wrong with you, Ben Adams? Have you lost your mind? Don't you realize she's talking about—"

"Yessiree!" He shoved Rita through the open door. "Mm-mm! I can practically taste your cube steak already. You are making mashed potatoes and gravy with it, right?"

"Don't I always?" Hands on hips, she glared out at him, then sighed. "I guess if you're that hungry, I'll start serving." She leaned to look around Ben's shoulder. "Nice meeting you, Reese." To Ben, she hissed out a whisper, "I don't know what you're up to, Ben Adams, but I don't like it."

"Serenity Island!" Reese said, causing Ben to jump just as he settled into his rocker with some very steamy fantasies of what he'd like to do in the rocker with Reese. "That's the name of the property." She frowned. "I think. I know the hotel was named Serenity House. Maybe the island has another name?"

He pretended to ponder for a few minutes, then said, "No, I think I recall an old hotel out on the island in the bay. And, now that you mention it, I think you're right. I think it is called Serenity Island." Hell, he didn't think it, he knew it. Certainly glad Rita had gone inside, he hoped Reese would stop talking about it by the time they went in for dinner.

"Looking for someone, Rita?" Ben concentrated on drowning his scoop of mashed potatoes in the thick, aromatic milk gravy to take his mind off the shorts and halter top Reese had changed into before dinner. He'd like to cover her in gravy and kiss it off. All over her hot little body. He licked his lips. "This gravy smells fantastic. You outdid yourself this time."

Rita smiled, her face lighting up. "Thanks, Ben, but you haven't tasted it yet. And yes and no. I guess I was just hoping. We have four other guests, the Mills brothers. At least, I think they're brothers. They aren't very sociable. They leave every morning, after breakfast, with their tackle boxes. Other than the breakfast buffet, they haven't eaten in the restaurant since they checked in."

Reese looked around the restaurant attached to the hotel, oblivious to the fact she was practically flashing her nipple at him. "It's filling up fast. If they don't get here soon, they won't get a table." She took a bite of the tender meat and had to bite back a moan. "Oh, Rita, this is fabulous! It's a good thing I won't be staying long. I'd gain weight!"

"You could afford it." Rita smiled. "How do you stay so thin? I enjoy eating too much!"

Reese swirled a bite of meat in her mashed potatoes and

gravy. "I don't eat much at home. Seems like I'm always running late. Then, at work, I'm too busy most of the time. Plus, I walk a lot."

"Yeah," Ben chimed in with a grin, picturing her walking. Naked. "She wanted to walk to the courthouse earlier."

Rita's robust laugh filled the dining room. Ben wondered if the pink flush spreading up Reese's neck went lower. Like across her surprisingly decent rack. Decent for someone so skinny, for sure. Wait. He had to stop thinking about sex with her. It wasn't his goal. His goal was to scrape up enough money to prevent her from buying his island.

Wiping tears of mirth from her eyes with the edge of her ruffled apron, Rita grinned down at his dinner companion. "I don't care if you're used to walking a lot or not, that would have been quite a hike!"

After Rita and Ben's laughter subsided, Reese swallowed her last bite of mashed potatoes. "It's pretty far from here, I take it?"

"Oh, it's not all that far," Rita assured her with a pat on the shoulder. "As the crow flies, that is. But on foot, you'd have to walk a winding path through town to get there. A five-minute drive would take a good forty-five minutes to walk. Plus, there are a lot of little hills. I've walked it a time or two and wouldn't recommend it," she added as she walked away.

"I don't suppose busses run from here to there?"

Ben chuckled. "Now, why would you want to take a bus when you have a limo right here?"

Reese shot him a deadpan look. "Maybe because I've ridden in the *limo*."

"Aw, c'mon. I didn't even charge you for the broken seat belt." *Lean this way a little more. I want to see your tits.*

"It was broken before I even touched it! You already admitted that." To his disappointment, she leaned back and glared at him.

"Will you two stop arguing?" Rita hustled over to the table with a rolling cart bearing several pies and a towering chocolate cake. "You need a dessert. It'll calm you down."

She had no idea how *uncalm* he was at the moment. Especially below his belt.

"I have strawberry rhubarb pie, apple pie, peach pie, and lemon meringue," Rita continued, oblivious to his sexual turmoil. "I also have my fudge suicide cake. You can get any of them à la mode, except the meringue." She took a huge, lethal-looking knife from the tray below and smiled. "Which will it be? It's included with the price of the meal, in case you were wondering."

Reese honestly couldn't remember eating as much as she'd ingested since arriving in Sand Dollar. Hand on her full stomach—fullness had to be the reason she felt a flutter there when she looked across the table—she said, "Oh, thanks, but I don't believe I'll have any. I—"

"Don't insult the cook." Ben smiled at Rita. "We'll take a small slice of each pie, with ice cream, please. And, of course, a big ole piece of cake. To share." He winked at Reese, who sat in numbed shock. "You can thank me later."

Reese bit back a groan as she lumbered up the stairs. So full, she felt she might roll back down the stairs. She took comfort, though, in knowing if she did, she'd take out the irritating man behind her.

"Hand me your key."

Paused to catch her breath at the newel post, she glared at him through her lashes. "In your dreams."

"Hardly. You're not my type. I'm just trying to be hospitable. After the way you chowed down, I figured it took all your strength just to digest it and walk up the stairs."

Knowing to pick her battles, although it galled her to know

he was right, she fished the card key out of the pocket of her shorts and slapped it into his palm. "Knock yourself out. I mean, thank you," she amended when he scowled back at her.

"Stop smiling at me like that. It creeps me out." He turned to open her door and she stuck out her tongue. "I saw that. Real mature."

"What? How did you see me?" She trailed him into her room and dropped onto the upholstered chair by the bathroom door.

"I saw your reflection in the brass plate on the door." He opened the little refrigerator and peered in. "Did you drink all the beer already?"

"There wasn't any beer. I . . . Wait! You were up here earlier." Her eyes narrowed. "Was there beer in there then?"

"Maybe. Maybe not." He pulled her to her feet, not stopping until they were chest to chest—well, okay, maybe it was closer to chest to abdomen—his arms securely around her. "Let's change the subject."

She struggled. A little. "What are you doing? Let go of me."

"I like this outfit better than the garb you had on at the airport." He swayed back and forth, making it difficult for her not to brush against him.

"Well, I was told dinner was casual. It's warmer here than in Houston." Walking shorts and a dressy halter top had seemed like a safe choice. Eyes wide, she looked up at him. "I was dressed appropriately, though, wasn't I?"

"Uh-huh. You have real nice legs for such a skinny, short person."

"Gee, thanks." Her palms flat on his chest, she pushed, but he remained plastered to her.

"I do have a question, though. I wondered about it all through supper." The tip of his index finger brushed a fiery trail along the plunging neckline of her top.

Her nipples immediately stood at attention, but she'd be darned if she'd let him know how his touch affected her.

Licking her dry lips, she swallowed. "Wh-what's that?"

Reese's posture relaxed. Ben wondered if she was aware she'd snuggled a little closer.

He should leave her. Now. But the enticing glimpses of nipple she'd taunted him with throughout their meal haunted him. All the reasons he should walk away marched through his fevered brain.

Whether she knew it or not, she was in Sand Dollar to ruin his life by taking the one thing he wanted most, his grandmother's island.

By the time he'd realized Gram had neglected to pay property taxes for years before her death, and that he'd also been remiss in the years since she'd passed, he owed way more in back taxes than he could cough up. Which was why he was busting his butt to scrape up the back taxes by working as a taxi and limo driver, doing any odd jobs that came his way. Hell, he'd even prostituted his beloved boat by running a charter fishing business in addition to the commercial fishing he did himself.

He had been running on empty emotionally for longer than he'd care to admit. That had to be the reason Reese Parker was having an effect on him.

The scrawny woman in his arms was so not his type, it was laughable. Yet, he felt drawn to her, anyway. Go figure. Just proved how desperate and horny he had become. Maybe it was a case of any pussy in a storm. Yeah, that had to be it.

Now she wanted to know what he'd been thinking about during their meal, he'd tell her.

"I wondered if you had on anything under that pretty little blue top." Ignoring her little gasp, he pushed on. "Then, when you leaned down to lick the last of the fudge frosting from your plate—"

"I did not lick my plate!"

His hips bumped his erection against her bony pelvis. Instead of shoving him away, she bumped him right back. She was feisty.

He liked that.

"I can think of a few other things I wouldn't mind seeing you lick. . . ."

"I'm going to ignore that. Back to our conversation. You said something about when I bent over?"

With a grin, he nodded and dipped his finger below the edge of her top, eliciting another gasp. The tip of his finger grazed a puckered nipple and his grin stretched. "I saw the edge of these." He flicked his fingernail over the erect tip of the first one, then the other breast.

Reese's breath hissed through her teeth, but she didn't move.

Taking that as a good sign, he ran his fingertips up under each strap, then shoved them down to her elbows, baring her perky little breasts.

To his continued delight, though they were definitely perky, they weren't all that little.

He reached out and plucked the hard nipples, squeezing them, rolling them between his thumbs and forefingers until she whimpered. "You like that?"

Blinking, she nodded.

"What else? Do you want me to do more?"

Swallowing, she gave a curt nod. "Suck—suck them," she said in a raw whisper.

Instead, he drew the top back to cover temptation. He wanted nothing more than to take her in his mouth. But he knew he wouldn't want to stop there. And maybe he couldn't stop there.

Too much was at stake.

He needed to keep his wits about him. And his dick in his pants.

"If I sucked your tits, I'd want to do more." He tweaked her still erect nipple through the silk and stepped back. "We don't know each other well enough for that. Not yet, anyway."

A blush bloomed on her chest, then rose to her cheeks. "Maybe I didn't want you to do anything more."

"Liar."

6

Reese stood, legs clamped tightly together, her rigid nipples aching, long after the click of the door to her room told her Ben had gone.

She didn't want to do anything more. Not anything sexual, that was for sure. Really. She was just lonely, being in a strange town with no one she knew. That had to be the only reason she'd reacted to someone who was so totally opposite of anyone she'd ever been attracted to before. Ever.

Dazed, she took a leisurely shower, letting the hot spray hit her square in the face. Afterward, still wide-awake, she wrapped her robe tightly around her and reached for her phone.

Tucking her feet under her on the end of the soft couch by the window, she tried to block her encounter with Ben from her memory while she waited for the connection.

"Paige? Are you busy? You weren't asleep, were you?"

Her friend's husky laugh vibrated against her ear. "Of course not! Bailey and I were just sitting here talking about you, wondering how you were doing. How was the flight?"

"No comment." She pulled her robe closer and lowered her voice. "Paige, I'm in foreign territory here and I'm worried. . . ."

"Beer?" Rick waved a longneck his way when Ben stepped onto the porch.

Ben hesitated less than a second before dropping to the chair and grabbing the cool bottle. "Thanks." He twisted off the cap and took a long draw.

"You know what she's here for, don't you?"

Eyes fixed on the waves rolling to shore, Ben waited a beat. "Yeah."

"If you don't want to haul her around, I could probably find someone else."

"What? And miss gouging her for the fares? Nah, I can take her. 'Sides, I need the money." He took another swig.

"We're all sorry the fund-raiser wasn't more of a success."

"Hey, you tried. I appreciate it. But, Rick, bottom line is, I should have known better. No, hear me out," he said when Rick looked like he was going to argue. "Gram used to beg me to use my degree to make something out of myself." He grinned. "Well, something more than a glorified beach bum, as she used to say. But did I listen? Hell no! Life was a party and I was determined to be its honored guest. I was too busy having fun to realize when the old girl was declining. Guess I saw just what I wanted to see."

"That's how she wanted it," Rick said softly. "She didn't want to be a burden to anyone."

"I know. I get that. But I should have noticed. She was my family. The only family I had left. I saw just what I wanted to see when I visited. And I didn't visit nearly as often as I should have, and you and I both know it. I should have at least checked to make sure her finances were in order and she was paying her taxes, for God's sake! It just never occurred to me. Then, after she was gone . . ."

"Don't beat yourself up. Miz Winnie wouldn't have wanted you to do that. She was a proud and private woman." Seeing how quickly his friend was drinking, Rick handed him another beer.

"But after she was gone—"

"You were pretty torn up."

"Stop making excuses for him, Rick!" Rita stepped onto the porch, letting the screen door slap shut behind her. "That's been Ben's problem. Everyone always made excuses for his behavior. Even Miz Winnie, the last time I was out to see her, did it." She slapped Ben's shoulder, none too gently, as she walked to the cooler and took out a beer. Lowering to sit on her husband's knee, she offered a small smile to Ben. "Ben, honey, it's time to grow up. Some life lessons are hard to learn. This may be one of them. Hard as it is for you, maybe you need to come to terms with the fact you may not be able to save Winnie's island." She took a sip and swallowed. "How's the tax money coming along? Did Rick tell you we're planning another barbeque and bake sale next week? I'm just praying the tropical storm they're predicting misses us."

"Yeah, he mentioned it earlier. I appreciate it, you know. I just don't think it's going to be enough, if what we made last time is anything to go by, even without a storm." He uncapped his beer and tilted the bottle to his lips.

"We tried to get the Mills brothers to charter your boat for their fishing, but they said they'd rented a boat already." Rick handed his empty bottle to his wife and stroked her hip beneath the edge of her apron.

"Thanks. I know you tried."

They watched the surf for a few minutes.

"For what it's worth," Rick began, breaking the silence, "I figured you'd take our newest guest out to the island. Who better to show her around, right?"

"Damn straight," Ben said, still watching the water. "Plus, I could use the money. Thanks, Rick."

"Ben, not to tell you what to do, but do you think it's a good idea to take to the open water with a storm brewing?"

Ben's bark of laughter startled some nearby seagulls. "Damn it, Rick, you're getting old. You know that storm will probably miss us altogether, just like always. And besides, I plan to be back before it gets here. Assuming it gets here, which I sincerely doubt."

7

After a long night, Reese made her way downstairs to the restaurant for breakfast. Maybe she'd feel more chirpy after she had some food and coffee.

"Oh! Excuse me, I didn't see you." Bumped up against the entrance of the restaurant, she watched the exiting tackle box–carrying men, all dressed in bright yellow rain slickers with some kind of logo on the back, then glanced out at the sunny morning sky. "Weird."

"Morning, Reese," Rita called from a nearby table, where she was pouring coffee for a couple. She hurried over. "Just take a seat wherever you want. The menu is printed on the place mat. Breakfast is included with your room rate. And coffee." She raised the carafe. "Juice is extra."

"Coffee is fine. Decaf, if you have it." After the night she'd had, she decided to cut back on her caffeine consumption. "With lots of cream."

Through the window, she watched the slicker-clad men make their way down the beach.

"I see you met the personality brothers," Rita quipped when

she returned with the coffee. "They're so strange." Shaking her head, her braid swinging across her shoulders, she pulled a face. "Don't say more than hello every morning, then head out, and I don't see them again until they come back, after dark, to hole up in their rooms. They're here, bright and early, the next morning—then it starts all over again."

"Maybe they just really like to fish." Personally, she didn't see the attraction, but a lot of people loved fishing.

"Maybe, but that's another thing that doesn't add up. At this time of year, fish practically commit suicide by jumping into the boat. Yet those men never have any fish. At least, none that we've seen."

While she waited for her breakfast, Reese contemplated the strange activities of the men. There was a possibility they were also here to bid on the island. But why the fishing disguise? Unless, of course, they were combining business with pleasure.

The logo on their slickers reminded her of something, but it danced out of her memory before she could make any connections.

"Why the frown so early in the morning?" Ben slid into the opposite side of the little booth and grinned at her. "How could you not sleep great, so close to the ocean?"

"I didn't say I hadn't slept well. Where do you come up with this stuff?" She glared at him, trying not to notice how cute he was with the morning sun glinting off his damp, freshly combed hair. It even looked as though he may have shaved. "And for that matter, I don't remember asking you to join me."

"Well, not in the biblical sense, no." His grin was unrepentant as he nodded his thanks for the cup of coffee Rita placed in front of him. He winked and reached for the pitcher of cream. "But I can wait."

She snatched the creamer from his hand. "Take your paws off my cream."

"There's enough for us to share." But he held up the pitcher to signal Rita to bring more, just in case, she noticed.

"Fine. And, for the record, you can wait until hell freezes over."

Thoughtfully stirring his coffee, he regarded her with a vague smile. "What are you trying to say?"

Was he that dense? "It means," she said, her voice escalating until she was shouting, "I'm *not* going to have sex with you!"

A collective gasp filled the little restaurant, then utter silence.

Heat crept up her neck as mortification washed over her.

Unabashed, Ben looked around at their fellow patrons and shrugged, holding his hands out, palms up. "I don't know where she gets this kind of stuff." To her horror, he did an eye roll and made a face. "She's just sexually obsessed with me."

"Sexually obsessed! I'll show him sexually obsessed." Reese threw a bottle of sunscreen in her tote bag, then dumped the rest of her granola bars. "Wait. What am I saying? That's exactly what he'd want me to do." She growled and stomped to her carry-on bag. A clean pair of panties and a change of clothes might be a good idea. No telling how dirty the old hotel would be. Plus, she might very well get wet. The old dock had no doubt seen better days.

A glance around the room confirmed she had everything she needed for her day's excursion. Her watch confirmed it was time to go down to meet her driver.

The sight of Ben draped over the desk, talking to Rick, caused Reese's steps to falter. Why was he still here? Unless . . . please, no.

"There she is now," Rick said with a smile. "I was just telling Ben, here, how you needed to get going if you hope to make it back ahead of the storm."

"Storm?"

"Don't worry about it." Ben draped his arm over her shoulder. "Damn thing will probably miss us. The weather service always makes a big deal, and then nothing happens."

A dip of her shoulder allowed her to escape his grasp. "What, exactly, is the weather service saying? If it's dangerous, I can always tell the charter to reschedule me."

"I told you, it's not dangerous." He attempted to steer her toward the door.

Planting her sneaker-clad feet on the hardwood floor, she locked her knees. "Please tell me he's not driving me to the marina."

Rick chuckled. "No need to drive. The marina's just out yonder. You can walk to it."

"Oh. Good." She shot Ben what she hoped was a dismissive look. "Do you know if the charter boat is ready?"

"Yes, I reckon it is, don't you, Ben?"

"Why are you asking Ben?" *Please don't tell me he's coming too.* "I'm perfectly capable of taking a charter to the island alone. I'll be fine." She backed toward the door.

The men exchanged looks.

Looks she didn't trust.

Come to think of it, she didn't trust Ben's grin either.

"Well," he began in a lazy tone as he sauntered toward her. "You may be fine, but I doubt you know diddly about navigating a cabin cruiser. I can see by your face, I'm right." Raking back his hair, he plopped a baseball cap on top of his head and gave Rick a brisk salute before turning back to Reese.

"A cabin cruiser? But—I mean—does that mean . . . ?"

"Yep! I'm your captain!"

Just shoot me now.

8

"Ben," Rick called from the porch as Reese's *captain* pushed her along across the sand. "I still think it's a piss-poor idea! That tropical storm's heading straight for us!"

"Bullshit," Ben growled under his breath. Louder, he yelled back, "No worries! Plenty of time! We'll probably be back before it even rains."

Reese attempted to hang back, but Ben was not taking the hint. "Wait! If there really is a tropical storm coming, maybe we should hold off on going to the island. I'm going to be here all week. I can wait."

"Yeah, well, I can't. Maybe I have more important things to do than haul your skinny ass around."

Jerking her arm out of his bruising grip, she whirled on him, fists planted on her hips. "Well, I wouldn't want to disturb your social calendar." She took a step back toward the hotel. "If you have so many important things to do, go on! I'm sure I can find another charter to take me out to the island after the storm."

"Wait." He grabbed her arm again and spun her around to face him. "I thought Rick would have told you. I'm it."

"*It?*" Talk about ego. Sure he was cute, but he wasn't really all that.

"Yeah. Most of the charters close down toward fall. I'm the only one left in operation. So, yeah, I'm it." Narrowing his eyes, he bent until they were nose to nose. "Take it or leave it, girlie."

"Don't call me *girlie.*" It was difficult to stand tall, with him looming over her, but she did her best.

"How about pain in the ass? Hmm?" Without waiting for an answer, he began propelling her toward a clubhouse-looking sort of place.

Good. Surely, there were other boats available, despite her escort's dubious assurance. She would ask someone at the club.

Only, she didn't get the chance, because Ben took a sharp left and continued propelling her down the boardwalk. Another left took her along a floating dock, past several boats with old tires secured around them as they bumped gently against the dock.

A lone boat bobbed in the water toward the end of the dock. A boat that could only belong to one person, given its disreputable state. It looked like . . . it needed a bath.

It probably smelled.

"Here we are! Watch your step."

"What's that stench?" She wrinkled her nose and tried not to gag.

"Oh! Sorry." He grabbed a cooler and dumped its contents overboard. "Old bait. Forgot to dump it." He took a bracing breath and flashed a smile. "Let's get going."

She glanced around the deck, which, to her surprise, was fairly clean and didn't appear to be in disrepair.

Thump.

Something hit her in the back, knocking her to her knees.

"Shit-fire-spit! I said I was throwing you the life jacket."

"You did not!" Knees throbbing, she pulled up to her feet and began unbuckling the straps. Lord knew, she'd probably need the dumb thing.

"I did so! I said heads-up!"

"Heads-up? Really." She jerked the jacket on and began trying to secure the straps. "What is that, sea talk for here is your life preserver? Hmm. Who knew?"

"Any fool would know—"

"Speak for yourself." A glance skyward didn't bode well. "Are you sure it's okay? Aren't those storm clouds?" The wind had kicked up too, she noticed as she held on to the rail.

Ben waved a negligent hand. "Nah, that's nothing. It's just a little overcast." He looked up and frowned. "But we should probably get going if we want to make it back ahead of the rain."

"Rain?" She had to yell above the roar of the engine. Ben refused to make eye contact, she noticed. "I thought Rick said there was a tropical storm headed our way!"

Shaking his head, he banked the boat in a hard left and headed out into open water. "No," he yelled back, "at the most, it's just rain."

The sky grew darker by the moment. Waves, made worse by the now fiercely blowing wind, tossed the boat in the air, then slapped it down.

Reese took a deep, hopefully calming, breath in an effort to fend off the impending nausea. It helped marginally, so she tried again. She was immediately rewarded by a face full of salt water as a wave jumped the edge of the rail.

Sputtering, she held on to the rail and proceeded to lose her breakfast.

"Some kind of fun, huh, Blondie? Hey, are you okay?" Ben yelled to be heard over the roar of the wind and waves. "Will you cut it out! You're disturbing the ecosystem!"

With one hand maintaining her death grip on the rail, she glared at him for the few seconds between her waves of nausea.

Finally—after what seemed like hours of tossing her cookies, then dry heaving—she slid to sit on the deck, still gripping the rail.

"Are we almost there?" she yelled.

"Shit!" Ben hunched his shoulders as though bracing for a blow. "Look out!"

Reese turned just in time to see a gray haze bearing down on the boat.

It wasn't a haze. It was a wall of water.

One second, it was in front of them; the next second, it engulfed the deck, drenching them.

Her fingers continued slipping, no matter how she tried to hold on. The force of the wind, combined with the torrential rain buffeting them, lifted her from the deck. Rain swirled around her soaked torso, slapping her ears, stinging her face, going up her nose.

The rail slipped from her clutching fingers.

Amid the cacophony of the storm, Ben's voice bellowed, but she couldn't make out the words.

Water—cold at first, then warmer—enveloped her, pulling her down.

Shouting every profanity he'd ever heard, Ben went full throttle, then banked starboard, the plume of water folding and falling back on him.

Where the hell was she?

As he anxiously scanned the angry water of the Gulf of Mexico, a little head broke the surface, then bobbed in the choppy waves.

Weak with relief, he backed off on the throttle, making tighter and tighter circles until he stopped.

Skidding sideways, he leaned out, practically prodding her with the pole. "Grab hold and I'll pull you back in!"

Just as he thought he was going to have to knock her out and drag her back, she reached for the pole.

When she was close enough, he leaned down and grabbed her forearm. Feet braced, he pulled. And pulled. Damn, who knew such a skinny broad would weigh so much?

9

She really, really didn't want to climb back up into that stupid boat. Death trap. Unfortunately, Ben seemed determined to drag her back aboard. Or rip her arm from the socket. It seemed to be a toss-up.

"Will you stop yanking on my arm?" Teeth clenched to keep them from chattering, she squinted through the torrential rain at him.

"Oh, pardon the hell out of me! I didn't realize you'd planned to levitate aboard." He hoisted her up and immediately let go of her arm, forcing her to scramble to grab hold of the rail to prevent being washed overboard again.

Something warm and heavy dropped over her shoulders. An involuntary yelp escaped before she realized it was a reasonably dry blanket. Her head jerked around in wonder at his sudden act of kindness.

He shrugged and actually looked somewhat embarrassed. "No point in both of us being soaked and miserable," he yelled over the roar of the wind and rain. He pointed to a door on the deck. "If you're through fooling around, I'd like to get on with our trip before the really bad stuff hits. Go down below and try to dry off a little. There are clean towels and blankets." He nudged her toward the door.

Really bad stuff? Could it get much worse?

Chilled to the bone, she didn't argue about the fooling-around part.

The first step, though, was a doozy.

Regardless of what the athletic store in Houston claimed, her deck shoes were obviously not nonskid. When the wet rubber hit the smooth surface of the steps, her feet flew out from under her, causing her to bump painfully down the next few stairs, landing with a bone-jarring plop in the rapidly growing puddle on the floor.

Stunned, she sat while the rain continued to pelt the top of her head.

"Geez, woman, were you raised by a pack of demented wolves? Shut the damned door!" Ben's bellow was immediately followed by the slamming of the door in question.

Aching, Reese pulled up on the banquette, holding on until she could stand without fear of falling.

Compared to the deck, it was really quite cozy.

Dim lights glowed overhead, bathing the little cabin in warmth. Honey-colored wood paneled the walls and ceiling. To her right was the banquette, easily able to seat at least six adults.

To her left was a little galley kitchen, complete with a cute little fridge.

Since her stomach chose that moment to announce its emptiness, she grasped the handle and pulled. The suction was strong, but after a couple of tugs, the door popped open, the interior light inviting her to take a look.

Beer. Wine. Orange juice—half empty and expired. A small carton of milk.

Even though the milk was not organic or skim or even low

fat, she licked her lips in anticipation. A tentative shake told her the carton contained at least a glass of milk.

Suddenly dying of thirst, she searched the cupboard for a glass, finally settling on a coffee mug.

The smell hit her a millisecond before a glob of spoiled milk hit the bottom of the mug.

"Shit!" A guilty glance told her no one had heard her cuss. Defeated, she dumped the spoiled milk down the drain and then sank to sit on the edge of the table.

The door above her smashed open, bringing in the roar of the storm and pelting droplets of rain.

"Hey, Blondie!" Ben-the-Politically-Incorrect yelled from above deck. "What the hell are you doing down there? Hey! You're getting my cabin all wet! Use a damn towel!"

The slam was immediately followed by a *whapping* sound as the boat hit a particularly large wave, and the door popped open and closed again.

The unexpected motion threw Reese up in the air, then deposited her on the floor. Pain raced up her arm from where her elbow had hit the edge of the table on her way downward.

"Yeah, Ben, I'm having some kind of fun now," she grumbled as she crawled toward the back of the cabin. Maybe if she kept low to the surprisingly clean and shining floor, her motion sickness wouldn't rear its ugly head again.

The boat chose that moment to lurch again, pitching her forward to whack her head on the frame of what she now saw was the bathroom door.

Blinking away the stars, she felt her way into the tiny bathroom, bumping her knee on the edge of the toilet.

A look in the hazy mirror above a child-size sink made her gasp. She honestly could not remember ever looking as bad as she looked at that moment.

Her hair was plastered to her skull. Her mascara had made a hasty retreat, leaving black streaks down her face, as well as beneath her eyes. She reached to rub at the streak, but it refused to budge.

Dang mascara had promised to withstand crying, rain, pretty much anything. What the manufacturer forgot to mention was it would transfer to places it was not supposed to be and then indelibly stick. Even the wet washcloth on the sink didn't make a dent in the mess.

She refused to think about what that washcloth had touched since it was last laundered. Still, she couldn't help recoiling and dropping the thing into the sink.

"Towels. You're down in this hellhole for towels. Stay focused," she whispered.

"What are you mumbling about now?" Ben's voice was directly behind her, by the open bathroom door.

Hand over her galloping heart, she glared at him. "What are you doing here?"

"I live here." His arms spread to encompass the little cabin. "Welcome to my home."

"I don't care where you live! I meant, what are you doing down here? Why aren't you up there driving the boat?"

"Engine stalled."

"Well, fix it! I'm paying you to take me out to the island—"

"*Well, fix it,*" he said in a falsetto voice. "If I could just *fix it,* I wouldn't be down here having this asinine conversation with you!"

Nausea washed over her and she wasn't sure if it was from the rocking motion of the boat or what her companion in her current fiasco had just told her.

Sinking to sit on the edge of the toilet, she gazed up at him, willing her tears to go away. "We're stranded?" she finally managed to say around the constriction in her throat. "Won't someone be looking for us? Surely, someone will rescue us."

"Don't call me Shirley." He grinned down at her. "Lighten up, it's a joke. As for being rescued, don't count on it. No one knows exactly where we are. Including me, at the moment." He scratched his chin. "Aw, don't look so shocked. Happens to everyone now and then. We were being tossed around pretty good. It's easy to lose your bearings."

Holding the sink, she stood up and backed him toward the hall. "You assured me you were the best, the only one to take me to the island."

"I said that?" He raised his eyebrows, blue eyes twinkling, and she had the distinct impression he was holding back a laugh. "I musta been drinking." He raised his hand. "Don't get me wrong, I'm good. Damn good. But I'm not sure I'd call me the best."

"Then what are you?"

"Available." His teeth flashed white in his tanned face. "And you were desperate. Great combination. It was a match made in heaven."

"Rick told me there wasn't anyone better to take me to the island." Valiantly ignoring the brush of her breasts against his chest, she wedged her way out of the bathroom.

"Yeah, well, Rick chose his words carefully. Bottom line, there flat-out wasn't anyone but me available." His warm fingers touched her lips, holding her mouth shut. "So, there really wasn't anyone better. He wasn't lying to you."

The boat must have hopped a wave because one second she was standing there, trying to decide how to get away from the man in front of her, and the next her feet left the polished floor. When she landed, it was against the warm human pad of Ben Adams.

His arms shot around her.

The boat rocked in the storm, rubbing her pelvis against his.

To her horror, he was not unaffected.

10

"That better be something in your pocket," she hissed.

"I don't have anything in my pockets." Realization must have dawned because a smile came to his face. "Oh! Sorry about that. No, wait. Why should I be sorry? You're the one who's rubbing all over me."

"I never!" Struggling, she couldn't quite touch her feet to the floor. "Will you put me down?"

He shrugged. "Whatever turns you on. I'm game. You're so skinny, I bet you have to run around in the shower to get wet."

She gaped, suspended in his arms.

"You said to put you down. It was the best I could come up with on short notice."

"Did your mother drop you on your head when you were a baby? I meant, let me go!"

He paused for a few seconds, then shook his head. "No, I don't believe I'm ready to do that yet."

With a sigh, she looked into his eyes, refusing to be impressed with the clear blueness of them. "Let's try this again.

Take your hands off of me and go back up and drive the boat. Please."

"I told you I can't do that. Not yet, anyway. Must've taken water into the manifold. It needs to dry out a spell."

"Dry out? Dry out?" She knew she was beginning to raise her voice—okay, she was more likely yelling in his handsome face. Not that she necessarily thought he was handsome. He wasn't her type. But there were some women, she knew, who might find him marginally attractive. "It's a hurricane out there! How could it possibly dry out?"

"First off, it's not a hurricane, it's just rain. Second, I know what I'm talking about when I tell you the engine is wet. I'd explain it to you, but it would take too long. The gist of it is we took on water where there should not have been water. Now we wait for it to drain out so we can restart the engine and be on our way."

"That's it?" It really wasn't too bad, being in his arms, but she felt kind of silly, just hanging there.

"That's it."

Her mouth hovered closer to his. All the reasons why it would be a bad idea to kiss him ran through her mind. First off, of course, he was so not her type. Second, he was her employee, of sorts. Third, he already needed a shave. Fourth, his eyes were too blue. Okay, she was starting to stretch for reasons why kissing him would not be smart.

Against her breast, his heart beat, its steady rhythm soothing her into a lethargic state. A sexually lethargic state, assuming there was such a thing.

"I want to kiss you." His voice was a low, intimate rumble that vibrated her chest.

Her heart rate accelerated, her breathing became shallow. "Oh?" Should she tell him to stop? Should she tell him she wasn't interested? Heck, who was she kidding? Every nerve ending stood at attention. If she tried telling him she wasn't interested, no doubt a big sign would flash across her forehead that said LIAR. Maybe she should just stop analyzing everything and lean into it. Let nature take its course. . . .

"Yeah," he said with a half smile, turning as he swayed from side to side. "But I'm trying to restrain myself." He dropped her to bounce on the mattress that filled most of the little back cabin. " 'Cause you smell like puke."

Mouth agape, she watched as he gave a jaunty little salute, then turned and made his way out of the cabin.

A few seconds after he disappeared above deck, the door opened again.

Scrambling to sit up and trying her best to look alluring, while not too eager, she was crestfallen to see her tote bag tossed to the table.

Immediately the door slammed shut, water dripping around the edge.

She found it easier on her stomach to stand than to sit or, heaven forbid, lay. With tentative steps, she made her way to the tote bag, then back to the bathroom. Thank goodness she always carried toothbrush and toothpaste for just such occasions.

Who said this trip had to be all business? She honestly couldn't remember the last vacation she'd taken.

When Ben Adams came back down, she'd be ready and waiting for him.

11

More relieved than he'd readily admit, Ben let out a sigh when the engine kicked over. Although it was still deep water, he'd dropped anchor just to keep them from drifting even more off course. After pulling up anchor, then double-checking their vicinity, he pushed the throttle down and headed for Serenity Island before he did something stupid. More stupid than he'd already done.

Hell, his stupidity knew no bounds these days. Despite his grandmother's pleas, he'd let his diploma gather dust while he played beach bum. When Gram had died, he was filled with remorse and tried to drown it in booze. He'd come out of his three-year drunk to discover not only had he neglected to pay the property taxes on the island, neither had his grandmother for a few years before her death. Now he could very well lose everything his grandparents had left him, and he had no one to blame but himself. He knew better.

Eyes squinted against the rain, he could barely make out the dark silhouette of the island. Swinging the boat starboard, he made for the dock he knew was there. If they could get there, and do what Blondie wanted to do, and get back, they may just make it to Sand Dollar before the worst of the storm moved in.

Stupid weather. How many times had everyone hunkered down for nothing? How was he to know this was the real deal? Of course, he'd never admit he'd made a mistake to the woman below. Not yet, anyway.

And, damn, he still wanted to kiss her. All over. Just goes to show how hard up he had become, to lust after a bag of bones like Reese Parker.

But she hadn't felt all that bony when she'd been pressed against his eager body.

"Get those thoughts out of your mind, Adams." He leaned forward, willing the boat to cut through the water at a higher rate of speed.

The sooner they made land, the better. If he'd stayed below a few minutes longer, no telling what fool thing he'd have done.

Reese smelled the minty freshness of her recently brushed teeth as she clamped her hand over her mouth and rolled from side to side on the overly soft mattress, where she'd fallen when the boat lurched forward.

Good thing Ben had not returned, she told her libido. Even though she knew he was not her type, she had no doubt they'd have ended up naked on the dubious cleanliness of the sheets she was currently wrinkling.

Yes, she was that desperate.

Watching the Dragon Lady and her playmate hadn't helped the situation.

Reese's love life was a barren desert these days. She listened to the rain pelting the boat windows and bit back a laugh. She'd almost ended her personal dry spell—literally and figuratively.

Her finger touched the motion sickness patch behind her

ear. Though only in place for a few minutes, it seemed to be working. Of course, she had nothing much left to throw up, so who knew?

A glance at her watch confirmed they should be at the island by now. Rick had told her it was about an hour from Sand Dollar, by boat, and it had been that and more. If they could make land soon, she might be spared the further humiliation of another bout of seasickness. Maybe.

She was certainly feeling groggy, all of a sudden, like she could almost take a nap. Must be the side effect of the patch, she decided, standing on wobbly legs to strap on her life jacket again before going up on deck.

Her deck shoes were cold and made little squishing sounds with each step.

"Ick," she said, gripping the handrail and taking tentative steps on the ladder.

A deep breath still did not sufficiently brace her for the wind and stinging wall of rain that slapped her in the face, knocking her back.

With a shriek, she swung by one arm when her feet lost their slippery grip on the steps.

Eyes trained on the dock ahead, Ben spared a second to glance back when he heard his passenger scream. Immediately he wished he hadn't.

Reese clung to the rail of the ladder, swinging by her arm, the other arm clutching her ridiculously oversize bag to her chest like she feared muggers.

The woman was, without a doubt, more trouble than she was worth.

When he was sure the boat wouldn't stray off course if he abandoned his post for a minute, he lunged for her, pulling her up and to him in one gut-busting movement.

Damn woman was going to end up giving him a hernia. Or

ulcers. Or both. Assuming she didn't make him wreck his boat first and drown.

"Why didn't you stay below?" He had to shout his question over the roar of the wind and rain. Through the mist, he could see the shape of the old dock. He breathed a sigh of relief. They were still on course.

"Rick said it was less than an hour by boat," she shouted back.

He chanced a quick look back over his shoulder. Seeing her huddled by the door, clutching her stupid purse, the life jacket snugged up to her chin, set off a riot of emotions deep within. None of them good.

She was bossy and generally irritating. She was skinny. She had way too short hair for his taste.

And, right now, he'd like nothing better than to strip her bare and lick her all over.

No doubt about it, he'd been alone too long, when someone like the drowned rat of a woman huddled on his deck aroused him.

And, son of a bitch, did she ever arouse him.

The question was, what was he prepared to do about it?

The answer was not a damn thing. Well, not a thing except take her for every dime he could wring out of her and hope the town could scrape up enough to help him pay the back taxes.

A movement to the side caught his attention. Reese was moving forward, scanning the water of the gulf like a little scared bird.

"What are you looking for?"

"The island, of course, I—oh!"

He refused to feel guilty for the roughness of his touch when he grabbed her, ignoring the fragile-feeling bones beneath his hand, and turned her in the opposite direction to make her look directly at the island. Then he pointed for good measure. "There it is."

"Sit!" he yelled as he navigated toward the bleached-out wooden dock.

"Excuse me?" She drew up, her bony arms clutching the tote in front of her like a shield.

Releasing the wheel for a second, he motioned to the bench built next to the anchor bay. "I don't have time to fish you out of the water again."

Pulling back on the throttle, he glided up to the dock and cut the engine.

"Stay!" he commanded, hopping to the dock to tie off, before dropping anchor for good measure.

"I'm not a dog!" she yelled over the rain.

He shoved her aside to drop anchor, then stepped back onto the dock. It only took a second to realize she was not following.

Turning back, wiping the rain from his face, he saw her digging around in her bag. "Now what are you doing? What are you looking for?"

"My umbrella," she answered, still intently searching. "I know I had one in here when I left home."

"Are you fucking nuts?" When she looked up at him, he waved his arms. "It's raining like we need to build an ark! We're soaked to the bone. What the hell do you need an umbrella for, at this point?"

Looking snooty as all get-out, she climbed up on the dock. To his further irritation, she shielded her eyes from the rain—it obviously was not against sunshine—and proceeded to do another three-sixty visual search.

Hands on hips, he glared at her. "Now what? Misplace the island again? I'll give you a hint." He pointed so hard it pulled the muscles in his shoulder. "It's about twenty feet that way. Walk to the end of this dock and you'll run right into it."

"No need to be obtuse," she said with a sniff as she pushed past him, almost knocking him into the churning water. "For your information, I was just trying to get my bearings. But I can't see Sand Dollar. Or any land, for that matter." Thin shoulders shrugged beneath the sunny yellow shirt plastered to her skin. "I guess an hour boat ride takes you farther than I imagined."

"Blondie, I have no idea how your imagination works and I have a feeling I don't want to know. But I will tell you one thing. You'll never see Sand Dollar from here." Leaning close enough to touch the tip of his nose to hers, he tried not to get sucked in by the pale blue of her eyes. "It's on the opposite side of the island," he said with a grin, then shoved past her to walk to the shore.

Casting a nervous glance up at the dark, ominous-looking clouds and getting a face full of rain in the process, Reese made her way to the end of the dock.

Ben paused on the path at the top of the hill leading to his grandmother's hotel and watched Reese pick her way along the jagged stepping-stones.

Damn, it was fun picking on her. More fun than it should have been. More fun than he'd had in longer than he cared to remember.

Damn the tropical storm for ruining his fun.

12

Prickly vegetation scraped at her arms and snagged her cloth-ing as Reese made her way cautiously up the steep walkway.

At one time, she could imagine, the hotel grounds had been magnificent. In a tropical-jungle sort of way, anyway. Would the Dragon Lady have the grounds cleared or try to preserve the island's historical integrity? She had a sinking feeling her boss would do the fastest, most financially expedient thing and bulldoze the whole mess under.

The thought made her a little sad.

Wait. What did she care? She was quitting after this trip. She'd never know what was or was not done to the island or the old hotel.

Right now, her job was to inspect the grounds and building and decide how high to bid on the property. Of course, then she'd have to get the price okayed by the Dragon Lady. Yet an-other reason to move on. Her career was at a standstill.

Her shoulders slumped. Rain pelted her head and back as her steps slowed.

Maybe Paige was right. Her job was a dead end and her career was nonexistent. Why had she stayed so long, allowed herself to become a virtual lapdog for Dorinda?

No more, she vowed, walking faster to catch up with Ben. Her steps slowed again when she noticed how nicely he filled out his shorts, the wet fabric clinging enticingly to the curve of his firm backside.

A sigh escaped her. At another time, in another place, they might have made a connection. Maybe even hooked up. She wasn't naïve. She knew there was something, some kind of spark, between them.

But, for now, she needed to focus on the reason she came to the island and do her job so she could go home and resume her life.

The stepping-stones curved. She had to concentrate to find the stones amid the overgrown grass and weeds. Were there snakes on islands? Snakes could swim, couldn't they? So, there would be nothing to prevent them from coming to an island, or even taking over one that was deserted. The thought sent a shiver through her and she hurried to catch up to Ben.

Lightning flashed jagging through the darkened sky. A boom of thunder immediately followed, shaking the ground beneath her feet. Could islands sink?

Another bolt of lightning lit up the sky, illuminating the huge structure in front of her. Dark and foreboding, it loomed, reminding her of the house at the Bates Motel in *Psycho*—only not in nearly as good a shape.

Its windows had, at one time, been boarded up. Now several of the boards swung in the wind, making the hotel look as though it were weeping plywood.

The wind chose that time to rip one of the pieces of wood off. It flew toward them, then landed to cartwheel down the walk.

Ben tackled her, rolling with her in the grass, weeds and mud. They came to rest at the base of the stairs leading to a wraparound porch.

"Are you hurt?" Ben breathed into her ear, his weight warm and secure against her, shielding her from the elements.

Wait. She didn't need protection. She was perfectly capable of taking care of herself. Wedging her hands between them to push on his chest, she grunted and said, "Get off of me!"

Immediately he stood. Cold rain drenched her anew. For a second, she sat, waiting for him to help her up. She was in for a long wait, because he never looked back as he made his way up the wide stairs to the covered porch.

Growling under her breath, Reese rolled to her feet with as much dignity as she could muster, given the circumstance, and brushed as much junk off her body as possible.

"You're welcome," he said in a frosty tone when she'd joined him on the porch.

"What? You think I should be thanking you for knocking me down and rolling me in the mud and Lord knows what else?" Wiping the wet hair back from her eyes, she glared at him.

"No, but I thought maybe you'd be grateful that I saved your sorry ass out there."

"Excuse me? I didn't realize my ass, or any part of my anatomy, was in jeopardy." Her eyes narrowed as she fired back his earlier words. *"It's. Just. Rain."*

"It's a tropical storm. Haven't you been listening to the weather reports?" He reached to pull on the board covering the entrance. It came off easily in his hand. "What the hell?"

Reese paused in midsearch of her tote and looked up. "Problems, *Bwana*?"

"Ha. Ha. Funny." He glanced down at the piece of wood, then around the lawn fronting the hotel. "Someone must have been here. This board wasn't secured."

Cold fear gripped her. *Don't panic. He probably wants you to panic so he can make fun of you.* She swallowed around the rapidly rising lump in her throat. "Someone," she squeaked. "Someone like who? A criminal? Kids? Teenagers?"

Personally, she liked the idea of teenagers. She could cope with teenagers. Teenagers would be here on their own agenda, maybe to drink or make out with their dates. Drinking and making out sounded pretty tame, not to mention good, at that moment.

"How the hell should I know?" Ben's voice brought her back to the situation at hand.

The front door squeaked ominously as he slowly opened it and peered into what looked like the lobby.

His hand on her chest stopped her from following. "Stay here."

Yeah, like that is going to happen.

Cautious steps took them into the cavernous room. With the windows boarded over and the darkness of the stormy day, it was difficult to see much of anything.

Reese alternated between looking down, ever vigilant for critters of any kind, and scanning the room.

Ben stopped, head alert, listening.

Reese ran into his back.

He caught her before she totally lost her balance and fell.

"I told you to wait outside," he said in a low voice.

"Why?" she whispered, to prove she could be as covert as anyone. "Do you think whoever it is could still be here?" Eyes wide, she looked around. Against her ribs, her heart beat a frantic tattoo. She wouldn't be surprised if Ben could hear it.

A movement by the door caught her eye.

Before she realized it, a scream ripped from her throat as she hopped onto Ben's back, clutching his neck for all she was worth. If someone or something ominous was lurking, they'd have to go through Ben to get to her.

Not very honorable, but there you have it.

Ben made a gurgling sound. Gasping, he pried her hands from his throat. "Shit, woman! What the hell are you doing? Get off of me!"

Instead, she tightened her knees and pointed a shaking finger at the white apparition floating by the door. "It moved," she hissed in his ear.

"Shit-fire-spit! Hell yes, it moved! We left the door open." Dislodging her, he stalked to the door and slammed it, then pulled the sheet from an ornate coatrack by the door. "Satisfied? I promise, the killer coatrack won't get you."

Arms wrapped tightly around her ribs, she chewed on her lip. "Well, how was I to know that? You started it, anyway, scaring me by saying someone had been here."

"Well, someone has." He glanced around. "But they're gone now, I guess." Arms wide, he turned in a circle. "So, this is it. Can we go now?"

"No! We can't go now. I need to take measurements, examine the facilities. You know, inspect things."

"What things?" Hands on hips, he glared at her. "You have no idea, do you? No, you don't, I can see it on your face. Blondie, if we don't get a move on and haul ass back to Sand Dollar, we're going to have to hunker down and wait out the storm right here."

"You told me the storm wasn't going to hit us."

"I was wrong." He shoved his hands in the pockets of his cargo shorts. "Doesn't happen often, but I'm man enough to admit it when it does." He walked to a large white lump and tugged off another sheet to reveal a couch and sat down, crossing one bony ankle over his knobby knee. Scooting down to a slouch, he closed his eyes. "I'll wait here while you look around. Make it quick."

* * *

After he heard her leave the room, Ben jumped up and looked out at the churning waters of the Gulf of Mexico.

"Son of a bitch!" He pounded his forehead against the door-jamb. The channel would be impassable now.

The gurgling of his stomach had him clenching his jaw. He sure hoped his grandmother was still in the habit of keeping a fully stocked pantry when she passed.

They weren't going anywhere for a long time.

13

Reese sneezed as another gust of wind wafted who knew how many layers of dust into her face. Digging in her tote for a tissue, she made slow progress toward the back of the hotel. At least, she thought it was the back.

All the dark paneling wasn't helping the situation. Her hand idly grazed the woodwork as she made her way down a long hall.

A door in the paneling stubbed her finger. A cautious peek revealed nothing but darkness. Flipping the switch on the hallway wall did absolutely nothing, as expected.

Ahead of her, a faint light glowed. Heart in her throat, she fumbled in her bag for her pepper spray in case the light turned out to be their intruder. Just as her fingers closed around the coolness of the spray can, the hall opened up into a small room, weak light spilling in through the uncovered bay window.

"Are you about finished?" Ben's voice, directly behind her, startled a scream out of her. Before she could stop, she reacted. Taking a step back, as she'd been instructed, she fired the spray.

"Argh! Damn it, why'd you do that!" Ben was doubled over, making gagging sounds.

"Oh! I'm so sorry! You scared me, and I guess I just reacted." Tentatively she touched his back, but he jerked away. "Is there anything I can do to help?"

"You've done enough," he said in a raspy voice.

"I think I have some eyewash in here." Reese dug around in her bag, but she kept grabbing the wrong things.

Ben staggered to a sink she hadn't noticed on the far wall and spit, arms braced on either side of the sink, shoulders slumped. Finally he spoke without turning. "Why would I need eyewash?"

"Gee, I don't know, maybe because I sprayed pepper spray in your eyes?"

"Wrong." He straightened and wiped his mouth with the back of his hand. "You sprayed me in the mouth. And whatever it was, it wasn't pepper spray." His eyes widened. "Shit. Have I been poisoned? What did you spray me with?"

"I don't—well, I mean—" She looked down at the can clenched in her left hand. "Oh."

"Oh, what? *Oh, isn't this funny* or *oh, he's going to die*?"

"Don't be such a baby. You're not going to die."

"Because . . . ?" He advanced on her, not stopping until he'd backed her against the paneled far wall of the room.

She held up the spray can, grinning when he flinched. "Because it's just breath spray."

"So, I just have terminally fresh breath?" He leaned closer, said breath wafting over her.

With a swallow, she tried to hide her smile. No telling what kind of mood her recent mistake had him in, so she didn't want to irritate him. "Um, yeah, I guess."

"Let's check it out."

Before she could take a breath, his mouth covered hers, his cool mint breath refreshing to the heated interior of her cheeks.

Greedy for more, she opened wider. His tongue explored her teeth, her palate, before rolling with hers.

Weak in the knees, she leaned against the wall, allowing Ben to hold her up.

While he kissed her, his hands explored the contours of her face, traced her ears, stroked the sides of her neck.

Somewhere in the foggy recesses of her brain, Reese tried to remember if she'd ever been kissed as thoroughly.

Too soon, Ben began pulling back. Her greedy mouth followed, hating to lose the warmth of his kiss.

When he'd finally severed the connection, he straightened, a smile playing on his glistening lips. "I think you're safe to take off the life jacket, for now."

Crap. So lost in his kiss, she'd totally forgotten she still wore the soaked preserver.

Deciding to play it cool, she grinned at him and said, "Are you sure? You said, before, it was just rain, and it turned into a tropical storm. I'm not sure I can trust your judgment."

As though she'd slapped him, the smile left his face and he stepped back toward the hall.

"I'm going back to the boat to make sure it's secure. I have a rolling cooler, so I'll bring back some supplies."

"Supplies?"

"Food. And blankets. Maybe a flashlight or lantern. Toilet paper." At her surprised look, he laughed. "We're gonna need it sometime and I don't know about you, but I don't want to wait for that time to discover the old hotel doesn't have any."

"Good point." She cleared her throat. "Do you need any help?"

"No thanks, Blondie, but I can take that life jacket back, if you're through with it."

Ben stood in the rain for a second, gripping the soggy life jacket and allowed the rain to beat down on him.

"Stupid, stupid, stupid!" he said in a growl. Still more than half aroused, he jogged down the path toward the dock, rain sluicing down his face, obscuring his vision. What the hell had he been thinking, to kiss his meal ticket like that?

So what if he was horny? So horny, in fact, he threw all the assets that had ever attracted him to women out the window to pant after a skinny chick who obviously thought she was better than him. That was pretty fucking horny.

He grinned at his mental choice of words.

If the damn storm wasn't roaring down on them, he'd seriously consider whacking off on the boat when he went back for provisions.

And speaking of provisions . . . on deck, he threw open the door and hopped down into the cabin. The cooler was right where he put it, in the closet next to the bed. Rolling it out, he proceeded to unload the contents of his refrigerator and most of the cabinets. Grabbing his duffel, he reached into the bathroom and grabbed his toothbrush and some toothpaste. His hand hovered over the razor for a second; then he decided to leave it. Maybe a beard would keep Blondie from allowing him to get too close.

Her response to his kiss earlier flashed through his mind. She hadn't seemed to mind the growth of hair on his face.

Grabbing a box of condoms, he tossed it into the duffel. Just in case.

He may not have ever been a Boy Scout, but he liked to think he lived by their motto: "Be prepared."

14

Reese listened to the quiet of the house while the storm roared and battered the exterior of the old hotel.

Kissing Ben had been a very bad idea. Just recalling the way she'd felt in his arms made her damp. Damper than she'd been from the weather. A totally different kind of damp. And restless.

Now he was telling her they were trapped there until the storm passed. How long would that take? More important, how was she going to keep her hands and lips, not to mention other body parts, away from him?

And did she really want to do that?

"Concentrate," she whispered, making her way back to the front of the hotel, trying to decide if she wanted to go up and check out the guest rooms or wait for Ben to return.

"Ha! Assuming he actually does come back!" He'd wasted no time in hightailing it back out into the elements. What would she do if he decided to wait out the storm in the relative safety of his boat?

Testing the first stair, she decided it would hold her weight and took a cautious step. On the third step, she turned to look through the transom above the front door, hoping to catch a glimpse of Ben. All she saw was dark gray sky and rain swirling around the hotel.

Determined, she pushed onward, not stopping until she'd reached the top of the stairs. Pausing to catch her breath, she gazed down into the lobby.

It must have been quite lovely in its time, she mused. Even now, with a protective layer of dust coating everything, she could detect the glow of its well-worn plank floor. A little to her left, centered over the lobby, hung a dusty, cobweb-draped chandelier.

She squinted. It was hard to tell, with the dust encrusting the cut-glass globes, but she thought she saw lightbulbs. That meant the hotel had electricity, or did at one time. Definitely a plus.

After staring at the chandelier for a few minutes, trying to envision it cleaned up and assigning a value to it, she moved down the carpet runner of the main hallway.

The first room to her right was empty. Large, even by today's standards, she thought it would make a great guest room. Well, duh, she chastised herself, the place had been a hotel. Of course, it would have at least adequate guest rooms.

She walked into the room and turned, trying to envision it with furniture. The old rose-print area rug had definitely seen better days. A peek under one corner revealed the same beautiful hardwood floor as downstairs. Unless the floor beneath the rug had hidden damage, it wouldn't even need refinishing. Unfortunately, the closet was small, and there was no en suite bathroom. Still, it had definite potential.

Dorinda had not mentioned whether she planned for each room to have facilities or if she planned for guests to share. Reese knew B&Bs were arranged either way, so not having a bathroom for each guest wasn't necessarily a deal breaker.

Although she, personally, did not like sharing.

Thoughts of sharing reminded her of her life back home, and a wave of loneliness rushed over her.

Maybe she could get a signal upstairs. She'd tried in the little breakfast room earlier, with no luck. She dug in her tote until she found her Blackberry and held it close to the window.

No luck again. No signal.

Dropping the phone in her bag, she trudged across the hall to see an identical room to the one she'd just left. The third room was smaller, but had furnishings, so it might have just appeared smaller. As she opened the door to what she was sure was another minuscule closet, she gasped in surprise to find a full en suite bathroom, complete with a huge claw-foot tub.

A bath. She'd kill for a bath.

A glance behind her confirmed Ben had not returned, so she made her way to the tub and twisted a squeaky faucet.

Nothing happened. Not even a drop escaped the curved dusty lip.

"Well, shoot." Although she knew it was probably impossible, for a second she'd hoped she was wrong. In spite of being soaked for hours, she felt grimy and would have loved to soak in a nice, hot tub of water until she turned all wrinkly.

A bump echoed up from the lobby area. Her heart tripped, then began beating frantically.

"Lu-cy, I'm home!" Ben's irritating voice boomed up the stairway.

Taking her time, she walked to the open railing. Ben stood just inside the door, dripping on the old floor, clutching the handle of a large rolling cooler. His other hand held a duffel bag. A strap of some kind of backpack dug into his shoulder.

"I'm up here," she called down. "Do you want to come up and explore the rooms with me?"

He plopped back on the sofa he'd used earlier. "Nah, I've seen them."

"You have?"

"Um . . . . sure. When I was a kid, we came here a couple of times."

It was difficult to tell in the growing darkness, but he seemed uncomfortable.

She remembered the kiss they'd shared. Again. Maybe it was better if Ben stayed on another floor from her while she was looking at bedrooms.

Restless, she continued her inspection, determined to ignore the rub of her bra on her aching nipples—nipples that hadn't ached in a very long time.

Not until she'd met Ben Adams.

15

Ben glanced around for a spot to stash the economy-size box of condoms he'd retrieved from the boat. Of course, if he made a few more blunders like he'd almost just made, he wouldn't have to worry about it, because Blondie wouldn't let him within ten feet of her.

He paused, midsearch, to wonder if she was a natural blonde. With her fairness, she probably was, but he'd still have a hell of a good time finding out.

And, speaking of his meal ticket, why hadn't she come downstairs yet? What was taking so long?

Keeping an eye out for her shapely ass in those god-awful tropical-print Capri pants and her screaming yellow shirt, he climbed the stairs and began a search of the guest rooms.

The idea of peeling Reese out of her soggy clothes held more appeal with each step. His dick twitched, doing its version of a happy dance at the thought of ending its current dry spell.

With each step, his erection grew. Hell, he knew he should have relieved some pressure back at the boat.

Where the hell was she? It was getting more and more un-comfortable to walk.

A soft sound drew his attention.

At the end of the hall, a glance in one room revealed noth-ing.

What he saw at the next door took his breath and damn near brought him to his knees.

Reese's wet clothing lay in a pile near the door. On the old iron bed, she lay sprawled on his grandmother's old Sunbonnet Baby–patterned quilt.

She was naked.

Weak light filtered through the old window, spotlighting the erotic show taking place on the bed.

Eyes closed, Reese was pinching, rolling, and tugging her erect nipple while she pleasured herself with the other hand.

Riveted, scarcely breathing, he watched her private sex show.

The slap of her hand echoed in the quiet room. Her plump lips parted, revealing her darkening engorged labia. Her small hand stroked the glistening tissue, rubbed the clearly distended nub. Harder. Faster.

Her breath hitched, her slender back arching off the sagging mattress.

Ben grabbed the door frame to keep upright. His cock tried to escape through his zipper.

Damn it, he knew he should have stuck a condom or two in his pocket before coming upstairs.

Would it have mattered? Would Reese have been as recep-tive to his touch, as she was to her own?

He closed his eyes, breathing deeply through his nose while he fought for control.

In his mind, he saw her standing in front of him, smelled her arousal.

With a shy smile, she'd tug down his zipper and slip her small hand into his boxers to measure his length and hardness.

He'd pump in her hand and she'd lick her lips. Next thing, his shorts and underwear would be around his ankles. Reese would be kneeling in front of him, taking him into her hungry mouth.

His muscles flexed. The soft tissue at the back of her throat would caress the tip of his penis, bringing his excitement to a fever pitch.

She'd smile, pushing her more than ample breasts—and this was where he knew he was dreaming, because there was no way someone that skinny had boobs that big—to surround his cock, encouraging him to thrust between them.

Close to exploding, he'd pick her up and carry her to the bed. But before he could lay her down, she would produce silk scarves and insist he tie her to the bed first. Since he knew he was dreaming, he went for it.

Wet. She would be so hot and so wet, it would be difficult for him to stay inside.

He'd increase his pace, slapping her pelvic bone with his, with each forceful thrust. Deep inside, her canal would contract, milking him. Against his palms, the flesh of her smooth ass would quiver with her excitement.

She screamed.

And it wasn't in a good way.

She screamed again.

He opened his eyes to see Reese practically climbing the headboard, the old quilt clutched around her nudity, her eyes wide.

"What the heck do you think you're doing?" Her shriek would break the old glass in the windows if she didn't tone it down a few decibels.

"Me? I was just . . ." He noticed the direction of her horrified stare and looked down. "It's not what you think," he began, covering what remained of his dignity, as well as his erection, and pulling up his drawers. He didn't speak again, until he'd zipped his cargo shorts. "Like I said, it's not what you think. Well, okay, it probably is. But, hell, you were laying there, buck naked, getting off. What did you expect?"

Wrapping the quilt tightly around her, she took slow steps toward the pile of clothes and picked them up. Then she backed away. "How about privacy? You were downstairs. You said you didn't want to explore. How was I to know you'd sneak up here?"

"Sneak! Sneak? I walked normally up the stairs and down that hallway. I can't help it if you were so busy masturbating that you didn't hear me."

"A gentleman would not have stayed and watched." She was fumbling around under the quilt, probably trying to get dressed.

He snorted. "Like I told you before, I'm no gentleman." His grin was unrepentant. "And, admit it, you were putting on quite a show. Any red-blooded male would have watched." He made an adjustment. "For what it's worth, I liked what I saw."

She stared, then blinked a couple of times while her mouth opened and closed. "I. Don't. Care. It was an invasion of privacy."

Dressed now, she carefully replaced the quilt.

"Hey, you saw me too. I'd say that makes us even, Blondie." Damn, he was so engrossed, he forgot to check to see if she was a real blonde. There was no way she'd agree to another peek, not with the way she was glaring at him. No point in even asking.

"Yeah, I saw you." She shoved him aside as she strode from the room. "I wasn't impressed," she shot over her shoulder.

16

Chest heaving, Reese leaned against the closed bathroom door. How could she go back out and face the grinning hyena that brought her here?

Heat seared her cheeks at the memory. What on earth had she been thinking? It was so unlike anything she'd ever done. Now she knew why, and planned to never do anything like that again. *Ever.*

Not that she'd never masturbated, she had. Well, maybe once or twice. But it had been in the privacy of her own home, not in the deserted room of a dilapidated old hotel, with a stranger watching.

Her moan echoed from the tiled walls as she sank to the floor.

Now what?

She couldn't stay in the bathroom for the duration of her stay at the hotel. Her head clunked against the door. For good measure, she did it two more times. Maybe it would knock some sense into her lust-crazed brain.

Straightening her still damp-clothes, she stood. She had a job to do and, by golly, she was going to do it.

Ben watched her approach with weary eyes, straightening to his full height as she came closer. "You're not going to do anything crazy, are you, like hit me or get hysterical again?"

With a sniff, she regarded him through narrowed eyes. "I'm not the violent type, but don't push it." Walking imperiously past him, she headed for the last room, near the top of the stairs. "And I was not hysterical. You just, well, caught me by surprise."

"I'll say." He followed her at a distance, wanting so badly to add he'd caught her with her pants down. But he didn't have a death wish.

"Oh!" Her gasp had him picking up the pace, worried she may have stumbled onto something unpleasant or dangerous, like a bum or a wild animal. Yeah, it was an island, but it happened sometimes.

"What?" He skidded to a stop and bumped her farther into the room. "Sorry. What is it?"

"The room. It's beautiful." Making a slow turn, she checked it all out.

Ben had to drag his gaze from her and look at the room, hoping he could do it without her realizing he'd seen it before. Many times, in fact.

It was his grandmother's room.

The realization brought a sharp pain of loss, causing his breath to catch for a second. Briefly closing his eyes, he could smell the faint scent of the perfumed dusting powder Gram always wore. It had always reminded him of home. Of safety. Of love.

He'd been a damn fool to leave when he had, and an even bigger one to stay away for so long. His resolve tightened.

He would say anything, do anything, to keep his grandmother's island and the old hotel she loved. Anything.

Reese walked to the window seat and lowered reverently down until she sat in the very spot he'd last seen his grandmother sitting, almost five years ago. Reese looked out the window with almost exactly the same expression his grandmother had had too, which was really kind of creepy.

He cleared his throat. "Yeah, it's nice, isn't it?"

"It's more than nice," she replied in a hushed voice, "it's almost spiritual. Magical. Can't you feel the love? It's like it's pulsing in the air." She inhaled deeply and Ben zeroed in on her chest, wondering if the ample bust he'd envisioned had really been a figment of his imagination.

She had no right feeling anything in his grandmother's room. It was like Reese was violating *his* privacy.

"Blondie," he said, deliberately sounding harsh. "I think you're probably feeling aftershocks of a different kind of pulsing." The grin he flashed was as close to a leer as he could get.

She blinked. "I don't know why I bother. It's not like someone like you could possibly understand."

His eyes narrowed. "Someone like me? What the hell is that supposed to mean?" Arms crossed to keep from shaking her, he leaned against the post of the bed. "Try me." At her widening eyes, he shrugged. "Hey, I can be as touchy-feely as the next guy."

"Touchy-feely? Really?" She did an eye roll, which had him clenching his teeth.

"I was just asking you to explain. Shit, what's your problem? Is it that time of the month or something?"

Her gasp gave him a little satisfaction, he maintained, even if he did feel more than a little guilty for throwing out such a typical macho piece-of-crap line.

"Okay, I'm not even going to dignify that with an answer. You want to know what I find so special about this room? I'll tell you." Hopping up, she paced from one end of the large bedroom to the other. "Well, for one thing, it's huge. For another, the furniture is gorgeous, obviously good quality and well cared for, as well as the correct scale for the room. All of this equates to a marketable guest room."

"Cut the crap. Even I know that's not what you meant."

He watched the movements as she crossed her arms and rubbed her hands up and down her arms. Was she cold? Did he care?

"You're right," she said after a few seconds. "While those things are well and good, they're not what got to me." She shrugged, the movement causing the wet fabric of her knit shirt to pull into a peak on top of her shoulder, then stay there for a second before slowly lowering. "It's kind of hard to explain. There's a warmth in the room, almost like an aura—"

"Are you saying it's haunted?" He looked around. He hadn't thought about ghosts.

"No, nothing like that! Look how the flowers on the bedspread match the flowers on the curtains, how the color of the paint matches the background of the spread just so. It's the obvious attention to details that got to me." She ran a fingertip over the well-polished, smooth wood of Gram's dresser. "It was obviously well taken care of by the previous owner. It makes me wonder what happened to her. And, yes, before you ask, I know it was a woman. I can feel it, see it." She gave a little laugh. "I even thought I imagined I could smell her when I first walked in. The room just feels, well, I don't know how else to explain it, except it feels safe, warm, inviting. . . ."

He'd always felt that way about the hotel, this room in particular. Of course, he couldn't tell her that.

A deep breath brought the faint scent of his grandmother and a surge of regret and sadness, which almost drove him to his knees.

17

"I'm telling you, Bailey, something is wrong!" Paige threw her robe into the open suitcase on her bed and stalked to the closet. "Aren't you even worried? It's not like Reese not to call."

"Of course, I'm worried." Bailey edged to sit on the mattress, next to the suitcase. "I guess I'm just kind of surprised you are."

Walking back out of the closet, clothes draped over her arm, Paige stopped and stared. "Bailey Ryan, I can't believe you're sitting there, being so calm, when our best friend could be in trouble!"

"Yes, she could be. But, Paige, she's on an island, away from the stress of her crappy job. She could also be basking in the sun, sipping an umbrella drink. The auction isn't until next Monday. She's probably thinking she really pulled one on the Dragon Lady by convincing her she needed to go ten days ahead of time to scope it out." Bailey's smile was a tad wobbly. Truth be told, she was worried every bit as much as Paige. "Maybe we're looking at this all wrong. Think about it. Maybe

Reese would have called if she had had a problem. But maybe, just maybe, she's having too much fun to contact us."

Paige dropped the wad of clothing into her suitcase and glared. "Are you serious? Does that sound like something Reese would do? No, it does not! And you know it too, Bay." Paige gripped her shoulders and gave a little shake. "C'mon. Call in sick and come with me. I'll write a doctor's note. We can go, check on Reese, and be back in a week, two tops. And we both know two heads are better than one. It would be expedient for both of us to go." She nudged her friend. "Well?"

"Okay." Bailey sighed. "But I can't stay for more than a couple of days, a week at the most, or I'll never get caught up on my workload."

"Woo-hoo!" Paige pumped her fist in the air and gave Bailey a one-armed hug. "Sand Dollar will never be the same!"

The windowpane cooled Reese's forehead. She idly watched as her breathing made a little patch of fog.

Outside, the rain continued to pour, the wind roared, the gray sky turning darker as night approached.

Just looking at the dismal scenery made her cold, despite the warmth of the hotel. Ben had found some wood stored in an enclosure on the back porch and built a fire in every fireplace. After the smoke had cleared, it was really quite cozy.

Thought of Ben's odd expression when she'd laughingly called him a Boy Scout for being so prepared made her a little uneasy. Why would he have such a strange reaction to being compared to a Boy Scout? It didn't make sense.

Unless he was really a serial killer.

Or a serial rapist.

Or both.

Heart hammering, she looked down, scanning the area around

the hotel for an escape route or somewhere to hide out, if needed, until she could be rescued.

Rescued. Yeah, like that was going to happen. Rick had been adamant that Ben was her only transportation.

Maybe Rick was in on it.

And, if so, what about his wife?

"Get a grip, Parker," she muttered, squinting through the drips coursing down the outside windowpane. What was orange down there? Scanning as far into the overgrowth as she could see in the dwindling light, she made out several more orange spots, reflecting the low light. Must be some kind of plant, either the flowers or the leaves turning for the impending fall season.

"Hey, Blondie!" Ben's voice echoed in the empty hotel hall. "Did you fall asleep up there?" Pause. "Or did you decide to finish what you started earlier?" There was a definite laugh in his voice.

Great. Now she had to listen to his stupid sexual innuendo all night.

"Very funny," she said as she descended the stairs. "I was just looking out at the weather."

"Oh, yeah?" he looked back from poking at the logs in the gigantic fireplace in the lobby. "And?"

"And nothing." She joined him by the fire. "It's still raining with no sign of letting up." She took in the glow of the room. "Where did you find all the candles?"

"Same place I found the matches. Most of them were in the big drawer in the back room. But there are candles and matches scattered all over the place, in just about every drawer you open."

"Hmm." She grinned up at him. "Must have been owned by Boy Scouts. Get it? Because they're so prepared?"

"Yeah, I get it. And I wish you'd drop the Boy Scout references."

"Why? What do you have against Boy Scouts?"

"Nothing! Just drop it."

"Ooh. Touchy, touchy. I'm hungry," she announced. "I have some snacks in my tote bag. Want to share?"

"Thanks, but I found a bunch of canned food out back. Thought we could heat it over the fire."

After they'd dined on green beans, cured pork chops, and sauerkraut, Ben heaved a sigh. Leaning back against the couch cushions they'd stacked by the fire, he rubbed his full belly.

"That was pretty good."

"Yes, it was—maybe you really were a Boy Scout." He cut her a look. "Sorry. I'll try to refrain. So . . ." She looked around the dark room. "Now what?"

"Now we heat water to wash the dishes."

"How?" She stood and followed close behind as he made his way toward the kitchen, carrying the candle.

"Same way we heated our dinner."

"But—oh, sorry," she said when she bumped into him as he stopped to set the candleholder on the table. "What I meant was how are you getting the water? I tried a faucet and it didn't work. I assumed there was no running water in the whole place."

"And you assumed right, Grasshopper." Grabbing her wrist, he led her toward the back door. "Watch and learn."

Digging in her heels, she tugged. "I don't want to go out in the rain again! I'm just now drying out."

"No problem." He struck a match and lit another candle, this one on the ledge by the back door. "There's a pump on the back porch." He arched an eyebrow. "The enclosed back porch."

"But there's no power—"

"Not necessary. It's not an electric pump."

She watched as he poured a small amount of water in and primed the chipped red-painted old pump attached to a tin sink on an obviously homemade counter. To her right stood two wringer-type washing machines. "I wonder if that's how they did the laundry for the hotel."

"What?" He glanced over his shoulder. "Oh, yeah. I mean, I guess."

He finished filling a bucket and lifted it with a grunt. "Grab that candle and close the door for me, will you?"

They made slow progress, avoiding most of the sloshing from the bucket.

"There's some dishwashing liquid in that cabinet, grab it and squirt some in," he said. When she turned questioning eyes on him, he forced a small smile. "I checked stuff out while you were upstairs earlier."

After she'd added the liquid, he set the bucket on the table. "I'm going to fill another one to rinse the dishes in. We can heat them at the same time."

"How?"

"There's a pot rack in the big fireplace in the lobby. You can hang two things at the same time. Didn't you watch when I cooked?"

"Um, I guess I didn't pay much attention." That would be because she'd been too busy watching his butt.

"Now what are you doing?"

Looking back from the bay window, she frowned. "I'm trying to get a signal. I need to make some calls."

"Who do you need to call?"

"My friends Paige and Bailey. I know they're probably worried about me. I haven't talked to them since right after I checked in yesterday."

"Blondie, you're in the middle of nowhere. Hard as it is to believe, there isn't any signal of any kind. You didn't notice a television. There's a reason for that."

"But what did people do if there was an emergency? Smoke signals?"

He paused and pumped the second bucket of water, then turned to answer. "I don't know," he lied. "There's a good-size dock. They probably had boats someone could take to get help or go to the doctor or hospital. What's your problem? Is it so difficult for you to go without modern conveniences for a day or two?"

She straightened and glared at him. "If you can do it, I can do it."

Oh, yeah, it was turning out to be an interesting night.

18

All conversation stopped when Paige and Bailey walked into the restaurant of the Sand Dollar Inn.

"Two?" A smiling woman in her midthirties with dark hair walked up to the hostess stand and picked up some menus.

"Yes!" Bailey shoved past Paige, then looked back apologetically. "After the ordeal to get here from the airport, I'm starving!"

That caught the woman's attention. "You wouldn't, by chance, have a reservation here?"

Paige nodded. "Yes, I'm Dr. Benvent. I reserved a double. This is—"

"Ms. Ryan?" The woman was looking flustered. "I don't understand. I sent Rick to pick you up hours ago. Where is he?"

"Right here," Rick said as he walked up behind Paige. "I had a little car trouble. Then it took me a while to find them, since they were wandering around. Looking for me, I suppose." He took a deep breath and patted his stomach. "But we're here now and I'm ready to eat."

"Since when do you pull the *doctor card*?" Bailey whispered as they followed their hostess.

"Since I'm tired and ready to leave this Podunk place before we've even seen our room, much less found Reese." She shrugged. "I figured it wouldn't hurt and maybe we might possibly get faster and better service. You did say you were starving."

As the woman showed them to a table by the window with a great view of the water, people began resuming their meals and conversations.

Well, most of them did.

"Paige," Bailey said in a whisper, leaning across the linen tablecloth, "I think the guy over in the corner is checking you out."

"How do you know he's not checking *you* out?" Paige continued staring at the menu. She'd noticed the man, all right, as soon as she'd entered the dining room. What living, breathing, heterosexual woman wouldn't?

"Um, because he's staring directly at you." She nudged Paige's menu. "Maybe he'll ask to join you," she said in an excited voice.

Paige took a deep breath, closed her menu, then blinked at Bailey. "Ri-ight. And then he'll let me strip him and fuck him, right here on the table." Bailey gasped, eyes wide. "Oh, come on, Bay, like any of that's going to happen."

"I'd have to insist you buy me a drink first," a smooth, deep voice drawled from directly behind Paige.

She swallowed and glared at Bailey.

"It's him, isn't it?"

Bailey nodded, her wild red hair flying around her head like living flames.

A heavy finger tapped Paige's shoulder. "I'm right here and I can hear you."

Shit.

She closed her eyes briefly. No point in prolonging things.

Turning in the padded chair, she looked up, way up, at the man standing next to her chair.

Well, it would not do for her to remain seated, allowing him the dominant position, would it?

After carefully folding her napkin, she stood and extended her hand.

"I suppose," she said with a small smile—which was absolutely not a flirtatious one, despite what Bailey may try to claim later—"if we're going to do that, we should introduce ourselves. I'm Dr. Benvent."

His big, warm hand was dry and slightly rough when it enveloped hers and gave it a hearty shake.

"Oh, yeah? A gen-u-ine doctor?" He flashed a blazing smile that was cleary as phony as it was white. "Well, golly. Imagine that."

She ground her teeth, carefully maintaining her smile. Something about the look in the hunk's eyes told her he was making fun of her.

She hated when that happened.

"And you are . . . ?" Thank goodness she finally managed to find her voice.

"Oh, pardon, ma'am." He pumped her hand again, tightening his grip when she attempted to disengage her hand. "I'm Brett McAllister." He leaned closer, his full golden brown eyelashes framing sparkling green eyes. "But you can call me *Doctor* McAllister, if you'd like."

"Paige, he's a doctor too!" Bailey gushed inanely.

After shooting her friend a look, she returned to gazing into Dr. Dreamy's eyes for a second before giving herself a mental shake. "Yes, I heard," she told Bailey, without breaking the all-important eye contact. Or the handshake. "I'm an internist. What type of doctor are you, Dr. McAllister?" Probably a veterinarian.

She noted a faint flush on his clean-shaven cheeks.

"Got me." He spoke in a less hick-sounding voice and grinned. "Oh, I'm a doctor, but it's a Ph.D."

"Ah." She nodded. "I see. What type of doctorate?"

That grin was back, in full wattage. The grin that made her weak in the knees. And damp in other spots she'd prefer not thinking about at that particular moment.

The rough pad of his thumb caressed the back of her hand. Her pulse raced.

"Animal husbandry," he said in a low, intimate voice. A voice so smooth, it made her mouth water. It made her nipples harden.

"Have y'all decided what you'd like?" The woman was back, pen poised over her pad. "Oh, hi, Brett. Are you going to be joining the ladies tonight?"

Under his breath, in a voice so low only Paige could detect it, he murmured, "Define *joining.*"

Paige jerked her hand away and reclaimed her seat. With a flourish, she picked up her menu. But instead of the daily specials and other tempting items, all she could see was an image of her and Brett, naked, writhing on the linen tablecloth.

She slammed the menu shut and looked up at him in horror.

He had the nerve to wink as he pulled a chair over and sat down.

"I believe I will, Rita, if that's okay?" Bailey nodded her agreement, despite Paige's meaningful kick under the table.

"Ouch." Brett frowned at her.

She bared her teeth in what she hoped passed for a repentant smile. Then again, what did she really care?

After they'd given their orders, Brett rubbed his big hands together and grinned at Paige. "Well, Doc, what do you think? Should we wait until after dessert or just fornicate right here while we wait?"

19

Dishes done and put away, Reese and Ben sat by the fire while the storm continued to rage.

"I haven't noticed any leaks," Reese said, "how about you?"

Damn well better not be any leaks. He'd spent the better part of a summer replacing the roof a few years back. "Nope."

He yawned and stretched, lowering his arm to rest on her shoulders. Not very original, but it pleased him to see she didn't shirk him off.

For show, he rubbed her upper arm. "Still cold?"

"No, I'm really comfortable. Why?"

"Well, if you haven't found any leaks and you are comfortable, I think we can agree it's safe to remove the life jacket now."

"What? Oh! Well, I just wanted to be prepared, you know, in case there was a flash flood or something."

He regarded her for a moment, hoping she wasn't going to make another Boy Scout reference. The condoms he'd stashed under the cushions made him feel guilty, which was stupid. "If we had a flash flood up here, a life jacket wouldn't help you."

Reese unbuckled the vest and he helped her take it off. "I guess I don't need it now." Their gazes met. "I have to be honest. I thought it would work as protection. You know," she continued when he just stared at her, "an added barrier between us? After what happened?" She pointed upward.

"I told you I wouldn't bring that up again. Didn't you believe me?"

"Well, yes, I guess. It's just that, well, we're the only ones here. Anything could happen. . . ."

"Oh!" Paige's teeth clicked against Brett's as he slammed her against the wall of her hotel room. His hand snaked beneath her skirt and tugged until he'd stripped off her thong and tossed it aside.

For that brief second pause in the action, she was eminently grateful to Bailey for deciding to get her own room.

Then Brett was back, shoving her skirt up around her waist, his hardness bucking against her eager wetness as he bumped her against the cool plaster of the wall.

"Strip," she demanded in a hoarse whisper. "I want to watch every inch as it's bared for my pleasure."

Sure, she'd used that line a few times. And it had always worked with predictable success. Men loved to feel lusted after, and were only too happy to play stripper for her.

Of course, she'd never been with anyone like Brett.

He paused and looked down at her, the soft glow from the hallway doing amazing things for his chiseled features.

He stepped away and closed her door, then flipped the lock.

More turned-on than she could remember being in recent years, she struggled to maintain her breathing as he slowly stalked toward her, his green eyes glowing with intent.

"You first," he said in a low voice that stroked her senses and made her wet. Wetter.

Without waiting or asking for permission, he pulled her to

him for another carnal kiss she felt all the way to the soles of her now-bare feet.

The zipper of her skirt echoed in the quiet, the only sound in the room except their labored breathing.

The skirt fell to the floor.

Before she could step out of it, he lifted her with one iron-muscled arm around her waist.

With his free hand, he unbuttoned her blouse, then pushed it from her shoulders, where she shrugged it off.

Her bra was next and he popped open the front closure with an obviously experienced hand. Tugging it down, he tossed it aside.

Hanging from his arm, naked, she was at a definite disadvantage. Just as she was about to try to form the words to say something, anything, his hot breath fanned her nipple.

Immediately his heat encompassed her breast as he sucked greedily, not stopping until he had it and the upper part of her breast deep in the wet heat of his mouth.

Shocked, she almost came then and there.

Locking her legs around his lean waist, she rubbed her aching center shamelessly against the hard ridge on the front of his jeans.

He switched his attention to the other nipple and she whimpered.

Desperate to get closer, she clawed at his shoulder, tearing at his shirt until the buttons gave way.

With a growl of frustration, she pushed at the shirt.

He lumbered to the bed and placed her on the mattress, following her down, never relinquishing her nipple. Worrying it with his teeth, he removed his shirt and dropped it to the soft carpet on the floor.

His mouth left her. Temporarily. Before she could utter a protest, he shucked his pants and, naked, climbed fully onto the bed. As he moved toward her, he pushed her knees back until they hugged her ears, exposing her completely.

She knew she should be embarrassed, she thought, as the cooler air of the room fanned her wetness. After all, they were basically strangers. But she found she couldn't work up that particular emotion. All she felt was sexy, erotic, potentially orgasmic pleasure.

The next thought gave her pause.

It felt right.

Then Brett lowered his head and softly blew against her exposed flesh, sending ripples of pleasure coursing through her body, puckering her nipples.

The first swipe of his tongue made her jerk. The whisper of his breath as he again blew on her wetness made her muscles vibrate with pleasure. As a physician, she knew it was physically impossible to die from sexual pleasure. Then his tongue probed her and she forgot to think for a long time.

20

When Reese returned from brushing her teeth, she saw Ben had made a pallet in front of the fire.

"What are you doing?" She tried to keep her tone of voice neutral. After all, she was more attracted to Ben than she'd been to anyone in a very long time. And she was horny.

And she'd seen him naked.

Well, okay, not technically naked. Just his erection. But, despite what she'd said, it had been pretty dang impressive. Or else she was desperate. Or both.

"Find everything okay?" Instead of answering her, like a normal person, he looked at the fire.

"All I needed was some water. There was plenty in the pail by the sink. Would you like to borrow some of my toothpaste?" On the off chance they kissed again, she wouldn't mind not tasting beer.

"Already did." He flashed a smile. "Thanks. I used my own toothbrush, in case you were wondering."

"No, I—really. When did you do that?"

"While you were upstairs covering the furniture."

Sinking to sit next to him, she resisted the temptation to snuggle against him. It wasn't like they were on a date or anything. Heck, they didn't even particularly like each other.

"I still don't know why you insisted on doing that," he grumbled, leaning back on his elbows.

"We're not one hundred percent sure the roof doesn't leak. I'd hate for the furniture to get ruined. Besides," she said as she pulled one of the quilts over her and settled into the soft bedding, "I was the one who uncovered everything. I felt sort of obligated to replace the dustcovers."

He grunted in reply and lay down, hands behind his head, to stare at the ceiling.

The fire crackled and popped. Outside, the rain continued to pelt the hotel. Reese could hear the steady stream of water running down the ancient drainpipes. Try as she might to ignore the urge, it became impossible.

"Ben?"

"Hmm?"

"Do you think the toilets work?"

A rude-sounding laugh escaped him. "Not damn likely. You told me you tried the faucets. No water means no water, Blondie. Anywhere." He rolled to his side and looked down at her. "Oh! I get it. You have to go." He shrugged. "There's an old outhouse out back."

"But it's raining. And dark."

"I brought some flashlights. Aw, hell, come on." He stood and pulled her to her feet. "I'll go with you and carry the flashlight. You can hold a blanket over your head."

"What do you mean, you'll go with me? I don't think so, mister! I don't know how they do things in Sand Dollar, but I do not use coed toilet facilities!"

His laughter echoed in the lobby. "Relax. I'll wait my turn. Or use a tree while you're in the outhouse."

Her shudder earned another laugh.

* * *

The rain seemed louder by the back door. They stood, poised on the back porch, protected from the worst of the rain by the overhang of the roof.

Despite the urgency she felt, she hesitated. "I think it's raining harder."

Beneath their quilt, she felt his shoulders shrug. "Doesn't really matter. If you gotta go, you gotta go." He flicked on the large flashlight he held in his right hand and circled her shoulder closer with his left arm. "C'mon, let's get this over with so we can get some sleep."

"Are you sure that's the place?" Holding back, he halfway dragged her down the stairs.

"Pretty sure."

Cold, wet clumps of grass tickled her ankles as she stumbled along, trying to keep up with his longer strides. At least, she hoped it was grass.

"Here," he said when they stopped in front of a door of a building the size of a large shed. "You take the flashlight. I'll wait here."

Praying she didn't find anything that wasn't supposed to be in there, Reese eased open the creaky door of the old outhouse. It didn't smell fresh, but probably because it hadn't been used in many years. It didn't smell as foul as she'd anticipated either.

"Snakes," she said in a loud whisper, "I'm coming in. I just need to use the, um, facilities, and then I'll be out of your way. Okay?"

"Who the hell are you talking to?" Ben threw open the door, causing her to jump and scream. Rain pelted her face.

"Snakes," she answered, casting the flashlight beam around to make sure she was alone.

"Quit clowning around. There are no snakes. Now hurry up!"

The door banged shut. The beam of the light touched on the

plank walls. Someone had actually tried to decorate the outhouse at one time, as was evidenced by the framed pictures hanging from nails. The wood of the actual facility was sanded smooth and varnished, with somewhat modern toilet seats on the holes. From the high ceiling hung a single lightbulb and she wondered if the former owners had used it for the servants.

Were those voices she heard in the distance?

Bang, bang, bang!

She shrieked and dropped her flashlight.

"Hey, Blondie! Did you fall in?" Ben's strident voice set her teeth on edge as she crawled to retrieve her light.

"No! Don't you dare open that door! I'll be right out."

She bit back a smile a few minutes later when she noticed he beat tracks to get into the outhouse. So much for his macho talk about using trees. Although she'd love to run back inside, she pulled the quilt closer and waited. It was only fair, since he'd waited for her.

A little blooming bush by the corner caught her attention. Closer inspection failed to reveal the identity of the flower. No surprise. She'd never been big on horticulture. Still, it was pretty and smelled nice. Sort of like honeysuckle.

Casting the beam ahead, she made her way around the outhouse, checking for other flowers. Maybe she could pick some and put them in a vase. Surely, a hotel would have vases. If not, she knew the cabinets were well stocked with glassware. She could always use a glass . . .

The spot of orange she'd seen from the upstairs window snagged her attention and she walked toward it.

The next second, her foot connected with nothing but air. Before she could scream, she was waist deep in a hole. Her ankle throbbed, and if she hadn't cut her knee, she was sure it was pretty badly scraped.

Oh, ick. Mud closed in on her, oozing around her hips, slithering up her pants legs.

At least, she hoped it was mud slithering up her pants.

The outhouse door banged against the exterior wall. Ben rounded the corner, his flashlight beam bouncing crazily.

"Reese!" His voice boomed over the rain and rumbling thunder. The lightning immediately followed, making the area bright as day for a few seconds. "Damn!" He ran to where she was mired down in the wet, smelly mud. "Are you okay?"

"Do I look okay?" Dang, she sounded bitchy. "I'm sorry. I didn't mean to snap. It's just that I was already cold and wet and generally miserable, and then I fell in this stupid hole."

He shone the beam around. "Wonder what the hole's from?"

"How the heck would I know? I'm cold and muddy. And I need help getting out of here. Could we possibly continue this discussion inside, by the fire?"

"You're not planning to track all this mud into the hotel, are you?" Even as he asked, he tugged her arm, slowly releasing her from the sucking mud.

"Wait! It ate my shoe!"

"Leave it. We'll come back out when it gets light and find it."

"But it will be all muddy—"

"It's not going to get much muddier."

"Oh. Good point. What about the quilt? I really hate to leave it out here in the elements."

He picked it up and held it at arm's length while it dripped mud as they walked. "I'll hang it on the rail on the back porch. Now what are you doing?"

Jaw clamped to keep her teeth from chattering, she turned her face toward the torrential rain. "Trying to get most of the mud off before I go in."

No doubt, Reese Parker would be the death of him. He watched rain sluice over her, slicking the clothing to her like brightly colored shrink-wrap. He felt his own clothing begin to tighten in certain areas.

What was she thinking? Was she deliberately teasing him? A man could only take so much in one day.

Of course, what he'd really like to do would be to strip them both, and rub up and down on each other in the rain until they were both clean. And so primed they were ready to fuck in the mud.

Undoubtedly, Ms. Parker would not share or appreciate his idea.

"Quit fooling around and get inside." Damn, that sounded harsh. "Reese, I don't think you really want to be standing out in this storm like that." When she looked at him, he added, "You're making the perfect lightning rod."

By the way her eyes widened, he knew the second his words sank in.

Slipping and sliding, she scrambled to the back porch.

"I didn't even think about that!" Eyes wide, she stared up at him, her teeth lightly chattering.

"Let's get you inside so you can warm up." He was pleased he sounded sincere and concerned. It was really a miracle ... considering he only had eyes for her nipples as they made intriguing little tents in her wet knit shirt.

21

"Oh-oh-oh!" Paige gripped the bedspread, holding on. Brett had her bent over the footboard of the iron bed in her room at the Sand Dollar Inn and was currently pounding into her from behind. Her breasts jiggled, tickling her ribs. Brett's sack slapped her engorged clitoris with each powerful thrust.

She wiggled back as much as possible, wanting more, on sensory overload.

When Brett proved ready for round two, almost as soon as they caught their breath from easily the most orgasmic sex she'd experienced to date, she'd briefly wondered if he'd somehow gotten hold of Viagra. But something told her the stud servicing her so enthusiastically and creatively was all natural. No doubt about it, country boys knew things. Things no one in her vast experience had seemed to know.

Reese crossed Paige's mind, and she wondered if her friend was experiencing multi-orgasms too.

Then Brett's talented fingers reached around to find her nub and tugged on it, and she forgot about everything but the here and now.

* * *

"If you want to finish rinsing off and maybe rinse your clothes, I can pump a couple of buckets of water for you," Ben offered, slamming the back door against the elements. When she looked back at him in obvious surprise, he shrugged. "The bathtub drains still work. I figure you can pour the water down the drain when you're done."

She nodded. "Thanks. That would be great. Does it matter which bathroom I use?"

"The room you used earlier," he said, biting back a grin when she averted her eyes, "has the biggest bathroom. There should be plenty of towels in the cabinet next to the tub."

On the third stair up, she turned, making her peaked nipple right at his eye level. "How do you know that?"

Shit. How did he know that? Probably because that's where his grandmother had always kept towels. But he couldn't tell her. "Ah, I looked around before." He winked and smiled. "While you were otherwise occupied."

She reacted exactly as he'd expected. "Bring the water up there, then."

He watched her flounce up the stairs, intrigued by the slight jiggle, as well as the way the printed fabric lovingly hugged the globes of her sweet ass.

"Yes, ma'am." When she'd disappeared, he made his way down the hall to the back porch. "Cool down, buddy, or you'll be able to carry one of those pails without using your hand."

As soon as Reese heard Ben enter the back porch, she scurried back down the stairs to grab a candle. When she'd made her grand exit, she'd forgotten all about the lack of electricity.

The storm was louder upstairs. Despite heat rising, it was noticeably cooler, as well.

She picked up the pace. In the bathroom, she set the candle on the little chest by the window. Just as Ben had said, there were about six towels neatly folded in the tall cabinet at the end of the tub. She extracted a fluffy white one, then paused.

Now what? She couldn't very well strip and wait for Ben to bring the water. Sure, he'd already seen her totally naked, thanks to her earlier uncharacteristically stupid impulse.

The very thought of what Ben saw brought a heated blush to her neck and cheeks.

Wait. It was a hotel. A fairly nice hotel. It wouldn't have been unusual for it to have robes for its guests.

A fairly thorough search of the room yielded nothing. The few ladies' garments she'd found in the drawers looked like they'd belonged to an old lady. Not only were they not Reese's style, there was something... personal about them that was off-putting. Who would have stayed at a hotel and left intimate items of clothing?

A knock on the bedroom door interrupted her musings.

Before she could open the door, it opened and Ben walked in, carrying two sloshing buckets of water. He strode past her and set them on the tile of the bathroom with a clunk.

He was clean and his hair was standing in wet spikes. Obviously, he'd taken a few minutes to bathe.

Rotating his broad shoulders, he looked at her. "You don't realize how heavy water is until you try carrying two bucketfuls up a flight of stairs."

He pulled the floral shower curtain around the claw-foot tub. "Go ahead. Get in."

"Excuse me? I don't need you to bathe me, thank you very much." She narrowed her eyes. "That's your cue to leave."

"Oh, get over yourself, lady." Narrowing his eyes, he glared right back. "I planned to pour the water over the shower curtain for you, but if you'd rather do it yourself, be my guest." Turning on his heel, he started for the door.

"Wait!" She stopped him with her hand on his arm, ignoring his body heat. "I'm sorry. I misunderstood. Please. Stay. I'd appreciate it if you'd pour the water." She stepped into the tub and drew the curtain, then peered out. "You won't peek, will you?"

"Believe it or not, not everybody is hot to jump your bones. Besides not being my type, you're too skinny for my taste. Relax. You're safe."

Nodding, she shut the curtain again.

Even though he could hear the storm continuing to rage, the wind roaring, the rain pelting the windows, he could have sworn he also heard the unmistakable sound of Reese Parker taking off her clothes.

Damn, he really didn't want to hear that.

"Okay, I'm ready," she said from behind the curtain.

Pulling the little chair his grandmother had called her slipper chair to the side of the tub, he climbed up with the first bucket of water.

Her little gasp when the cold water hit gave him a perverse sense of satisfaction. He stepped down to get the second bucket.

At that moment, lightning stuck, illuminating the room. Through the thin shower curtain, he had a perfect view of Reese's silhouette. Her naked silhouette.

His cock sprang to full attention.

Before he drew his next breath, he'd stripped and was reaching for the curtain edge, the bucket in his other hand.

He figured he could always use the galvanized bucket to ward off her attack, should she take offense.

"Faint heart ne'er won fair maiden. . . ."

His grandmother's words ran through his mind.

That may be the case, Gram, he told her silently, *but this particular fair maiden may beat me until my heart actually stops.*

22

Reese jumped when cool air, even cooler than the air in the enclosure, swirled around her wet torso.

Another flash of lightning illuminated the Greek god climbing into the old tub with her.

Her mouth went dry while other parts of her anatomy grew moist.

Did she want to turn him away? Despite their differences, he was sweet and kind and funny. Not to mention smoking hot. It had been a long, dry spell, sexually, for her. But she knew she should probably pass on whatever he was offering.

She just wasn't sure if she had the willpower.

Ben actually looked stunned as he visually swept her body, as though he didn't know what to do next or where to focus his eyes.

"Ah, I'm, I mean . . ." He swallowed. "Need any help?"

Well, that was a unique opening line.

"I thought that's what you were doing, Ben, by pouring water for me." She narrowed her eyes. "From the other side of the shower curtain. What made you change your mind?"

As much as she tried to force her gaze upward, she just couldn't help it. Her eyes had a will of their own. And they were intently cataloging Ben's . . . assets.

Suddenly big hands blocked her view.

"I'm sorry," he said, backing to the edge of the tub. "I didn't mean to—well, okay, I did mean to, but I won't."

"Ben, you're babbling." Regardless of his discomfort, she refused to cover her nudity. He was the one who had barged in on her shower—he deserved to be embarrassed. It also gave her a small thrill of pleasure to note his body had a definite positive reaction to hers.

"Yeah, I know." He glared at her as he lifted his foot to step out of the tub. "I—shit!"

One second he was starting to step over the lip of the tub, the next instant his big bare feet were in the air. His hands left their modesty protection and his arms flailed.

"Ben!" She grabbed for his arm, his leg, anything, to stop the progress of his fall.

Somehow they became tangled in the floral shower curtain, ripping it from its hooks to land in a heap of wet skin, tangled limbs, and exerted breathing.

"Ow."

"What do you mean, *ow*? You fell on top of me! You may have broken my tooth with your hard head." Ben shifted and she had to quickly grab hold of his warm chest to keep from falling to the tile.

"Shit-fire-spit, woman! Let go of my chest hair!"

Shifting again, she felt his entire body stiffen.

"Your knee," he gasped, "move your knee. Easy!" He sucked in air through his teeth, which, now that she looked at them, looked perfectly fine.

Easing off the intriguing warmth of his body, she pulled on the shower curtain until she could wrap it around her nudity.

Spread-eagle on the floor, Ben's chest rose and fell with his labored breathing while his hands massaged his wounded . . . masculinity.

She really had to bite her tongue to keep from offering to take over that particular duty.

For some reason, she got the impression Ben was probably not in the mood anymore.

"Let's forget about all this and just try to get some sleep, okay?" Suddenly tired, she tugged at the sagging shower curtain, kicking it out from under her feet as she walked out of the bathroom. "Does it matter which bedroom I use?"

Behind her, she heard the unmistakable sound of Ben getting to his feet and moving around in the bathroom.

She waited until she'd heard the echo of his zipper before turning to face him.

The look of obvious sexual hunger on his face was almost her undoing. She could so identify with what he was feeling.

If she were Paige, she'd already be horizontal with her hunky guide. But Paige had always been way more adventurous than either Reese or Bailey. Unfortunately.

"None." Ben's gruff reply stymied her.

Before she could question him, he said, "I don't want to waste our firewood by keeping more than one fireplace going. We may need it if the storm stalls out for a while."

"Stalls out?"

He nodded. "Yeah, you know, stalls, as in hangs over the island before it moves on. Storms have been known to do that." He closed his hand around her wrist and tugged her past the dustcover-clad bed toward the door to the hallway. "We better stick to my original plan of sleeping in front of the fire in the lobby. It'll be warmer and conserve wood." He paused again at the door and looked down at her, his expression clear of any remaining lust. In fact, she had no idea what he was thinking. If anything.

"I don't suppose you brought any clothes in your magic bag?"

Straightening, she tugged her arm from his grasp. "Actually, I did. I have some clean underwear—"

"Great. Me too. Let's go put it on and try to get some sleep."

After a second of standing with her mouth hanging open, she trotted to catch up with him as he headed for the stairs.

"Wait just a minute! Are you telling me you expect us to sleep together in just our underwear?" True, most underwear covered more than the average bathing suit. Why—oh, why— had she allowed Paige to talk her into buying those stupid thong panties?

"Our clothes are wet and still kind of muddy," he shot back over his shoulder as he made his descent. "There's no point in getting the quilts and blankets all messed up. Especially since we have no way of cleaning them and don't know how long we'll be stuck here."

"Oh. Good point." Dang, she hated when that happened.

Standing by the warmth of the fire, she watched Ben rummage in his big bag, waiting until he'd left the room to get her clean undies out of her own tote. Casting a nervous eye toward the closed door of the hall, she quickly changed and scooted under the warm covers.

Ben gently banged his head against the door frame. In spite of standing in the darkened hall, with no heat, in nothing but his boxer briefs, he felt on fire. And he wasn't sure there was a damned thing he could do about it.

He peeked through the crack in time to see the shapely creamy white ass of his meal ticket as she bent to step into her panties.

He squinted his eyes, trying to determine if she was smooth all over.

The leopard-print thong had his cock springing with renewed interest.

For a few seconds, he admired the slight jiggle of her buttocks.

"Well, shit," he whispered. The industrial-strength sports bra she'd pulled on negated the sexiness of the panties. Who dressed like that? Why couldn't she have a sexy bra that matched the thong?

Reaching down, he squeezed his erection. Hard. Grabbing a towel from the butler's pantry, he wrapped it around his waist and made his way into the lobby.

Thankful when she turned her back to him, he dropped the towel and slid beneath the covers, not stopping until he felt her body heat.

The smooth skin of her butt grazed him, causing him to jerk back.

She looked back at him, over her shoulder. "Is it okay that I hung my clothes on the edge of the hearth to dry? You don't think it's too close to the fire, do you? Or do you think I should move them? I—"

"Hush." He put his hand over her mouth. "I haven't had time to answer your first question. Can you be quiet for a minute and let me answer?"

She nodded and he eased his hand away, thankful she hadn't bitten him.

He glanced at the fire. Her clothes were hung far enough from the flames to not be in danger.

"Faint heart ne'er won fair maiden. . . ."

He scooted a little closer.

She didn't move or protest. He considered it a good sign.

Slow and easy, he dragged the tip of his index finger up her bare arm.

She didn't scream and jerk away, or, worse, grab and break his finger. Another good sign.

Encouraged, he leaned to brush his lips on the cap of her shoulder.

A little shudder was her only reaction.

He placed a little kiss at the base of her neck. Then he kissed his way to her ear. "Your clothes are fine where they are," he whispered, then stuck his tongue in her ear.

She gasped and jerked, her bony elbow firmly connecting with his right eye.

"Shit! Why did you do that?" Rolling to his back, he held his injured socket.

"Oh, Ben!" She was leaning over him, her soft breasts squished against his forearm. "I'm sorry! You startled me! And I'm ticklish. Move your hand so I can see if I did any damage."

"No." He drew in a deep breath and let it out slowly. "I'm okay."

Reese chewed her lower lip. No doubt about it, she wasn't cut out for wild, spontaneous—much less, uninhibited—sex.

Ben's kisses had felt nice. Good. More than good. She must be really hard up if someone who obviously didn't like her, who had been rude to her ever since they first met, only had to kiss her arm and neck to turn her on.

She'd never done an impulsive thing in her life. It was just her and Ben in the old hotel. No one would ever know if she decided to take a walk on the wild side.

Unless Ben told. He didn't seem like the type, but then, she had no idea what kind of guy would kiss and tell.

Did she have the nerve to find out?

Why not?

She started by placing tiny kisses on his cheekbone, then made her way to the hand covering his eye. Prying his finger back, she playfully looked through to his eye.

"Let me see if I gave you a black eye," she whispered. "At least, give me the chance to kiss it and make it better."

"How do I know you won't punch me again?"

She would have taken offense, but she saw the smile tugging on his full lips. "You're just going to have to trust me," she said in the softest, sexiest voice she could muster.

He moved his hand. Before she could blink, it was cupping her bottom.

On his side, now, facing her, he said, "I like your underwear." He ran his finger under the back strap. Up and down. Up and down. Ever so slowly.

She swallowed. "Thanks."

"I vote, to conserve our meager clothing, you just wear this while we're on the island." When she stiffened to keep from rubbing against the erection poking at her, he hurried on. "You're pretty pale. Think of the tan you could get."

"True, I'm pale, but it's raining, Ben. Wearing a thong won't help me get a tan. Nice try." She grazed the tip of his nose with her teeth. "Any other reason I should do that?"

He pretended to think. "Okay, how about just inside? You can wear clothes outside."

In answer, she reached down and snapped the elastic at his waist. "What about you?"

"Me? I'm willing to negotiate," he said against her lips as his mouth descended.

For a few seconds, she couldn't remember to breathe, all she could do was feel.

His lips were warm and soft against hers. She opened wider and their tongues danced an intimate tango.

He gathered her close. She could feel the beating of his heart against her ribs. Their breath mingled.

His slight stubble rubbed against her chin as the kiss went on and on. She knew, with her fairness, she'd have razor burn the next morning, but it was a risk she was willing to take.

Ben tugged on her sports bra, his fingers roaming, pushing and pulling against the solid elastic. Finally he pushed his hand under the wide band on the bottom, not stopping until he cupped her bare breast, the sports bra wadded up around her armpits.

The pressure of his hand when he squeezed felt like heaven. She did a little happy dance up and down the ridge pushing against her pelvis.

He groaned, his big hands circling her ribs to push her higher and higher until his mouth closed over her aching nipple.

With a blissful gasp, she arched her back, pushing her breast deeper into his mouth.

His free hand smoothed down her stomach, circled her hip, petted her thigh, not stopping until his finger slid under the wet centerpiece of her thong to pet her excitement.

"Take this off," he said in a growl against her breast. He pushed on her sports bra.

She reluctantly eased away from his intimate touch to sit back on her heels, pulling the bra over her head and flinging it away.

The room immediately brightened. She turned and gasped to see her bra going up in flames in the fireplace.

"Forget it," he said, massaging her breasts with both hands as he pulled her back to him. "I like you much better like this, anyway."

What the heck. Her bra was history now.

Lowering down to his waiting mouth, she all but purred when he drew her nipple back into his wet heat.

"How about this?" she asked in an excited whisper, directing his hand to the thin edge of her thong.

He growled—honest to goodness growled. She bit back a smile. She'd never had that effect on a man.

"Leave it," he said between licks to her distended nipples. "It's sexy and I can work around it."

"Oh?"

To demonstrate, he laid her back on the quilt and spread her legs. With a wink, he pushed aside the damp thong and took a sexy, leisurely lick before letting the thong return to its place. Her breath caught at the warm, velvety smoothness of his stroking tongue.

She wanted more. She wanted him to do it again. And again. Her heart hammered, trying to break out of her chest.

Shaking, she reached for the tented front of his knit boxers. After clearing her throat, she said, "Well, I don't think I can work around these."

She pulled and tugged. Ben obediently lifted his hips so she could get the boxers off and get an unobstructed view of the hardness that had made her mouth water.

But, at the last second, she chickened out. She'd see it soon, up close and personal. Brazen as she was trying to be, it was somewhat humiliating to realize she just didn't have it in her to take that step yet.

Eyes nearly closed in what she hoped was a sexy look, she slithered up his long legs, allowing her breast to drag along his roughened tan skin. The effect on her sensitive nipples had her panting by the time she'd stretched out along his length.

She slid her hand down, maintaining eye contact and a smile. Then gasped.

Little Ben was already sheathed and ready for action.

23

Paige rolled over and reached for her farmer lover. Her hand encountered cool sheets.

A knock on her door had her pulling and wrapping the sheet around her nudity as she navigated through the litter of clothes.

Pausing with her hand on the cut-glass knob, she looked down at her less than proper attire. "Who is it?"

"Paige?" Bailey's voice sounded as though she were whispering against the crack of the door. "It's me. Are you alone?"

Paige opened the door and regarded her friend. Obviously in the relaxed beach-themed mood, Bailey wore a bright yellow Capri outfit embroidered with perhaps a hundred hot pink flamingos. Her bare toes sported hot pink polish with tiny yellow polka dots. The little prisms on her yellow flip-flops jingled merrily with each step she took as she entered the room.

Bailey looked at the nest of clothes on the floor, the bra dangling from the bedpost, then back at Paige.

"Aren't you going to turn on a light?" Bailey's voice screeched like fingers dragged down a chalkboard.

All the alcohol she'd consumed the previous night throbbed a dull drumbeat in Paige's skull.

"Don't need one," she muttered as she shuffled back to the bed and flopped down. "Your ensemble is bright enough to light up the room."

"Are you hungover?"

She cracked open one eye. "Stop shouting. No, I'm not hungover. Just still enjoying the buzz." She shifted and winced at the surprising ache between her legs. "Among other morning-after delights," she muttered.

No sunlight peeked around the edges of the shades, she noticed.

"What time is it, Bailey? It's still dark!"

"Don't get excited, I waited until I knew you'd be awake before I came down to your room. And it is kind of dark, but I doubt it will improve much." Bailey shoved aside Paige's suitcase and sat down on the small sofa. "When I was down to breakfast, Rita said the tropical storm that was predicted was moving in. She and Rick think Reese and her guide are trapped out on the island and probably won't be back until it blows over."

"Great." Paige rolled to her side and propped up on one elbow. "Did the informative Rita and Rick happen to say when that might be?"

Bailey shook her head. "No. I got the impression it has something to do with wind speed, which seems sort of variable." She flashed a bright smile. "So, since we're here for the duration too, what shall we do today?"

Ben rolled to his back and frowned at the familiar feel of his morning boner.

Down, fella, he silently chastised. Being prepared last night had done him no good whatsoever. And that was putting it mildly. It was a safe bet his bedmate wouldn't be pleased to meet Mr. Happy first thing in the morning either.

"Now what?" Reese's soft voice practically screamed seduction in the gray dawn.

Remembering her scathing comments when she'd called off their hot and heavy session the night before, it was easy to drudge up sarcasm.

"Now what?" he repeated, with an edge to his voice as he rolled over and propped up on his elbow to stare down at her. "You pretty much canceled any what, or chance of what, last night." He narrowed his eyes and leaned closer, feeling pretty smug when she shrank back. Good. Let her be wary of him. After the stunt she pulled last night, she deserved to feel awkward or guilty. Or both. Hell, even afraid wouldn't stink.

Pulling the quilt higher, she sat up and blinked. "I meant, now what do we do? Do you think it's safe to head back to Sand Dollar?"

In answer, he pointed upward, where the sound of the rain pounding on the roof echoed in the lobby. "What do you think?"

"You're the expert. That's why I hired you."

"True. But I was also all that was available." He stretched, biting back a smile when he saw her eyes widen at the action. For good measure, he scratched his belly and yawned, then added a grunt.

Just as he was wondering if scratching his balls would be the coup de grace to put her over the edge, she spoke.

"About last night . . . I'm, well, I'm sorry."

He stopped, midscratch. "About what?"

"Well, I didn't mean to lead you on. I mean, I should have known better."

"What? You reckon if you screwed a low-class jerk like me, I might take it for something more than a casual fuck?" He snorted and jerked on the quilt, pulling her closer. "You think I'm so hard up for a piece of ass that I'd fall on my knees and beg you to marry me?" Leaning until they were nose to nose, he glared straight into her wide blue eyes. "No fucking way."

"No! Of course not." She shrugged and he did his damn best not to drool or give in to the impulse to lick her smooth skin. All over. "I was just, um, I guess, surprised, last night." She waved her hand in a vague gesture. "You know, you were already, um, *prepared.*"

"I like to be prepared," he said, on his knees, advancing across the quilt until he had her backed against the hearth. "For anything."

She shivered when he dragged the tip of his right index finger across her shoulder and then traced her collarbone.

"Ordinarily," he continued in what he hoped was a lazy, only mildly interested drawl, "I'd tell you to drop the quilt and let's get back to where we left off last night."

"B-but? I'm sensing a *but* in there." Her breathing was shallow, and her voice low and husky.

He really was trying not to notice her breasts moving so enticingly beneath the old quilt with each breath she took.

"You were the one who called a halt last night, so I'm not going to make the same mistake twice. Next time, you make the move." So close now he could feel the warmth of her skin, smell her arousal, he waited a beat. Then another. Then, with slow, deliberate movements, he tugged the quilt until it fell around her knees, then walked his fingers up until he closed his hands over her breasts. Beneath his right palm, her heart hammered.

On their knees, they faced each other. He ignored her subtle hint when she inhaled, filling his hands, silently asking for more.

His lips barely brushed hers. He leaned back and slowly released her breasts, brushing her erect nipples with the pads of his fingers as he severed their contact.

"You want more." She glanced down at his obvious tent.

"Don't you?" he countered.

She broke eye contact. "Maybe."

He couldn't resist. Reaching out, he gave both nipples a tiny pinch, gloating at the hiss of her indrawn breath. "Liar. That's more than *maybe*. So . . . what's holding you back?"

"You," she whispered. "You were right when you said I was afraid. But not because I think you will read too much into whatever we do." She swallowed. "I'm worried I will."

His snort echoed. "Right. I'm such a catch. You wouldn't want to let a stud like me get away."

Her tentative smile clenched his heart.

"Now," he said, pulling her into his arms, trying not to sigh at the contact of her smooth chest to his, "I get to tell you, *I'm really a billionaire recluse, looking for the one woman in the world to make my life complete,* right?"

She bit back a giggle, which he found totally adorable.

"That would be nice," she said with a shy smile.

"No shit. Too bad it's not true." Then he wouldn't have had to scramble for money to save the island and his inheritance. He wouldn't have had to watch what he said and did around the woman in his arms. He wouldn't have had to pretend to be something he was not.

Because he wouldn't have met her.

Swaying back and forth, he ran his fingers under the sides of her thong. "Damn, I love these panties." He trailed a row of kisses up the side of her neck. "I wouldn't object if you took them off, though."

"I—I can't."

"Are they laminated to your body? What do you mean, you can't?"

"It wouldn't be fair. To you. To either of us. Ben," she said, reaching for him when he dropped his arms and moved away, "we just met. Regardless of what I let you believe, I'm not a one-night–stand person. I'm in Sand Dollar on business. I'll only be here for a week or so. I know, I know, you aren't looking for forever. But what if I am? You only want me because I'm convenient. Sex between us would just be something to do until the storm passes. What if I did something stupid and fell in love with you? Or, worse, what if you fell in love with me? Don't you understand how that could mess up everyone's life?"

"You're interested," he persisted. "And I know you're horny." He winked and smiled. "I can help you with that problem." He held his hands up, palms out. "No strings attached. Just two people giving each other pleasure." He hooked his thumbs in the elastic edges of her thong and gave an experimental tug.

When she didn't protest, he tugged again, until he slid the minuscule underwear down to her knees.

Bare. She was erotically smooth all over. With the tip of his index finger, he traced her exfoliated seam. His pulse kicked up at the feel of moisture.

Barely touching her, he stroked her, spreading her liquid excitement.

Wordlessly, she widened her stance.

When he paused, she grasped his wrist and pulled his hand between her legs.

He met her fiery blue gaze. "Tell me what you want me to do." He leaned closer, lightly massaging her distended nub.

She whimpered and pushed her wet folds against his hand.

When he didn't immediately respond, she pushed on his wrist, moving his hand to pet her labia.

Her eyelids drooped. Her slim hips moved in a seductive pattern against his fingers, begging for more.

"Tell me," he managed to say again in a gruff whisper, "tell me what you want."

"You," she said, her voice only slightly louder than air. She pushed on his hand and moved her hips harder.

He wiggled his fingers, flicking her wetness. His cock strained against the fabric of his boxers, intent on its target, like a heat-seeking missile.

He shoved his finger into her heat, the pad of his thumb massaging her nub. He pushed higher. "Open your eyes, Reese. Look at us. Look at me." When she finally lifted her lids to look at him, relief washed through him.

They were both going to end their dry spell.

24

"Tell me," Ben urged again, his finger buried deep inside her aching body.

Lordy, if he kept whispering to her like that and wiggling his embedded finger, she was going to embarrass them both and come all over his hand.

"Tell. Me. What. You. Want." His breath was hot against her ear.

It's not that she didn't know the words. Heaven knew, she'd heard Paige say them enough. And, also thanks to Paige's sometimes graphic descriptions, she was also pretty sure what she wanted. More turned-on than she remembered ever being in her life, Reese found her only problem was getting her throat and voice to cooperate enough to verbalize her desires.

With his other hand, he rolled her nipple. Between her legs, she grew slicker. Her muscles began to tremble. How much more of his sensual torture could she take before she collapsed in a quivering puddle of need?

Swallowing, she finally managed to croak out, "No words."

Executing a little shimmy against his marauding hand, she pushed his finger deeper. "Just action. Please," she managed to say in a desperate whisper.

A whimper escaped her when he withdrew the tantalizing warmth of his hand and fingers.

Almost frantic, she grabbed the waistband of his underwear.

He grinned and wordlessly stepped out of them, his erection was huge, the head of his penis dark and shiny.

"Stop looking at me like that, darlin', or it will all be over before we begin." He grinned and patted her butt. "Turn around and hold on to the mantel for a little bit. Do you trust me?"

She could only nod and do as instructed.

The warmth of the fire heated her naked flesh, caressed her nipples.

Behind her, Ben closed the distance, his warmth branding her back, his erection searing her upper buttocks, where it lay against her spine.

He moved slowly, up and down, creating a sexy friction. The hard points of his nipples dragged up and down her back, causing her nipples to pucker tighter.

In slow motion, his hands caressed her hips, gliding around to trace her pelvic bone, sliding downward.

Fascinated, she watched his tanned forearms against the pale skin of her belly. His palms cupped her femininity, heating her as surely as if she'd straddled her favorite heated vibrator. Gently he moved his hands, petting her. She'd read about this phenomenon, but she still gasped when his actions caused her labia to bloom, opening for him, their damp furrows dark with the circulation of her excitement and glistening in the firelight. It beat the heck out of her vibrator.

With one hand, he gently pushed back, causing her labia to part more. Using his index and middle finger, he parted her farther while the fingers of his other hand stroked her dampness, spiraling her excitement until her breathing grew ragged, her nipples ached and the muscles in her thighs quivered.

"Shh," he said against her ear when she tried to speak, to tell him she wanted more, so much more. His teeth worried her earlobe, causing a resurgence of moisture to shine her exposed flesh and drip onto the slate of the hearth.

"So pretty," he said on a breath in her ear. "But I want more. Is that okay?"

Weak with desire, she finally managed to give a faint nod.

Before she could protest the removal of his hands, they petted her legs farther apart. In a heartbeat, he slid between her legs to sit on the hearth while she stood above him, a foot on either side of his lean hips.

His hot hands stroked up her legs, then again gently pushed her labia apart, exposing her to his rapt gaze.

He lightly blew on her dampness, the action causing a shiver to streak through her and pucker her now-aching nipples.

Pushing the soft tissue together, he traced every fold with the tip of his tongue. Just as she was about to tell him she wanted more, he opened his mouth and sucked her into his heat.

He continued massaging her, pushing her more fully into his voracious mouth, all the while alternately rubbing and plucking her nub to screaming awareness.

Every nerve ending in her body vibrated. Her knees grew weak. Her nipples puckered into aching points.

He slid two fingers of his other hand deep into her and wiggled them at the same time he took a little nip of her soft tissue before resuming his suckling.

On sensual overload, she dug her nails into his shoulders, locking her knees to remain upright. Deep breathing only did so much.

Her climax roared through her like a tsunami, drowning her in sensation and never-ending pleasure.

She may have screamed.

Her lungs were paralyzed. It took a tremendous act of strength just to drag oxygen in and out. She knew her muscles were the consistency of pudding. Oh, yeah, what she'd just experienced was worlds away from her best vibrator experience, with or without heat.

Surely, she was too spent to remain standing. . . . Oh, right, the tightness at her hips was Ben's strong hands holding her up, the pads of his thumbs drawing lazy circles on the sensitive skin just below her hip bones.

Wait.

A tiny spark of excitement flared into a flame of desire within seconds. Her breathing accelerated. Her nipples puckered.

And when Ben pushed his sheathed erection into her, she was more than ready.

She was eager and willing.

25

Finesse flew out the window as Ben pumped into Reese with reckless abandon. How long had it been since he'd been so turned-on? Hell, how long had it been since he'd even been with a woman? That had to be at least part of his excitement.

Reese Parker was different. Deep down he knew it. And, also deep down, he knew she could spell trouble for him and the future of his grandmother's island.

But, right now, buried deep in her wet heat, he didn't care.

With a growl, he slammed into her one last time and did his best not to howl his frustration. It should have lasted longer. He should have made sure she'd climaxed at least once before he got off.

Was Reese Parker the kind of woman who would allow do-overs?

Damn, he hoped so.

When his breathing was somewhat under control and he was reasonably confident his knees would support his weight, he leaned forward to lick the side of her neck.

She giggled and scrunched up her shoulder, trapping his face in the fragrant cocoon of her smooth shoulder and neck, her flowery fragrance washing over him, surrounding him. Drowning him in sensation.

He wanted to kiss and lick every inch of her body, then do it all again.

But he'd just taken her, standing up, against the mantel of the lobby fireplace in his grandmother's hotel. How would she react if he tried for an instant replay?

She struck him as the kind of woman to make love to in a bed, surrounded by flowers and candles. He wanted to make her scream, and he wanted to take all day and night doing it. Doing her.

Serious thoughts for so early in the morning.

"Hungry?" He eased from her solace and reached for his underwear in the suddenly cold lobby. A feeble light filtered through the clouds, telling him it was definitely daytime. "There're quite a few canned things in the pantry and fruit-house out back."

"More stuff to char over the fire?" A tentative smile curved her lips as she modestly pulled the quilt around her again.

Momentarily distracted by the smoothness of her skin, he fought the urge to tell her to forget covering up. Not in front of him. Hell, he wanted her naked, 24/7, for as long as they were together. Even if they weren't fucking. He just loved to look at her.

"What?" He made what he hoped was a discreet adjustment. "Oh, uh, no. At least, I hope not. I saw a generator out back. Thought I'd see if I can get it started, while the rain has eased up a little."

"I thought the hotel had been closed years ago. Would a generator still be hooked up?"

"Sure. It runs on propane, which was delivered on a regular basis." At her amazed look, he shrugged. "That's what I was told, anyway. And, since propane doesn't evaporate, it's a pretty safe bet there's at least enough left to run the stove and water pump for a little bit."

"And you know how to start it?"

"Sure. The battery is solar powered, so it's just a matter of flipping the switch—"

"How do you know all this?"

Shit. How would he know it? "I told you, I spent a lot of time here as a kid." He shrugged again. "You know how boys are, exploring everything. Besides, it's the only way an island this size could get electricity, by generating it. It just makes sense."

She nodded. "Maybe to you." With a wave of her hand, she sat down on the sofa he'd pulled close to the fire. "If you don't mind, I'll just wait here."

Flip-flops on, he headed toward the back door.

"Wait!" she called to him with a laugh. "Are you planning to go out in just your underwear?"

His smile was relieved. For a second, he'd thought she was going to ask more questions. His knowledge of the island and the reason were no secrets, and he planned to tell her. Later. He stuck up his foot. "Nope, I'm wearing shoes. Don't look so shocked. It's not like anyone will see me, and this way, I won't have to worry about getting more clothes wet. Be right back!"

The rain had slacked off from semityphoon status to a steady downpour. Ben had seen it before, so he wasn't fool enough to believe the worst of the storm had passed.

Within seconds, his boxers were drenched and sagged low on his hips as he made his way around the hotel to the shed housing the generator. The pump controls were right where he remembered, next to the door. The generator looked just as he remembered, so he could only assume it was functional. He unlocked the control box and flipped the switch on the solar battery. In seconds, the generator roared to life. They would have to conserve, since he had no idea how much fuel remained, but at least they could use the bathrooms and the occasional light. He knew Reese would appreciate that.

Humming, he ducked his head against the intensifying wind and made his way back to the porch.

The old hotel seemed suddenly big and empty. Reese pulled the quilt tighter and looked around the lobby. It truly had been, and could again be, spectacular. All it would take was a little work. Well, maybe more than a little. But it would be worth it.

Though not large by hotel standards, it would be a huge B&B. Possibly too huge. Try as she might, she couldn't picture the Dragon Lady running a place that large. Or any bed-and-breakfast, for that matter. It was so out of character.

Not for the first time, Reese wondered about her boss's sincerity at wanting a change of career. Could sending Reese to the auction have been a ruse to get her out of Houston? And, if so, why? To her knowledge, no deals were pending.

A huge clunk echoed through the hotel. Reese could have sworn it jarred her bones.

"Oh, no!" She scrambled from the sofa and skidded down the hall toward the back porch. "Please, please, please," she fretted under her breath as she ran for the back door, "don't let Ben have blown himself up!"

A leap from the back porch landed her in Ben's arms as he rounded the corner.

"You're alive!" Relieved, she clung to his broad shoulders and rubbed her cheek against the firm, wet skin of his chest.

"Sorry to disappoint you." He set her on her feet on the rough planks of the porch and then hopped up, wiping his hands on the leg of his boxers.

"What?" Where was the passionate guy of a few minutes ago? Had she read it all wrong? Was she, after all, just a convenient way of passing time on the island during the storm? Was she that out of practice with men that she hadn't seen it?

"Lighten up." He brushed a kiss on the end of her nose and pulled her along as he walked into the kitchen. "I was just kidding." He glanced back over his shoulder. "Unless you were trying to off me back there." He made a show of rubbing his chest. "You hit me pretty hard."

He couldn't possibly be serious. She deftly ignored the seductive sight of his bare chest, glowing in the weak light.

And she refused to allow her gaze to wander any lower.

For now, anyway.

"You're kidding . . . right?"

At the entrance to the lobby, he whirled on her, pulling her tightly against his—she now realized—aroused body.

"What do you think?" His low voice was a half whisper/half growl as he rubbed his excited lower body against hers. His hands briefly skimmed her nakedness, beneath the quilt, before he pushed it away to land at their feet. "Although, now that I think about it, you definitely have a killer body," he said with a grin, and an outrageous wiggle of his eyebrows.

Although she'd love to jump into his arms and continue what they'd started, she had to be serious. They hardly knew each other. Sure, they had great chemistry, or whatever you wanted to call it, but she was only here for a few days, until the auction.

To start something they had no intention of finishing would be counterproductive, and could quite possibly have disastrous ramifications in the long run. So, pleasant as it had been, it couldn't happen again.

Darn it.

How could she put all that into words without sounding cold or harsh or just plain uninterested?

She couldn't.

Instead, she reluctantly picked up the quilt and wrapped it

around her nudity. She forced a yawn. "Do you think we have enough power to run water for a bath?"

He stared at her for a few seconds. "Sure. I guess. The pipes probably have some air in them and maybe a little rust from sitting for so long. Tell you what," he said when her shoulders slumped. "I'll go up and take a quick shower, to get things going. Then I'll run the water until it's clear for your bath and call you when it's ready."

"Thanks." She smiled a smile she really didn't feel and walked to sit on the sofa. "Sounds like a plan."

Of course, a better plan would be to share his shower, but she knew that wasn't a very good idea at the moment.

Avoiding further intimacy was her idea, and she was sticking to it.

Even if it killed her.

26

Paige's head was throbbing by the time she left Bailey in the restaurant. Good Lord, was it really only a few minutes past noon? They'd gone on an excruciatingly long and boring tour of a local dairy barn, culminating with a seemingly never-ending demonstration of churning butter. Who the hell churned butter these days, anyway?

During their excursion, the drizzle had morphed into a torrential downpour. They were lucky they hadn't drowned on their trek back to the hotel.

Soaked and exhausted, she'd made her excuses to her friend and trudged up to her room. Even fantasies of what she and Brett could do to fill the stormy day couldn't warm her. Besides, after her nocturnal activities, all she was really interested in was a long nap under the soft, warm blanket.

Her purse landed with a dull thud on the rug, next to the door. Without turning on the light, she flipped the privacy lock and stepped out of her soggy sandals. The leather soles were already beginning to separate.

"Great. That's two hundred bucks down the drain. Literally." She unzipped her shorts and let them drop to the floor as she began peeling her halter top off over her head.

Goose bumps rose all over her body and she wondered if the air conditioning was on.

Suddenly heat covered her bared breasts at the same time she was pulled roughly against a hard, muscled male body.

A naked and fully aroused male body.

Her brain had just processed that as her lungs filled with air for her first scream, when Brett's voice whispered in her ear, "About damn time you came back."

The chill immediately left as heat streaked from her core to her extremities.

His big hands spun her to face him a nanosecond before his demanding mouth covered her surprised one.

A whimper of delight escaped from deep in her throat. She opened wide to accommodate his marauding tongue. A little hop pushed her higher in his embrace and her legs clung to his lean waist.

He growled, the sound low and feral. Primitive.

Her back slammed against the wall, his kiss all but devouring her, while his erection bumped wildly against her wetness.

With a frustrated roar, he tore her thong from her, tossing it like a piece of annoying tissue that was keeping him from his present.

The next instant, he was buried deep within her as they grunted with each penetrating thrust.

Reese sighed and sank deeper in the rapidly cooling water of the claw-foot tub. She'd have loved to have a really hot bath, but just couldn't wait for the old water heater to do its thing. The cooler air of the bathroom, compared to the warmth by the fire in the lobby, would make the bathwater seem hot when she finally decided to get out of the tub.

She glanced at the locked door and tried not to feel guilty.

Ben had already taken a shower. If he joined her in the tub, she knew it wouldn't be for bathing or water conservation.

Her soapy hand found her swollen clitoris and toyed with it, her breath catching at the intimacy of the touch. It felt good. Too good. No doubt her sleeping hormones had roared to life.

Too bad Ben wasn't there to help.

No, wait, that wasn't right. Backing off had been her idea. And she knew it was probably for the best.

But . . .

She sank down until her nose barely cleared the water and rested the soles of her feet on the edge of the tub, her legs spread.

She idly stroked her swollen folds, watching as her nub swelled from its hood. She'd never watched herself being pleasured, and it sort of embarrassed her.

But it also excited her. A lot.

Swirling soap around her breasts, she thoroughly massaged them, then slowly drizzled water from her washcloth until they were clean, her nipples standing in alert peaks, tingling in the cooler air.

Ready for Ben's eager mouth.

No! Not yet, anyway.

Thoughts of Ben brought her hands between her legs again.

What was wrong with her? Had she become a sex addict?

Her hand moved faster, rubbing her slick folds, pinching her clitoris.

Water sloshed as her hips began to undulate. Faster. Harder.

Her breath caught when the first wave of pleasure washed over her, setting off aftershocks all over her body.

On sensual overload, she arched her head back and promptly took in a mouthful of water.

Choking, she floundered, slopping water all over the tile floor as she slipped and slid on the porcelain, trying to catch her breath.

Ben pounded on the bathroom door with enough force to splinter the wood.

"Reese! Reese! What's going on? Are you okay?" *Bang, bang, bang.* "Reese! Answer me!"

Finally she was able to make a sound other than a cough. "I'm fine. I just breathed in some water. I'll be out in a sec."

Ben was standing right outside the door when she opened it, after she had wrapped a towel around herself. His Adam's apple bobbed when he swallowed. He licked his lips.

After what had just transpired in the tub, her legs were already wobbly. All it would take for her to forget her stupid idea of abstaining would be for him to make a move. Any move. Heck, even an indication he might make a move.

She took a deep breath and slowly exhaled. It helped somewhat. "What's up?"

"What's up? I heard all kinds of water sloshing and then you choking. I thought you were drowning!" Hand shoved in the pockets of his cargo shorts, he looked at the floor, then met her gaze. "Why did you lock me out?"

Okay. Good question. Too bad she didn't have a good answer. Well, she had thought she had a good answer, but abstaining didn't seem like it was such a good idea now.

Just looking at Ben standing there, chest bare, his shorts riding low on his lean hips, made her mouth water. Other places were feeling pretty moist too.

Decision made.

"I didn't mean to worry you." She stepped closer and walked her fingers up his firm pecs. "I assumed you weren't interested in sharing my bath, since you already took a shower."

"Right." He slid his arm around her, tugging the towel until it fell at their feet, then groaned when she rubbed her nipples on his chest.

After a long and thorough kiss, she looked up and smiled

while she tugged at the zipper of his shorts. "Why am I naked, and you're wearing these?"

He smiled back, his teeth white in the dimness. "I can fix that." He pulled a handful of condoms from his pocket and tossed them on the nightstand, then shucked his shorts and underwear in one movement.

"I do like how you're prepared, after all."

Gathering her in his arms, he playfully nipped her neck, earning a shriek of laughter. "And I like the way you smell." He took a gigantic exaggerated whiff. "Mmm. Fresh and clean."

She shrieked again when he tossed her on the old bed, its springs creaking with their weight as he followed her down.

"I think, though, I need to check."

"Check what?" She tried to back away a little, but he was having none of it as he held her ankles.

"To make sure you did a good job." He ran his hand down her leg, then back up, pulling her to him by her foot.

His kisses on each toe tickled, but he held her still as he trailed his tongue between each toe. When he sucked on her big toe, her giggling stopped.

Arousal, hot and heavy, slammed into her. Her breathing became shallow.

Their gazes met.

How embarrassing was it to get turned-on by having your toes kissed?

She struggled to regulate her breathing while he gave her other foot the same treatment.

Toe sex, that's what it was. Who knew?

Then he kissed his way up to her inner thigh, and she forgot to breathe entirely.

Leisurely licks took him to her core and had her panting for more. Literally.

"Pretty." His breath was hot against her exposed flesh. "Give me your hands. Feel. Feel how wet and slick you are for me?"

Embarrassment heated her cheeks, but she did as he asked.

He arranged her hands until she was holding her labia open for whatever he wanted to do to her.

His tongue probed her. Briefly. Too briefly.

She tried to pull him back.

He grinned up at her. "Don't let go." He again arranged her hands. "Keep them just like that. Trust me. You'll see. You'll like it."

He proceeded to lick, suck, and probe her with his tongue, sucking her to at least three screaming orgasms—she lost count—while he pinched and rolled her distended nipple.

She wanted to reciprocate, she really did. But he didn't give her a chance, even if her thoroughly sated body would have obeyed her commands.

When he'd sucked what surely must have been her last orgasm from her, he planted a smacking kiss on her cherry red folds and reached for a condom.

She watched, amazed at the size of his erection.

But he'd been wrong about one thing. She hadn't liked what he'd done to her.

She'd *loved* it.

"The wind." Ben's breath was still labored from their last session. They lay snuggled beneath the old quilt on the bed, too exhausted to move back to the lobby for a while. While they panted, Ben continued to touch her, petting her breast, tweaking her nipples, kissing her wherever he could reach.

Reese sighed and snuggled closer. "What about the wind?"

She liked having sex with Ben. Besides being a fantastic lover, he was fun. And thoughtful. She'd noticed he made sure she'd climaxed at least once before he came. And she loved that he liked to snuggle. No *wham, bam, thank you, ma'am* with Ben Adams.

A wave of sadness washed over her. If he lived in Houston, he'd be the perfect boyfriend.

He nodded toward the window. "It's picking up again." The treetops waved wildly, loose leaves flying. If possible, the sky looked even more ominous. The rain pelting the windowpane increased. "I need to go move the boat."

"Where?" She didn't remember seeing anything other than the dock. Did boats have garages?

"To the protected side of the island, by the beach. I can't risk the storm tearing it apart at the dock."

She nodded, attempting to wrap her tired brain around what he was saying. "Why didn't you do that to begin with?"

He exhaled and rubbed the back of his neck, as though he were struggling to hold his temper as he sat up on the side of the bed. "Because the dock is on that side. When the hotel was built, it was considered to be the more scenic side. Probably," he added. "And it's an easier walk to the front of the hotel. But the opposite side is the sheltered side, the one that faces Sand Dollar." She admired the line of his arm, the firm muscles when he pointed toward the window facing the back of the hotel. He bent to look into her eyes, his warm palms on her bare shoulders. "Trust me. I know what I'm doing. And I need to do it sooner rather than later."

"Then why are you asking my permission?" She pulled the quilt up and wished he'd just go so she could have a little time to give herself a pep talk on why having sex with him again had not been the best idea of the century.

And so she could remember all the reasons why a relationship with him would never work.

27

Ben bent and leaned into the wind as he made his way down the slope to the dock, where his current home was being thrown against the old wood by the crashing surf like a discarded bath toy. Rain pelted him, stinging his eyes. But he didn't need to see what Mother Nature was doing to know his boat needed rescuing.

He'd just untied the bowline, when a gust of wind took him over the edge of the dock and deposited him into the churning water. Even beneath the water, the storm howled.

Spitting salt water and obscenities, he bobbed for a few minutes, not needing to tread water, thanks to the movement of the choppy Gulf. Another wave crashed into him, washing him high enough to grasp the starboard rail and flop down onto the decking.

Panting, he lay with the rain stinging his face for a few seconds before rolling to his knees and struggling to his feet.

Irrational as it may be, he couldn't help but feel at least part of his problems stemmed from Reese Parker.

For one thing, if he hadn't ferried her to the island, he wouldn't be in his current predicament.

For another, if he hadn't been seduced by her, he would have had more strength to do what he needed to do to get his boat, and only source of shelter, out of the storm.

He took out his frustration on the anchor chain. It felt good to work off some of his anger hauling the anchor up.

Anger? Was he really angry? And, if so, with whom? While Reese was a good candidate, he had to be honest: She couldn't have seduced him *if* he wasn't willing. And eager. Okay, maybe also a little hard up, not that he wanted to admit it. And, face it, she wasn't the only one doing the seducing.

So now here he was, fighting the storm and the Gulf of Mexico to stay afloat long enough to seek shelter. That was his goal, his motivation, for the time being.

He fired up the engine and motored out into open water. The power of the waves made it doubly important to keep his distance from shore in order to prevent crashing on some of the sharper rock formations surrounding the northern tip of the island.

Wind buffeted his boat, rocking it violently, when it wasn't tossing it up and down.

He bit back a smile as he navigated the turn toward the bay side of the island. Reese would be tossing her cookies if she was with him.

Soon the old diving platform came into view through the rain and he bore port and pulled back on the throttle.

"What the hell . . . ?" Through the gray downpour, a fishing boat bobbed in the waves, tied to a leg of the old platform.

He racked his brain, trying to remember if he'd spotted it when they passed on their way to the dock. Surely, he'd have noticed another boat on a deserted island. *His* deserted island.

Trespassers should not only be tried and prosecuted, but shot.

The bow of his boat bumped against the platform and he cut the throttle, scanning the beach for the boat's owner.

Another thought hit him. What if the owner of the boat was also scoping out the island with the intent of bidding on it? He had enough to worry about with Reese.

Reese. Shit, he'd left her alone in the deserted hotel. Naked and alone in the deserted hotel. The unlocked deserted hotel.

Where the hell was the owner of the damned fishing boat?

The water was too shallow to risk getting closer to shore. He'd have to tie onto the platform like the fishing boat and hope for the best. After securing the rope, he stood on the undulating platform, anxiously scanning the deserted beach. Where the hell was the boat owner? If he hadn't gone inland or, worse, to the hotel, he had to be close by. The only shelter Ben remembered was a small cave he used to play in as a kid. His grandmother hated the cave and always threatened to have it filled in. If it wasn't snake infested, she'd maintained, it was at the very least unsafe. With a wry grin, he noticed she'd never destroyed it.

If the owner of the boat was anywhere nearby, he was probably holed up in the cave. He hoped.

After only a second of hesitation, he hopped into the fishing boat and pulled the starter rope. The little motor whirred to life. Ben scanned the beach, waiting for the unseen fisherman to run along the shore, yelling about him stealing the boat.

Only the sound of wind and rain and surf filled the humid air.

Untying, he pointed the craft toward shore and opened the throttle. Waves slapped against the hull, pitching him off the hard metal seat and then slamming him back down. When no one came running, he continued until he'd run the little boat ashore.

Cutting the engine, he hopped out and scanned the area once again. Seeing no one, he bent into the rain and headed toward the mouth of the cave.

Reese finished making the bed and paused, listening for Ben's return. How long did it take for him to move and park his boat?

Sighing, she leaned her forehead against the cool glass of the window and listened to the wind and rain while she looked out over the property behind the hotel. After she'd located the roof of the outhouse, she tried to figure out where she'd seen the flowers blooming. Again, orange showed through the dreary, rain-soaked scenery. Soon she spotted another and another.

Squinting, she looked to the far left and thought she saw another spot of orange. She knew it wasn't flowers. What the heck was it, and why were there so many of them?

In the bathroom, she pulled the little chair close to the tub and climbed up. Using her fingertips, she pulled up until she could peek through the high window. But from that angle, she found it was difficult to see much.

She dragged the chair to the bedroom window and climbed back up.

Suddenly she knew what she was looking at—sort of.

"It's some kind of a grid," she whispered, her breath fogging the windowpane. But why? What was the purpose?

"Ben!" Her voice echoed. Jumping from the chair, she ran for the hall and yelled again. "Ben! Are you down there?"

Nothing.

Practically tripping in her haste, she ran down the curved staircase.

The lobby was vacant.

"Ben!"

The kitchen was cold and empty.

He wasn't on the wraparound porch. Ditto with the back porch.

What the heck could be taking him so long?

She had a feeling the grid was important, and maybe Ben would know why.

Grabbing the old quilt they'd dried on a peg by the back door, she wrapped it around and over her head like a colorful poncho. She stuck her feet into her cold, semiwet, and muddy deck shoes and leaped off the back porch.

It took a few seconds to get her bearings. If the hotel faced the Gulf of Mexico and the "safe" side of the island was the opposite, facing Sand Dollar, then she needed to head straight out from the back porch until she found water. Ben should be there by then, and maybe between the two of them, they could figure out what was with all the orange stuff.

Overgrown landscaping caught and tugged at her shorts, scraping her legs, as she slowly made her way into the vegetation. Every few minutes, she looked back, making sure she could still see the back of the hotel and that she was still going in a somewhat straight direction.

"Ow!" Her toe stubbed something hard, the pain vibrating up her shinbone.

It was a paving stone, shaped like the state of Texas.

A few feet beyond, she found two more, about a foot apart. A path! Of course there would be some kind of paths throughout the hotel grounds, if not the entire island.

Especially to direct guests toward the beach.

Practically skipping with excitement, she hopped from one stone to the next, checking her location every once in a while.

Through the haze and rain, a horizontal ribbon of deeper blue-gray edged the horizon.

Ben paused at the opening of the little cave and listened to the sound of male voices. He didn't recognize any of them. It was best not to take them by surprise. No need to jump to hasty conclusions, but he touched the fillet knife strapped to his waistband, just in case.

"Hello?" He edged into the darkness.

The voices quieted.

"Hello?" Ben repeated, walking slowly into the dimness. As he rounded a shallow curve, he saw four men, dressed in bright yellow slickers and waders, sitting around a small campfire.

They turned to look at him. The closest one stood.

"Hey," Ben said, forcing a relaxed posture. "Storm catch you by surprise?"

The standing man shrugged and grinned. "Naw, we sort of expected it. It's been predicted for the last few days."

"You must be hard-core fishing fanatics to face these kinds of elements." He smiled and extended his hand. "I'm Ben Adams, by the way."

"Clay Mills." The standing man shook Ben's hand with a firm grip and looked directly into his eyes.

Ben's grandmother had always said no one with something to hide would look you in the eye.

Ben prayed Gram knew what she was talking about.

He nodded.

Clay motioned to the other men. "This is T.J. Rutherford. The two misfits on the other side are Austin Packerd and Barry Lange." His smile faltered as he looked out over Ben's shoulder. "Wish the rain would ease up so we can get out of here."

"Fishing sucks right after storms," Ben said, and waited.

"Oh, we're not fishing," the man identified as T.J. said as he stood and turned to kick dirt onto the fire until it smothered.

"Oh. That's not your boat out yonder?" And what about the four tackle boxes lined up against the wall of the cave?

Clay followed his gaze and laughed. "I guess you're wondering about the tackle boxes."

"Yeah, it crossed my mind."

"Those are for samples," Austin said, picking up two and handing one to the man Clay identified as Barry.

"Samples? What are you, fucking Avon Ladies?" How stupid did these guys think he was?

All four laughed, but not like they really thought he was funny.

"I tell you," Clay said as he donned his hat and slapped Ben on the back as they all headed for the mouth of the cave, "sometimes I think that would be easier. Unfortunately, it's not anything that glamorous. We're here to take soil samples. After we tag them and log 'em in, we store 'em in the tackle boxes."

"Ah," Ben said with a nod. "I guess you have your reasons, but why the hell would you do it in the middle of a tropical storm?"

"No choice. We're on a deadline."

A deadline for what, they weren't saying. Ditto with the mysterious soil samples.

"Yeah," Austin chimed in, "and thank God these are the last ones."

Clay nodded. "Yep. We've been waiting for the storm to break, but it doesn't look like that's gonna happen anytime soon, so we're outta here."

They stepped into the rain and paused, all staring at the beached fishing boat.

"Hell of a place to dock your boat," Ben said with a smile. "I don't want to hold you men up, so—"

"Ben!" Reese appeared through the sea grass, then came sliding down the berm to scamper along the beach toward them, his grandmother's old quilt flapping in the wind. "Ben, I need to talk to you about—oh! Sorry, I didn't realize you weren't alone."

"Clay Mills." Reese shook his extended hand. "I was just telling your husband—"

"What? He's not my husband! He's just . . ." What was he? Her boyfriend? No. Her lover? Well, technically, kind of, sort of. But it wasn't any of this man's business. "My employee," she said for lack of a better way to describe their relationship.

It was probably wise not to glance in Ben's direction. She'd have to explain it to him later.

Standing to one side, she watched as the men shook Ben's hand and then pushed their boat into the water before climbing in. The motor caught on the second pull and they turned to head into the bay.

"Hey!" Reese turned and faced Ben. "If it's safe for them to leave the island in that tiny boat, it must be okay for us too, right?"

"Wrong," Ben said, his face hard. "They're amateurs. They won't make it beyond the tip of the island before the storm will force them to turn around."

"I don't understand. Then why did you let them go?"

He shrugged. "It's a free country. Besides, they'll figure it out on their own in a few minutes."

"Do you think they'll want to stay with us in the hotel?" She was just getting used to being around Ben. Did she really want to be around more men she didn't know?

"Hell no. They'll probably just hunker down in the old cave they've already been using until the storm dies down enough to head to the mainland."

"Those must have been the men from the hotel. You remember Rita talking about them? The weird fishermen?" Memories of the logo on the backs of their slickers flashed through her mind. Where had she seen that logo before? "I remember seeing them at the hotel. Don't you think they're the same men?"

Ben glared down at her. "Don't ask me," he said in a hard voice. "I'm just an *employee.*"

28

Paige avoided Brett's gaze as she entered the restaurant to meet Bailey for an early supper.

She'd known that he was there even if she hadn't seen him brooding in the corner when she walked into the dining room. It was like she'd suddenly developed a weird sixth sense where Brett was concerned.

She chanced a quick glance.

He had no right to be sullen. Sure, they'd had phenomenal sex, mind-blowing sex. But he didn't own her. And she wasn't some sex-starved, pathetic woman who was so grateful the hot farmer had given her a tumble that she'd want to be with him 24/7.

So, why was she feeling guilty?

"Don't look now," Bailey said from behind her menu, "but the hunky guy is back, and he's staring at you. Again." She slowly lowered her menu to stare wide-eyed across the table. "Oh, Paige! You didn't! Please tell me you didn't." Bailey's whisper was urgent. "Can't I leave you alone for a minute?"

Her shoulders slumped. "I knew I should have stuck with our original plan and shared a room with you."

Paige grinned as she picked up her wineglass and winked over the rim at Brett before taking a sip. She regarded her friend and swallowed. "Why?" She set the glass next to her appetizer plate. "Are you disappointed you didn't get to take part in a three-way?" She laughed at the look on Bailey's face, coupled with the pink staining her cheeks.

Her laughter faded, though, when she glanced over at Brett.

The fire in his eyes caused an answering heat to fill her, to moisten her thong. She shifted on the suddenly uncomfortably hard dining chair.

Why couldn't she have found someone like him closer to home? It would have been so much more convenient. She'd always preferred doing her sexual entertaining on her own timetable.

Brett made things . . . different. Complicated.

Exciting.

"If you are that interested," Bailey's frosty voice whispered, "why don't you go have dinner with him?" She shrugged. "I'm fine. It's not the first time you've done this to me, you know." She sighed. "Lord knows, you aren't paying any attention to our conversation."

"Hmm?" Paige broke eye contact with Brett and looked at her friend.

"Exactly my point," Bailey said with a prim nod. Her fingers were white where she gripped her water goblet.

"Bailey, don't be like that," Paige drawled. "You know if the situation was reversed, I'd wish you happy hunting."

"That's just it, Paige. The situation is *never* reversed! Whenever you're in the room, I somehow become invisible to anyone with a Y chromosome."

"I can see you," a startlingly handsome twentysomething

man said in a low voice. He dumped some steaming rolls into the partially empty basket. "You look good to me." He flashed Bailey a smile filled with blazingly white straight teeth.

Paige couldn't believe her friend was just sitting there, mouth slightly agape, while such a prime specimen was obviously flirting with her. Paige gave her a surreptitious kick.

"Ow!" Bailey glared at Paige and leaned to rub her shin.

"Thank the nice man for the compliment," Paige said through her teeth. "And introduce yourself," she added in a hiss.

In response, Bailey jumped up, extending her hand like a rabid conventioneer. "Hi! I'm Bailey—oh!"

They watched as the wineglasses toppled in slow motion, the deep red stain spreading across the white tablecloth.

A glance at Bailey's face confirmed her complexion rivaled the Merlot in color.

Instead of running in the opposite direction, the man's smile widened as he sopped at the escaping wine with a towel, while never breaking eye contact with Paige's obviously demented and socially inept friend.

"Hi, Bailey-o," he said with a grin. "I'm Travis."

"Is everything okay?" Rita hustled over to their table. "Oh!" She made a hand gesture to someone on the other side of the dining room. "We'll get that cleaned up for you. Meanwhile, Travis, would you show our guests to table twenty-three?"

Travis nodded and extended his elbow for Bailey. "No problem." He flashed another dazzling smile at Bailey. "Right this way, pretty lady."

With a sigh, Paige stood and began to follow. She was pleased to see someone flirting with her friend, she really was, it was just that it had been a long time since a male had ignored her.

Her progress was halted by the hard hand that grabbed hers as she followed Bailey.

Brett tugged until she leaned closer.

"Take a seat with me and let your friend have some privacy." His slow grin was followed by a sexy wink. "I promise I won't bite."

She snickered and dropped into the chair opposite him at the small table. "Tell that to my right buttock. It bears a definite mark to prove otherwise."

Not answering, he shrugged and poured a glass of wine from the bottle in the bucket next to the table. After he replaced the bottle, he met her gaze. Another slow grin emerged. "As I recall, you were eager and willing."

"Yeah, well, I never said I wasn't, I was merely stating a fact," she muttered, taking a sip of wine.

"Maybe I was marking my territory." When she stiffened, he reached across and held both her hands. "As were you. I have the marks on my back to prove it. And, for the record, I don't mind."

"What now?" She looked down at her hands, where his thumbs were stroking in maddening circles. She knew she should eat something, but suddenly her appetite took a hike.

The only thing she was interested in was devouring Brett.

"Are you hungry?" He threw some cash on the table.

She shook her head, but he was already out of his chair and reaching to help her up.

With flagrant disregard, he pulled her tightly against his excited body. Nose to nose, they stared at each other.

To her surprise, he nuzzled her nose with his.

"Let's go back to your room for dessert."

"Looks like your friend changed her mind about dinner," Travis said, dropping into the seat across from Bailey. "No need for you to be lonely."

"Travis!" Bailey leaned across and tried to look stern. "Aren't you going to get fired? I don't think you're supposed to sit with the customers."

He grinned and toyed with the silverware. "That would probably be true if I worked here."

"What? You served the rolls. Of course, you work here. Don't you?" Despite his angelic appearance, was he actually some kind of con artist who preyed on unsuspecting women?

"Relax," he said, and reached across to pat her head.

Great. She should have known. No man in his right mind would look twice at her when Paige was in the room. Bailey's jaw clenched at the thought of being pitied. *Poor Bailey.* How could she possibly compare with the uberglamorous Paige, aka Doctor Darling? Men always fell all over themselves around Paige. Why should Travis be any different?

"I don't know what I said to offend you, but by the look on your face, it must have been pretty bad. Let's start over." He extended his hand, careful to move the wineglasses out of harm's way. "I'm Travis," he said with a smile. "My sister owns the place. She's short staffed tonight, so I offered to help."

Relief washed through her. "You're Rita's brother?"

"Yes, he's my brother," Rita said, setting plates laden with food in front of them. "But I won't say he's being much of a help." Grinning, she placed a smacking kiss on top of his head. "But that's okay. I can handle it until Rick gets back from town." She pointed a finger at her brother. "But this is it. If you want dessert, you know where the kitchen is, go get it." With a wink, she turned and strode away.

"Eat. I want dessert. I highly recommend the banana pudding cake," he said with a smile.

A sudden mental image of Travis slathering the confection all over her naked body just about choked Bailey as she took her first bite of prime rib.

Sure, it would be messy and sticky. But she wouldn't mind it if he licked it all off. . . .

* * *

Every attempt Reese made at conversing with Ben on the hike back to the hotel was met with stony silence.

It gave her a lot of time to think. Had the slicker-clad men been on the island to scope it out before the auction? It wasn't totally out of the realm of possibility. Dang, she wished she could get a signal on her cell. The Dragon Lady needed to know she might not be the sole bidder.

Reese looked at the lush greenery and could easily imagine how attractive the island could be to visitors. Granted, the old hotel needed some updating and deferred maintenance, but it wouldn't be cost prohibitive.

Her pace slowed as the hotel came into view. It didn't seem nearly as creepy and foreboding as it did the day before.

Still, it was more than a stretch to imagine Dorinda as an innkeeper.

Something soft brushed across the top of her foot.

Make that slithered across the top of her foot.

The tail of the reptile had yet to disappear into the bushes when Reese's scream pierced the air.

Ben turned and ran back, shoving at the overgrown vegetation.

When he was within a few feet of her, she made a giant leap into his arms. Her legs wrapped around his waist while her arms threatened to cut off his air supply.

"Snake!" she screamed again, numbing the hearing in his left ear.

She leaned back, gripping both his ears to force him to look at her. "Snake!"

He hefted her up a little in the hope she would relinquish her grip on his ears.

She didn't.

If he set her back on her feet, she'd have to let go. But he wasn't sure he was ready to put any space between their bodies, despite how angry he'd been with her just a few minutes ago.

Oh, no. Fear crept up his spine as her frantic words sank in. "Did it bite you?" He began running his hands up and down her legs, as far as he could reach, checking for fang marks.

She plastered herself to him again, practically choking him. A shudder ran through her.

"No," she finally said in a tiny, pitiful voice. "I don't think so. It just creeped me out." She shuddered again and tightened her grip on his neck. "I have snake germs on my foot!"

She moved, hunching down in his arms until they were nose to nose. "And don't you dare make fun of me."

"Wouldn't think of it," he finally managed to say around the laughter threatening to escape. "Are you sure it was a snake?"

"Of course, I'm sure it was a snake! It was slithery and creepy and moved in a serpentine pattern along the ground until it disappeared into the bushes." Her gaze darted around before returning to him. "Did you know there were snakes on this island when you brought me here?"

Heaving a sigh, he lowered her to the ground. "Of course. Snakes are all over Texas. Islands are not exempt. But I didn't bring you here to scare you with them, if that's what you mean."

"I'm sorry." She scampered along next to him in her effort to keep up with his fast pace.

Sure he could slow down, but he found he didn't want to do anything to accommodate his current employer.

Just the thought of her calling him her *employee* set his temper to a slow burn. He wasn't a fool. He knew they were practically strangers, despite the intimacy they'd shared. Ships passing in the night, as it were. But hearing her refer to him as just an employee was a bitter pill to swallow.

His steps slowed.

Regardless of their relationship or lack thereof, she deserved to know the truth about him. Besides being the right thing to do, if she found out later, all hell would break loose, and that was abso-damn-lutely something he'd rather avoid.

Besides, he was a lover, not a fighter. Well, okay, he kind of liked fighting with Reese, but it was all in fun. A fact Ms. Parker would likely not agree on. Which was all the more reason to just tell her and get it over with before she found out and used it as yet another reason to distrust or hate him.

Funny. He glanced back at her trudging up the little path behind him, the ridiculous quilt flapping in the wind. Until he'd met Reese, he hadn't given a rat's ass what anyone thought of him or his integrity. And, for the life of him, he couldn't understand why he did now.

Must be getting old.

"What was your point in bringing the quilt?" He yelled to be heard above the renewed roar of the wind as she approached. "It's soaked. Not likely to protect you from the rain."

"Well, it's better than nothing," she said, brushing past him to start up the back steps.

"Like me," he grumbled, turning to follow her.

At the top of the steps, she whirled on him. "Will you stop with the pity party? I know I hurt your feelings when I told that guy you were my employee, but he caught me off guard when he called you my husband." Her eyes widened. "You didn't tell him that, did you?"

"No! I may be dumb enough to let you talk me into going out in a tropical storm, but I'm not stupid." He shook his head, opening the back door for her. "Get over yourself, Blondie."

Sputtering, she wrapped the quilt tighter and stalked down the hall toward the lobby.

Actually, he hadn't thought fast enough to tell the men she was his wife. At the time, he just wanted them gone. But he couldn't deny he felt fiercely protective of the skinny blond pain in the ass. Telling a group of strange men, trespassers on his island, she was his wife wouldn't have been a half-bad idea. Strictly as a means of protection, of course.

It wasn't like he was . . . what? Attracted to her? Well, hell yes, he was attracted to her. He'd like to lie and say it was just because of the enforced togetherness, any port in a storm. But, deep down, he knew that wasn't true.

But did it mean he felt something for her other than bone-deep lust and an affinity for her money? Maybe.

And that thought was enough to give him nightmares.

Reese was sitting by the fire when he walked into the lobby. She'd draped the quilt on the staircase rail.

"Look, princess, we need to talk." He strode to the railing and jerked the wet quilt down. "First off, not only is this thing wet, it's muddy, thanks to you playing Batgirl and running through the weeds, and Lord knows what else. Second"—he patted the handrail—"this is solid mahogany. It's survived for at least one hundred years. It would be nice if it could survive another day or two with you around. We do not lay wet things on it. Got that?"

"Yes," she grumbled. "I'm not a moron."

"I never said you were. You're just a spoiled rich girl who thinks everything is replaceable."

"Rich? What makes you think I'm rich?"

He had to hand it to her, she managed to look genuinely confused. Now he wondered what else she'd been faking.

"Of course, you're rich. Why else would you come way out here to bid on a whole goddamned island?" It was best to just lay everything on the table. Let the cards fall where they may, so to speak.

"You know"—hands on hips, she narrowed her eyes—"what I don't get is why you care. Why are you so angry with me? Are you planning to bid on it and don't want the competition?"

"First off," he said, wadding the soggy quilt and clutching it tightly to prevent accidentally reaching for her. Or, worse, kissing her. Just to shut her up, of course. "I don't care. Second, I'm not mad at you. Not for wanting to buy the island, anyway." He shrugged and tossed the quilt onto the tile of the kitchen. "I just thought we should be honest about everything."

"Honest? You want me to be honest? Okay. Yes, I'm going to bid on the island at the courthouse auction. You knew that. And I needed to scope out the island and the hotel. And," she continued is a low, slow voice, "the reason for that is because I need to be able to report back to my boss—that would be the woman who pays me to do things like this—whether or not I felt it was a wise investment. It's what I do for a living. So, that's why I'm here, but it has nothing to do with me, and I'm certainly not rich."

"Your boss, huh?" He moved a little closer. "So, is she rich?"

"Danged if I know." Reese managed a wry grin. "I'm sure she's got more money than me. Of course, it wouldn't take much, with the pittance she pays me." She touched Ben's hand. "I'm just doing my job."

"Pretty cool job, getting to travel around and buy stuff."

"Believe it or not, this is only the second time she's had me do something like this. Most of the time, my critical job skill is the ability to get her Starbucks order correct."

They settled onto the cushions by the fire. Ben pulled her close, his arm holding her against his warmth.

"It sounds like you're not very happy working for her." His lips brushed a light kiss on her temple.

"That's an understatement." She shrugged and tried to smile. "Which is why this is the last time. I'm turning in my notice after I get back. Well, as soon as I can find another job, anyway. Unfortunately, working for the Dragon Lady has provided luxuries I've discovered I can't live without, like eating and living indoors."

He chuckled. "You could always come work for me."

Leaning back, she widened her eyes. "I didn't realize you

did anything. I mean," she hurried on, "anything that requires employees. No offense." She kissed his chin. "What kind of pay are we talking about?"

He forced a pained expression. "Well, I can't afford to pay much right now. Okay, make that nothing. But the benefits are good."

"Oh, yeah?" She straddled his now very happy lap.

Nodding, he situated her in a more comfortable, and accommodating, position. "Eating and living indoors, for starters."

"Anything else?" Her breath was hot against his lips.

"Unlimited hot and varied sex."

"Unlimited, huh?" Her hips made a lazy circle, grinding their sexes together. "And, just to clarify, how varied are we talking?"

"Wherever, however, and whenever you want it."

29

The shrill sound of the house phone startled Bailey. Regretfully breaking the lip-lock she had going on with Travis, she stretched off the bed and grabbed the receiver.

"H-hello," she said, trying to sound normal, even though Travis was now sucking on one nipple while he squeezed the other one.

"Bailey, where are you?" Paige's voice sounded more breathless than Bailey's. "I came back to the restaurant and you were gone. Did you hook up with that hot busboy?"

"Travis." He looked up at the sound of his name, but she pushed his face back to her aching breast. "His name is Travis. He was kind enough to have dinner with me after my sex-crazed friend deserted me."

"Oh! Sorry about that, but . . . um, well, something came up."

Right, Bailey thought, *like Brett.* She may not be as experienced as Paige, but she wasn't naïve. Brett's smoldering looks in the restaurant had hot sex, ready and waiting, written all over it. And her friend Paige had never let an opportunity like that pass her by.

"So . . ." Paige continued—as Travis rolled Bailey to her stomach and trailed kisses down her spine—"I guess you're pretty tired now. You want to just meet tomorrow morning for breakfast?"

"Ah!" Bailey tried to regulate her breathing until she could hang up the phone, but it was kind of difficult with Travis's erection buried deep inside her.

Then he began moving.

"Yes—yes! I mean, sure, what time?" The mattress was beginning to bounce and she hoped Paige wouldn't hear the squeaks.

"What? Um, I'm really tired, so how about I give you a call when I wake up?"

Bailey meant to agree and tell her friend good-bye, but Travis reached around her and hung up the phone.

She really didn't mind.

Paige stared at the phone, then hung up.

"Okay," she said, walking toward her prey, who was naked and firmly tied to the guest chair. Her heart hammered beneath the thin silk of her bustier. The edible thong felt different against her engorged folds as she walked to Brett. The fire in his eyes sent a shudder of sexual hunger racing through her.

Climbing onto the chair, her knees on each side of his lean hips, she kissed him with reckless abandon, rubbing her silk-covered breasts against his firm chest. Against the moisture of her arousal, his turgid penis pulsed, its heat making her impossibly wetter.

She'd love nothing more than to sink onto his impressive erection, but the edible lingerie had been her fantasy, and Brett had been more than willing to accommodate her. He'd even let her tie him up.

A man after her own heart.

The thought gave her pause. Many former lovers would agree she had no heart, only an insatiable sexual appetite.

And, of course, they were right, she thought as she leaned back, putting her legs on either side of Brett's head.

The heat of his increased respiration excited her even more.

Grasping his wrists, she positioned his hands to cover her breasts. He needed no further instruction and immediately began fondling, kneading, and plucking her ripe nipples.

Summoning her strength, she arched up, hooking her knees behind his head, bringing her in direct contact with his mouth.

His tongue took an experimental swipe of the edible-thong crotch, sending shudders of need streaking to her extremities.

She tightened her legs and growled, "Eat me." Then gave in to the sensations racing through her body.

And her heart.

30

_____

"Are you okay?" Ben's voice came in huffs as he continued to pump into her. "It doesn't hurt?"

It took a second for Reese to realize he meant their position on the stairs, not the actual sex act.

In reality, their position was . . . interesting. It tilted her pelvis for a different angle of penetration. That angle caused an inferno of sensations to lick through her body.

A grunt was the only sound she could form as she wrapped her legs around his hips and slammed her pelvis up against his, delighting in the feel of his sweat-slicked skin against her breasts. Their abdomens met with a slapping, sucking sound.

Thunder rattled the windows, shaking the very foundation of the building. The effect was a vibration of the wooden steps at her back. Deep within, a tiny vibration answered the external stimulus. Her breath caught. Her nipples tightened.

Teeth clicked as their mouths came together for another searing kiss.

Her uterus contracted as the rest of her muscles followed

suit, and her climax washed over her, pulling her into its sensuous undertow.

Ben quickly followed, his spine arching, muscles rigid, a guttural sound escaping his throat.

When their heart rates slowed, Ben pushed up from her and grinned. "Wow. Was what we just had what they call make-up sex?" He gave a final, deeper thrust. "If so, I could get used to it."

It took great effort, but she managed to raise her heavy hand high enough to give his shoulder a weak slap.

"Not funny," she said, gasping the words.

"Oh," he said with a satisfied nod. "I get it. You missed me."

Pushing until she'd severed their connection, she pushed him aside and stood on the step. "Yeah, right."

He heaved a sigh and grabbed her hand before she could get away. "I don't want to fight again. Let's go take a shower to get the rest of the mud, and who knows what else, off of us. Then we'll see what we can find to eat. And, if you play your cards right, I just might let you have your wicked way with me again." He kissed the tip of her nose and tugged her up the stairs.

After their makeshift bathing, even the tepid water dribbling out of the old showerhead felt incredibly luxurious.

Reese groaned, tilting her face into the meager spray of water.

"Feels good?" Ben stepped into the shower and pulled her against his firm body as he swayed them from side to side.

"Um-hmm," she said with a smile, eyes still closed. "It's positively orgasmic."

"Nope. I can show you what orgasmic feels like."

And he did.

Reese rolled off Ben and flopped onto the pillow to look at the ceiling medallion. For several minutes, she concentrated on breathing in and out.

Something, an idea, buzzed around the periphery of her mind, just out of reach. What was it?

"Stop thinking so hard," Ben muttered next to her ear. "You're keeping me awake."

Instead, she rolled to face him. "I've seen the emblem on the slickers those men wore down on the beach. I just can't remember where."

He kissed the tip of her nose. "Probably when they were on their way out of the hotel in Sand Dollar."

"Right. But I remember thinking, back then, that I'd seen it before that. I just can't place them." She sighed. "I hate it when that happens."

"Don't worry about it," he said, pulling her closer and nuzzling her neck. "My grandmother always said, if you think about something else, what you're trying to remember will come to you." His hands rubbed up and down her bare back, finally settling low enough for him to grasp her butt. "I can help you take your mind off of it."

"Gee, thanks." Halfway into their kiss, she pulled back, breaking lip contact. "What did they say they were doing here? Do you think they're scouting out the island? Maybe they're planning to make a bid?"

Ben rolled to his back and pulled her to lie against his side. "Nah. They said they were here on business, taking some kind of soil samples."

"Why would they do that, if they weren't planning to make a bid?" Sitting up, she scooted to the edge of the bed and dug in her bag.

"Now what are you doing?"

Her shoulders slumped. "Crap." She held up her cell. "Still no signal."

"Let me get this straight." He sat up, the covers falling to drape his hips. "We have hot sex on the stairs, then again in the shower. Now we're naked, in bed, and you feel the burning desire to make a phone call." He gave a dry bark of laughter. "No doubt about it, I've definitely lost my touch."

Reese did an eye roll. "As you're so fond of telling me, get over yourself. It's not all about you, you know. I told you, I'm working. I'm here because of my job and part of that job is to keep my boss informed. To do that, I need to use my cell phone, only there's no stupid signal."

He ran his hand over his face and heaved a sigh. "Yeah, I get that. What I don't get is what you think you need to report. Nothing has changed. Other than our sex lives, which I doubt is any of your boss's business. Don't give me that look, Blondie. It's true. The auction hasn't happened yet. You haven't had much of a chance to scope out the entire property because of the storm. And, because of the storm, you're trapped out here. You were trapped yesterday and you're still trapped today. Hardly newsworthy."

She flopped back on the pillow next to him. "You're right. I guess I just feel guilty for not contacting her and telling her my every move."

His hand covered her breast. "Your *every* move?"

"Relax," she said, turning to slide her arms around his neck. "I don't plan on divulging any of *your* moves."

He bent and licked her breast, earning a shudder from her.

"You have a few moves of your own." His breath fanned her nipple.

She gasped when he began sucking and she gave a shaky laugh. "Yeah, well, I don't plan on telling her about those either."

31

"Son of a bitch!" Dorinda slammed down her phone, then slapped the top of her desk for good measure, ignoring the stinging in her hands. "Where the hell is Reese? Why the fuck isn't she answering her damned cell?"

Halston Conrad sank deeper into the leather sofa in Dorinda's office. "There is a tropical storm in her area, doll baby. It isn't out of the realm of possibility that cell signals have been disrupted." He twisted the massive signet ring on his right pinky. "Have you tried the hotel?"

"Yes, I tried it. They haven't heard from her in over twenty-four hours. We're going to have to fly down there."

"My jet is ready when you are. But there is only a small window of opportunity, due to the storm. All you have to do is say the word. Soon. And agree to my conditions."

His conditions were always the same. Not that she minded. She just liked to fuck on her terms.

She gave a curt nod and snarled under her breath. Damn Halston Conrad to hell. She'd tell him exactly what she thought of him, if he wasn't such a great fuck. His cock was enormous. Just thinking about it, even in her current frame of mind, made her wet.

And that irritated her too.

At her age, she had no time to allow sexual urges to deter her from her business goals. Unfortunately, that's how she came to be in her current dilemma.

Thanks to some unwise advice, she'd lost a substantial amount of her assets. Then along came Halston. And his enormous cock. He was a skilled lover, and she'd been alone for so long. The combination had been irresistible. After too many earth-shattering orgasms to count, everything he suggested had seemed like a good idea.

Which was how he came to own 49 percent of her company.

Now she was forced to play ball with him, as well as ball him.

She growled her frustration.

Jumping up, she strode to the couch, ripping off her suit jacket and camisole as she went. May as well enjoy what he had to offer. Nothing else was going right for her today. A mind-blowing orgasm might help.

It was all his fault she was in this mess, she reasoned. Her nerves were strung out. No doubt about it, she desperately needed release. Halston was ready, she noted by a glance at the obvious bulge in his designer dress pants. And she knew from experience he was willing and oh so able. Why not put him to work?

She wiggled until her pencil skirt bunched around her hips as she climbed to straddle his lap. "I need to relax," she said, pushing his head until he sucked her breast deep into his mouth.

It wasn't enough.

Visions of Reese Parker sipping mai tais and laughing at some innocuous comment made by a faceless man had Dorinda's muscles tightening. And not in a good way. "More," she said in a hoarse whisper, rubbing her aching core against the hard ridge in his pants.

After a quick pleasure/pain nip, he straightened, easing her back toward his knees.

Even the cooler air of her office felt erotic as it swirled around her wet nipples. Finally she found her voice. "Do you want me to take off the rest of my clothes?"

She hoped her legs would support her weight. Damn, she hated sounding breathless almost as much as she hated being so sexually needy.

Halston's thin lips curved into a knowing smile. "I can work around them, sugar pussy." With one hand, he unbuttoned and unzipped his pants, then freed his erection.

"Hurry," she breathed, blocking her hatred for his disgusting nicknames in favor of immediate and intense sexual release. She watched him reach into the drawer of the end table and begin opening the condom.

She whimpered again when he picked her up and moved her to his side. Her knees sank into the leather cushions.

"It's flavored," he said with a smile and a wave of his hand to indicate the bright yellow condom sheathing him.

Reaching around her hips, he gathered her close, his fingers plowing beneath the thin crotch of her silk thong. Talented fingers tunneled along her folds, exciting her to the brink, before sliding deep into her wetness.

The action caused her head to dip, bringing her up close and personal with her private joystick.

She took him into her mouth and took an experimental lick. Banana. At that moment, he shoved his fingers deeper, which pushed his penis to the back of her throat.

They groaned.

He withdrew his fingers, eliciting a whimper of need from Dorinda.

The stinging slap he delivered to her genitals only heightened her excitement. The next slap made her internal muscles convulse in spasms of pleasure. Her excitement dripped down her inner thigh.

On sexual overload, she attacked his erection, sucking and biting, reaching her hand down to jiggle and squeeze his testicles, while his fingers plunged back into her receptive body.

Determined to make him come before her next climax, she increased the tempo, her mind on nothing more than physical gratification.

Let the games begin.

32

Rita made a discreet adjustment as the screen door slammed shut.

Rick was drinking a beer while he sat in a rocker on the front porch and watched the rain.

"Just as I think the storm is moving out, it comes back again," she said, slipping onto her husband's lap and pulling his head into the pillow of her breasts.

Rick nuzzled her breast through her loose T-shirt for a few seconds, then looked up at her. "Storms are like that. They make everything and everyone edgy. You can feel it in the air."

He played with her nipple through the fabric until it pebbled for him.

"I see you're not wearing a bra. Musta missed that earlier." He plucked at the hardened tip, causing her breath to hitch.

"I just took it off before I came out here."

She squirmed on his lap, biting back a smile at her effect on him.

"That's not all I'm not wearing," she whispered in his ear, unbuttoning his fly.

He glanced around the deserted porch. "What if some of our guests come out here?"

"Most of them have already checked out. Travis is with the girl from Houston." She snickered. "Knowing my brother, we won't see either of them until tomorrow. And when I took fresh sheets up to remake a vacated room, the sounds I heard coming from her friend's room told me she's occupied for the night too."

Rick sighed when she gently ran her fist up and down his freed erection. "Things could change, you know."

"Are you saying you're not interested?"

"You're holding the proof that says otherwise." He ran his hand beneath her shirt to cup and squeeze her breast. "I'm just saying we need to either take this to our apartment or be discreet."

Rita grinned down at him. "That's why I wore a full skirt." She raised the hem, flashing him for a second, pleased to feel his penis surge within her grasp. "So . . . what do you say?"

"I say climb aboard."

Hefting her skirt, she straddled him. A sigh escaped as she settled onto his turgid flesh, not stopping until she'd taken him fully into her body.

Groaning, she made a little circle with her hips as she planted tiny kisses all over her husband's face.

Her tongue darted out to lick a trickle of sweat from Rick's cheek.

He groaned. Gripping her hip bones, he ground into her, causing an ache to swell deep within her.

He drew a shuddering breath. "Damn, I love to fuck you on the porch." He bent to bite her nipple through the knit of her shirt. " 'Course, I love to fuck you anywhere." Thrust. "Anytime."

"Yes-s-s." She arched her back, taking him deeper. "I just wish we didn't have guests. Then we could be naked out here."

She gasped at the fierceness of his thrust. "Easy. We don't want anyone to know what we're doing."

"I want you naked," he said with a growl. "Like we were during Hurricane Ike."

Just the thought of their sexual marathon during the last big hurricane had her slipping and sliding on his lap.

"I want that too," she finally managed to say, "but we can't right now."

"Then at least show me some pussy." Rick shoved at her skirt.

After a quick glance around, she pulled the edge of her skirt up around her abdomen.

He groaned and stroked the smoothness of her recently waxed skin, then stretched her labia open to get a better view of his penis plunging in and out.

"Lord, I'm going to come all over you! Look at what we're doing." His thumbs massaged her swollen clitoris, spreading her juices around.

It was more than she could bear. Spreading her legs a little wider, she plunged down on him, raised a few centimeters and came down forcefully again.

The wind and rain picked up, slamming across the plank flooring to douse them.

The storm had nothing on the force of their passion.

Bucking up into his wife, faster and faster, as he felt her orgasm begin to crest, Rick tore her shirt from her and bit down on one erect nipple as his climax roared through him.

The force of the storm's resurgence drowned out the scream of Rita's pleasure.

Thunder shook the floor of the porch, a fitting ending to their stormy interlude.

Gasping, she clung to him while he petted her back and continued to suck and lick her nipples.

When she could bear to speak again, she held his head tight

to her chest, willing her words to be heard through her body. "I'm beginning to worry about Ben and his lady friend. They should have been back by now."

"The Mills fishing group isn't back either," Rick said against her breast.

"Do you think they're all safe and together?" She idly plumped her breast with one hand and traced her husband's mouth with the tip of her nipple.

"Hope not." He licked the tip and blew on it. "I know Ben. And I saw the way he looked at Reese Parker." He sucked her breast deep into his mouth, silent for a few seconds.

"W-what do you mean?" she asked as her heartbeat accelerated again.

"I mean Ben wouldn't welcome company. About now, I think he's probably doing the same thing we're doing." To demonstrate, he ground his hips into hers.

"Really?" She did some grinding of her own.

Rick nodded and stood, gently lowering her to stand on the plank floor and then finally severing their intimate contact.

"Stormy weather makes stormy passion, sweetheart," he said, leading her to the porch railing, then gently pushing until her upper torso was wet with rain. He sluiced the drops from her breasts, holding her ponytail aside to lick and kiss the back of her neck until she was writhing against the rail.

The wind caressed her buttocks when he pulled her skirt up around her waist and she widened her stance.

"If they're not back by tomorrow morning or we haven't heard from them, I'll see what I can do about a search party," he said over the roar of the storm.

Rain stung as it pelted her face and bare breasts. Behind her, Rick stroked the fires of her passion higher with his fingers. He played with her slick folds, then plunged his finger in and out in a rapid succession that had her gasping. Her heart slammed against her ribs, making breathing difficult.

"But first," Rick's voice rose above the storm as he gripped her hips, "I need to do this."

He impaled her, banging her hips against the porch rail. She'd never felt so alive. Exhilarated.

Before bliss claimed her again, Ben flashed through her mind.

Wherever he and Reese were, Rita hoped they were having as passionate an experience.

"Oh-oh-oh!" Hands gripping the brass headboard, Reese reveled in the sound of the old bed bumping the wall with each of Ben's powerful thrusts. Who could have known she'd experience wall-banging sex? Even better, it was on a business trip. The thought made her smile.

If she could draw a deep breath, she'd marvel at her sexual activity. She'd had more varied and orgasmic sex since she'd met Ben than she'd had in her entire life.

"I don't know where you're at, but come back to me, darlin'," Ben said, gripping her ankles and placing them on his shoulders.

The slap of skin against skin played a duet with the banging of the headboard.

The new angle of penetration caused a twinge deep within her abdomen that caught her breath and ratcheted up her passion.

All thoughts except ones of immediate sexual gratification left her mind.

Her fourth orgasm slammed into her, drowning her in decadent pleasure.

Ben gave a roar of completion, his spine stiffening into an arch as he plunged into her one more time, then collapsed, his breathing harsh in her ear.

"Kiss me," he finally managed to gasp. "The way I feel right now, I may just die of pleasure. I need one more kiss."

Laughing, she planted a smacking kiss on his puckered lips. "You're such a drama queen."

Ben went limp, his weight pressing her into the mattress.

"Ben? Ben, are you okay? If this is a joke, it's not funny!" Just as she began to really worry, he growled and rolled with her until she lay stretched along his body.

She screamed, then punched his shoulder. "That was so not funny! You shouldn't fake stuff like that."

In response, he rubbed noses with her. "Who said I was faking? You're wearing this old boy plumb out, having your way with me."

"Right." She rolled to his side and snuggled close. The feeling of utter contentment was just from having another world-class orgasm, wasn't it? Of course. It was just a manifestation of having been sexually satisfied. Four times.

She couldn't keep the smile from her face at the thought of how many times she'd come in one afternoon.

"Are you ever going to tell me why you followed me clear to the other side of the island today?"

She pinched his nipple.

"Ow! Cut it out. Since you're not saying, I have to assume it's because you missed me so much you had to find me." He leaned closer and whispered, "And have your way with me."

"Yeah, right. I was so horny, I braved the elements to hunt you down."

"That sounds about right."

"Don't be smug. It's unattractive. Actually," she said, snuggling closer and yawning, "I couldn't wait to tell you what I saw."

"I'm listening."

"Remember that hole I fell into? The one with the orange plastic? Well, when I was up here, making the bed—"

"Ah-hah! I knew it! You had sexual designs on me."

"Will you shut up and listen! I looked out the window when

I was making the bed, and, okay, maybe I did think about us using it later. Maybe. Anyway, I noticed the orange again. Then I saw more. So I went into the bathroom and climbed up to look out that window, and that's when it hit me. Ben, it's some kind of grid! If you look at it from up here, it's plainly not a random pattern."

"What kind of grid?"

She sighed. "That's the problem. I have no idea. I thought maybe if the rain lets up, we could go see if we can figure it out."

"We can do that," he said, snuggling her closer. "Let's rest a spell and see how the rain is doing after we take a little nap."

Ben awoke to the rain continuing to pound on the roof. Beside him, Reese slept.

He eased away from her, relieved when she accommodated him by rolling over, her back to him.

With slow, deliberate movements, he got out of bed. Reese didn't move.

Guilt ate at him. Reese had told him why she was here. It had been the perfect opportunity to clear the air and tell her who he was and why he didn't want her to bid on his island.

Yet, for some reason, he'd remained stubbornly silent.

But what if Reese Parker wasn't even her real name? What if she had other reasons for buying his island? Had the soil sample guys taken samples of more than soil? Maybe that was the real reason Reese had come running after him. Maybe she and the sample guys were working together. Or maybe they worked for her and were doing some sort of soil analysis for her so she could decide if she wanted the island.

He had to find out.

Another glance told him she was still asleep.

Inching his way around the bed, he kept glancing at the naked woman, wishing he could just crawl back into bed with her and make love until he couldn't think of anything but her and the way they felt together.

But he had to know.

Bending, he picked up her mammoth bag, praying it wouldn't rattle and alert her.

It only took a second to locate her wallet. It weighed a ton. What did the woman carry in her wallet, gold?

A quick look confirmed she was exactly who she said she was and her corporate ID badge backed it up.

Curiosity kept him rummaging. How many lip glosses did one person need? Maybe she had chronic chapped lips or something.

Antinausea medication. He gave a silent snort. Yeah, like that worked. Antidiarrheal medication. Laxatives. Sinus medication. VapoRub. Antibiotic ointment. Several kinds of bandages. The woman was nothing if not prepared.

He paused, her cell phone in his hand. If she didn't have it locked, he might be able to scroll through her phone and find out if she'd been talking to anyone he knew.

"Ben? What are you doing? Are you going through my bag?" With each word, Reese's sleepy voice grew more awake and louder.

Oh, shit.

33

"Huh?" *Think, Adams, think.* "Ah, no! I mean, of course not!" Dropping the bag, he held up her phone. "I woke up. I thought I heard something. I thought maybe it was your phone, so I came over to check."

Her smile was breathtaking and made him feel lower than a snake's armpits.

Unmindful of her nudity, she ran to him and grabbed the phone. Her smile fell when she saw she still had no service.

"I don't know what you thought you heard, but it wasn't my phone." To be sure, she walked to the window and held it up. Nothing.

"Um, maybe it's running out of its charge and beeped?"

"Nope. The battery still has almost a full charge. Without use, it should last for at least a week."

Back in bed, he held up the edge of the sheet. "Well, I must have heard something else. Why don't you come back to bed? It's still raining. There's nothing else to do, so we may as well—"

"Make whoopee?"

"Well, I was going to suggest another nap, but I'm willing if you are."

"Sorry." She climbed in beside him and snuggled up. "I didn't mean to accuse you of anything. Either time."

"No problem."

"Ben?" Her voice pulled him back from the edge of sleep a few minutes later. "Are you awake?"

"I am now."

"I was just thinking. I mean, well, we've been pretty hot and heavy. Intimate, even . . ."

"Spit it out, Blondie. What do you want to know?"

"You're not married, are you? I mean, obviously, if you are, you're not happily married. But I just, I mean, I need to know—"

His hand covered her mouth. "Hush. No. Not only no, but hell no! I'm not married. Shit, woman, do you really have such a low opinion of me that you think I'd do the things we'd done if I had a wife?"

"Sorry." She snuggled back down, only to break her silence in less than a minute. "Ben?"

"What?"

"Have you ever been married?"

"Have you?" he countered.

"No. Have you?" Silence. "Ben?"

"Yeah, I was married. Once. A long time ago." He wished she'd forget it, change the subject, go to sleep. Anything but continue along her current conversational path.

"What happened?"

"We made a mistake and corrected it."

"Was she from around here?" she persisted.

"Yep."

"Has she remarried?" For some reason, she needed to know. Ben's clipped answers weren't helping.

"Yep."

"Does she still live in Sand Dollar?"

He took a deep breath. Just as she thought he wasn't going to answer, he said in a low voice, "You could say that."

"Do you ever run into her?" Why did she keep probing? Maybe she was looking for a reason to back off.

"Just about every day." Crap. She didn't need to hear that. But, then again, she had asked.

Swallowing her reluctance and what felt suspiciously like jealousy, she forced the next words from her mouth.

"Really? Maybe I've met her—"

"Oh, yeah, you've met her, all right." He looked her in the eye. "It's Rita."

Her heart seized along with her breath. To say she was shocked was an understatement. She wasn't sure what she'd expected, but it sure as heck hadn't been that.

On second thought, maybe she shouldn't have been too surprised. After all, Sand Dollar wasn't a big town. The dating pool was probably limited. But still, Rita and Ben?

Ben arched one eyebrow and said, "Surprise."

"I—I don't understand." His eyes widened and she hurried on. "I mean, obviously, I understood what you said. I just don't understand how someone who had been married could continue to be such good friends. You are friends with her, right?"

He nodded. "Rita and Rick are my two best friends. Always have been."

"But how . . . ?"

"The usual way." He grinned. "I'd be happy to give you a demonstration," he said, and bumped against her with his semierect penis.

"Stop joking around." Tucking the sheet around her, Reese scooted toward the other side of the bed. "I'm serious. I really want to know why you married and divorced Rita."

He scrubbed his face with his hands and heaved a sigh. "Of

course, you do." Propping his head up on one fist, he turned to look at her. "I don't suppose you'd be satisfied with the condensed version that we made a mistake and corrected it?"

She shook her head, wondering if she should accept the short explanation and try to get past the fact she may very well be falling in love with someone who was best friends with his ex-wife. Did she really want to be involved in something that had potential for heartbreak written all over it?

"We were young and stupid?"

She bit back a smile at the hopeful look on his face and shook her head again.

"Okay. Rick and Rita were hot and heavy all through high school and college. We all went to UT," he said as an aside. "Toward the end of our junior year, they broke up. Rick dropped out the next week. I—"

"Started dating Rita?"

He gave her a hard look. "Will you let me tell it?"

"Sorry. Go on."

"Come on back over here and let me hold you while I tell you. It would be easier without you looking at me."

He had a point. A bonus would be she also wouldn't have to look at his face while he told her the details about marrying another woman. A woman he still obviously had feelings for and had no plans to stop seeing socially. She scooted back across the mattress, stifling a sigh when he tucked her close to his side.

"That's better," he said, his voice rumbling through his chest against her ear. After taking a deep breath, he began talking. "Since we'd all been friends, Rita naturally began spending a lot of time with me, with Rick gone and all."

"Naturally." It was very hard to keep her body in a relaxed pose. Especially when she had to fight the urge to pinch him. Hard.

Oblivious to her misery, he continued.

"One night, we'd been to a party. Rita had a lot to drink. We both did. My apartment was closer than hers, so I told her she could stay there. I didn't want her driving in that condition."

"Of course, you didn't." Despite his surly attitude when they'd first met, she'd always known, or at least suspected, that deep down he was a good guy. Darn it.

"Are you sure you want to hear this?"

"I'm sure," she lied. "Go on."

"Rick picked that night to beg her to take him back. When she didn't answer her phone, he drove in to see her in person."

"And she wasn't home," she guessed, hoping she wasn't correctly guessing what happened next.

"That's right." She felt him nod against the top of her head. "So, naturally, he came to my place to see if I knew where she was—"

"Naturally."

"Hey, are you going to let me tell this?"

"Sorry." She traced the edge of his nipple with her fingertip. Maybe if she distracted him, he'd shut up.

No such luck.

Ben took a deep breath and exhaled. "I mentioned I'd had a lot to drink too, didn't I?" She nodded. "Well, I didn't hear the phone. He figured I was out too. Since he knew where the spare key was, he let himself in. He found us . . ."

"Found you? Were you lost? Oh, no, tell me he didn't . . ."

He nodded. "Oh, yeah, he did. We were together. Naked. In my bed."

Reese truly thought she may lose her lunch. At their age, it wasn't like either of them would be inexperienced. It was just that she preferred not knowing exactly who and what that experience was, or when it had happened.

"That's okay. You don't have to tell me any more. I get the idea." Not to mention a disturbing mental picture.

When she struggled to sit up, to move away, he tightened his grip, holding her plastered to his side. His naked side against her naked side. Dang it, she so didn't want to be there anymore.

"You wanted to know. You insisted. Now you need to hear it all."

Slumping back against him, she blinked back tears. Stupid tears. Her nose stung. If it started running, she would be beyond mortified.

"Go on. I can probably guess what Rick's reaction was, though."

Ben's chuckle echoed against her ear. "Truth be told, I was more horrified than him. And poor Rita!"

"What did Rick say? Did he beat you up?"

"I wish he had. I've beaten myself up enough for both of us over the past ten years."

"You two didn't fight?"

"Nope. Rick looked at each of us, nodded, and turned and walked out the door."

"And she followed him and explained and they got back together?" Maybe if Ben had lived the life of a monk ever since, she could forgive him a night with Rita. Wait. She didn't know him back then. She had no right to be jealous or hurt.

"Not hardly. He wouldn't talk to either of us for months. He blocked our calls and e-mail. By the time we came home for the summer, he was gone. He'd joined the navy."

"But eventually he forgave you both and came back for Rita, right?"

"Eventually. Hell, it might have happened sooner if—"

"If? If what?" And did she really want to hear it?

"If Rita hadn't found out she was pregnant."

A weight pressed on Reese's chest. Was she having a heart attack? Breathing was difficult and it took a second to realize it was because tears were choking her.

A baby. Ben and Rita had made a baby together.

"A baby?" she finally said in a squeaky voice. "A boy or girl? Does it live with them?" She hadn't seen a child anywhere around the hotel. Of course, she hadn't been there too long.

"No. Anyway, that's why we got married. There was no baby. She miscarried at five months. A boy."

"I'm sorry," she whispered.

"It's not like you're thinking. I can tell by the look on your face, you're pitying me."

"I feel sorry for anyone who lost a baby." Was there something he wasn't telling her? From the stubborn set of his jaw, it seemed likely.

"Rick came to his senses, but we were already married. And miserable. He and Rita started seeing each other—"

"That's awful! She cheated on you? And while she was carrying your baby?" How could anyone lucky enough to be married to Ben be so stupid?

"Hey, it wasn't entirely her fault. It takes two, you know. And, like I said, we were both miserable."

"How long were you married?"

"About four months. Maybe. We all knew Rick and Rita belonged together, so we went to Mexico for a quick divorce. Rick went too, and they were married there."

"Oh, Ben!" Crying now, she clung to him. "How did you stand watching her marry someone else when she was carrying your baby?"

He patted her shoulder. "It wasn't that hard. It was the right thing to do. Besides, it wasn't my baby."

"What?" Raising up, she swiped at her leaky eyes. Ben was actually smiling at her.

"Rita and I never had sex. That night, after the party, we were both too drunk."

"But you said he found you in bed together, naked."

He nodded. "He did. I'm not saying we didn't think about

fooling around, but we were too wasted to do the deed. Plus, our hearts really weren't in it."

"But—but then why did you get married?"

"To bring Rick to his senses. When it didn't work, we went ahead with it because . . . well, you know."

"What a mess."

He snorted. "Tell me about it. Like I said before, we were young and stupid."

"But you did it for the right reasons." She sniffed and smiled through her remaining tears.

"Maybe." He neatly flipped her to her back. Lying on top of her, he kissed away her tears. "And maybe," he said, insinuating himself between her legs, "I was waiting for you to come along."

34

Ben pounded on the bathroom door. "Hey! Why'd you lock the door?"

Reese smiled at her reflection in the medicine cabinet mirror and spit out her toothpaste. "Because I knew if we showered together again, we'd end up back in bed, and you said you had things to do."

"Maybe I meant you," he called through the door.

Laughing, she rinsed her mouth.

When she opened the door, he was leaning against the frame, looking so hot he took her breath away. How anyone with beard stubble, a faded T-shirt advertising a fishing charter, and wrinkled khaki shorts could look sexy was a mystery, but he definitely pulled it off.

"I was just going to take a hike to the other side of the island to make sure our *guests* aren't taking advantage of our generosity. Wanna come along?"

His use of the word *our* sent a secret thrill running through her. She'd never been part of an *our* before. It was sort of like they were a real couple.

She liked it.

* * *

"Will you slow down!" Reese tripped through the under-brush, scraping her legs in the process, in her attempt to match Ben's long, purposeful strides.

"Hey, I can't help it if your short little legs can't keep up," he called back over his shoulder as he continued to plow forward.

"I'm hungry," she complained when he paused and she was finally able to reach his side again. She looked down. "And I'm bleeding. Isn't there a better path somewhere around here we could use?"

"We're on the path, Blondie." His smile was white in the filtered light.

The rain had let up, but it still covered them with a fine mist. Reese followed Ben's line of vision to the deserted beach. "Maybe they're gone. It's not raining so hard now. Maybe we can get out now too?"

Mother Nature chose that moment to crank up the volume of the wind, immediately following it with a stinging sheet of torrential rain.

"Maybe not," Reese yelled through the noise of the renewed storm, answering her own question.

After a few more steps, she grabbed Ben's arm and pointed. "Look!"

A dark dot bobbed in the turbulent water between the shore and the platform anchoring Ben's larger boat. It looked like the fishing boat's occupants were doing nothing except holding on for dear life.

"Aw, shit-fire-spit!" Ben kicked off his shoes at the edge of the beach and ran for the water.

"Wait! What are you doing?" Reese's yells bounced back to her from the roar of the rain and surf. Her shoulders slumped as she watched Ben's strong strokes take him closer to the yellow-slickered men.

She sank to the sand, clutching Ben's Top-Siders to her chest. "Great," she muttered. "Now what?" She narrowed her eyes. "Don't you dare drown and leave me stranded here, Ben Adams!"

There was no way he could have heard her yelling, but he turned and waved back at her when he reached the boat.

After an interminable time, Ben crawled to shore, dragging the boatload of men several feet behind him.

Now in shallow water, the men jumped out and dragged the boat up on the beach.

"Were y'all stranded out there overnight?" Ben asked as Reese walked up.

The taller man laughed. "No, we didn't even make it that far, yesterday. We ended up spending the night in the cave again. When the storm appeared to be waning, we thought we'd try again."

"Well," Ben said, looking up, then out across the water, "this should be the last of it. We'll be socked in the rest of the day, but tomorrow should be clear. Meanwhile, I want to remind you, you're trespassing on private property. Due to the weather, you're welcome to take shelter in the cave, but I don't want to see you anywhere else. And I expect you to leave everything like you found it, and clear out as soon as possible. Got that?"

The man gave a curt nod and walked to join his teammates as they hauled their boxes out of the boat.

"C'mon, let's get out of here." Ben grabbed her elbow and half-dragged her along as he headed back into the vegetation.

"Was there a problem back there?" Reese stumbled, but he caught her.

"None that I know of, but I don't want to hang around and find out. Especially with you there."

"Thanks, I think." She grabbed his arm and turned him to face her. "Ben, I appreciate you being protective, but I'm a big girl. I've been on my own for quite a while and I'm perfectly capable of taking care of myself. Heck, if I can hold my own with the Dragon Lady, I can do it with just about anyone."

He stared, the muscles flexing in his jaw. "You talk a good game, Blondie, but I'm betting you never had to worry about being gang raped by your boss."

Oh, crap, she hadn't even thought of something like that. "What? Do you think that is a possibility?"

He answered as he kept walking, pulling her behind him. "They're strange men, Blondie, and you're a hot little number. From talking to them, I'd say they're pretty safe, but you never know."

"Better safe than sorry."

"Right."

The rest of the walk back to the hotel was made in silence, with Reese thinking about the logo on the men's slickers. She'd seen it before. The image danced in and out of her memory like an annoying gnat.

Finally, as they neared the back steps, it hit her.

"Ben!" She ran up the steps and grabbed the back of his shirt. "I remember where I saw the logo!"

35

"Any luck?" Paige dropped into the chair next to Bailey on the front porch of the hotel.

Bailey stuck her iPhone into the pocket of her rain jacket and sighed. "No. It's either nothing or it fakes me out with a ring before going to Reese's voice mail."

"Same with me. I just tried, by the window in my room." She smiled at her friend. "So . . . what did you do last night?"

Bailey grinned and looked down at her lap. "The same thing you did, I imagine."

"Oh, yeah? Way to go, Bay! I thought young Trevor was pretty cute."

Bailey threw a wry glance her way. "His name is Travis, and he's not all that young."

"Do tell." Paige raised her eyebrows as she crossed her legs, focusing her attention on her friend. "Really. Tell."

"No! We're not in junior high anymore, Paige. Besides, I'm not the kiss-and-tell type." She primly smoothed the skirt of her sundress.

"Okay, I'll tell," Paige said with a smile. "After our first tumble, Brett let me tie him up. Then I gave him a little—"

"Paige! Please. Really? TMI!"

"Hey, I was just trying to help." Paige settled deeper into her chair, her sandal-clad feet on the porch rail.

"By telling me the intimate details of your night of debauchery? Thanks, but I'll pass."

"Debauchery? You don't even know the meaning of the word. I could tell you about—"

Bailey held up her hand. "Please. I know you're much more, um, experienced in that area than me. Heck, you're probably more experienced than Reese and I put together. But, you know, there are some things I really don't want to know. Plus, it's a lot more fun finding it out for myself. Do you understand what I'm saying? Nod your head if you do."

Paige executed an eye roll. "Cute. Yes, I understand." She sighed and looked out at the angry gray surf. "What I don't understand is why the hell Reese let herself be talked into going out in this kind of weather."

"It probably wasn't storming when she left." Bailey took a sip from the water bottle on the table and set it down, idly dragging her finger through the wet circle on the slate. "Plus, you know Reese. Dragon Lady says jump and she asks how high. Reese probably wanted to gather as much information as she could, before the auction, so she could make the most informed bid possible."

"Yeah, that sounds like Reese. We need to get her over that tendency."

"I kind of understand it." She arched her eyebrow at Paige. "Not all of us have high-paying jobs, you know."

"It's not all about the pay. Well, okay, the pay is great, but I also love what I do. If Reese could say the same, I'd butt out and let her continue making a pittance. She's not happy, Bailey.

We both know it. But if we don't push her, she'll stay right where she's at and be miserable until she's old enough to collect her pitiful retirement. Assuming Dragon Lady even has those benefits."

"There are some things you need to figure out for yourself, Paige." She closed her eyes and took a deep breath. Exhaling, she met Paige's gaze. "And for right now, I plan to try to relax and enjoy what time I have here before we have to go back to the real world."

"It is kind of nice here, isn't it?" Paige looked out at the water. "I wish the rain would stop, so I can at least get in some quality beach time before we leave."

"I wish the rain would stop too, so Reese can safely return from Lord knows what's out on that deserted island."

"Yeah, well, there's that too."

"Are you shitting me?" Ben pulled Reese into the kitchen and reached for some towels from the stack by the door. "Are you sure? An oil company?" He handed her a towel and then shook his head. "Although that grid you saw could be from some kind of seismic testing. I know they do that when they're looking for oil and gas deposits. But . . . it doesn't make sense."

She paused after drying her face, thinking. "It doesn't? Didn't they tell you they were collecting some kind of samples?"

He nodded. "Yeah, soil samples. But there's no oil on Serenity."

Briskly toweling her hair, she asked, "How do you know?"

Okay, now would be as good a time as any to come clean. Of course, knowing he had enough money to stop the auction would make it a better time. No, it was past time.

"Reese, I . . . how about a cup of coffee or hot chocolate? There's still plenty of both in the pantry."

"Um, okay"—she followed him to the pantry—"I don't suppose there's any cream in there?"

"Nope. And, trust me, if there was, you wouldn't want it. I guess that means you want hot chocolate? And, before you ask, no, there is no whipped cream or—wait! Ah-ha!" He reached deep on the back shelf and pulled out an old blue tin canning jar. "Marshmallows." He shook the jar. The mini-marshmallows moved as one. "They may be a little stale, but what's to go bad? They're bound to soften up once they soak in the hot chocolate a little."

"Since I have no idea, we may as well give it a whirl. What can I do to help?"

"Tell me everything you know about this oil company. What was it again? H.V.?"

He turned on the faucet and they watched the water trickle into the kettle.

"H.C. . . . H.C. Worldwide, Nationwide? Something like that, with the word *Oil*." She closed her eyes, envisioning the logo on the door of the limo again. "Yes, I think that was it. It was printed above the logo, and in smaller print, under it, it said *A Division of H.C. Industries.*" She frowned. "At least I think that's what it said. Like I told you, I was kind of in a hurry. Ordinarily, I probably wouldn't have even noticed it. But it irritated me that it was illegally parked right smack-dab in front of the door to my building. I almost ran right into it when I left, which irritated me more."

"I still don't get why an oil company would be interested in an old hotel." He set the kettle on the stove burner and twisted a knob.

"I doubt it has anything to do with the hotel, unless it's sitting on top of an oil well. What do you remember about the island from when you came here as a little boy? Maybe we can figure out what's going on."

"Okay." He took her hand and drew her to sit at the table in the bay window of the kitchen. "I haven't been totally honest with you."

She drew back on her hand, but he held tight. "Excuse me?" Her voice was small and frightened-sounding. "What are you saying?"

"Shit-fire-spit, woman, stop looking at me like that! I'm not some criminal, if that's what you're thinking." He released her hand and dragged his through his hair, eyes closed.

"Then what, exactly, are you?"

Their gazes locked.

"The grandson of the late owner."

The teakettle began to make noise, breaking the silence of the big kitchen.

Ben got up and took down two mugs and began spooning hot chocolate mix into them.

"I don't understand," Reese finally managed to say. "Then you lied, before, when you said you weren't planning to bid for the island?"

"No, that's true. I'm not bidding." He gave a short bark of laughter to keep from choking on his words. "Hell, I barely have enough money to get by, forget buying a piece of property like Serenity Island."

"But would you, if you could?"

"Nope." *It's mine. All I would have to do is pay the back taxes and the damn auction wouldn't take place.* He'd tell her, but not just yet. The pity on her face already was enough to turn his stomach.

He plunked her mug in front of her on the old table and took the chair opposite her. "Well? Aren't you going to say anything? You always seem to have something to say about everything."

"Sorry. I was just thinking." She blew on the hot drink, then took a tentative sip. "Pretty good. But I think I'll wait to try out a marshmallow."

Ben held up his finger as he chewed. And chewed. "Good

idea. They're still a tad tough." With obvious effort, he swallowed.

"Okay," Reese began, "since this was your grandmother's place, I'm assuming you were out here quite a bit." He nodded. "Did you live here?"

"No. But I spent most of every summer out here."

"When was the last time you were here?" She took another sip.

"Hell, I don't recall. Maybe five years ago? I spent about a month, doing odd jobs for Gram and putting on a new roof."

"I take it you didn't have time to explore the island during that visit?"

"You got that right." He finished his cocoa and slurped up the marshmallow pebbles. "But as a kid," he said, chewing vigorously, "I knew every inch of the island."

She nodded. "So, in your opinion, there's no chance there is any oil?"

"I don't know where it would be. I—wait! I used to get into trouble all the time for getting this nasty goop all over me from the swampy place."

"The swampy place?"

He nodded. "Yeah, out on the north end. It never dries out and is full of really gross black mud that stains your hands and everything it touches—shit. I bet that's because it has oil in it!"

36

"What? Is there a problem? Why are you looking like that? Reese, cut it out! You're kind of scary when you have that look on your face."

"Hmm? Oh, sorry." She finished washing and rinsing their mugs and handed them to Ben to dry. "I was just thinking about what you said. You know, about the swampy area at the end of the island."

"It's a stinky place too." He made a face, wrinkling his nose. "I don't blame Gram for getting mad when I dragged in, covered in the mess. I remember one time, she had to burn my clothes."

"I bet they burned pretty easily."

He shrugged. "I didn't notice, but clothes usually burn with no problem. With or without oil, if that's what you're getting at."

Reese fished her cell out of her bag and held it up by the window. Her shoulders slumped. "Still no signal," she reported.

Ben held out his hand. "Let's go sit on the porch for a while.

The rain is coming pretty much straight down now, so we should stay pretty dry."

She trudged behind, allowing him to pull her along as her mind hopped from one worry to another.

Had Dorinda ever planned to open a B&B? Did she know about the soil testing? Was her boss possibly planning to move into the oil industry? And, if so, would that leave Reese unemployed? Sure, she'd been planning to resign, but did she have enough set aside to live on if her termination was immediate, before she had a chance to find another job?

Ben pulled her to stand in front of him on the porch, his arms wrapped snugly around her, his chin resting on the top of her head.

Reese tried to blank her mind and enjoy the feel of being in Ben's arms. Who knew how much more time they had left to be together?

"Relax," Ben said in her ear. "We're safe out here. Are you cold?" She shook her head and he gave her a brief hug. "Good. It feels good to be outside and not get pelted with rain." He rubbed her arms. "Don't worry, I'll get you back in plenty of time for the auction."

That surprised her. "I wasn't worried."

"Yeah, right." He pointed toward the water. "Look. If you try real hard, you can see a gradual lightening in the cloud cover. The heaviest rain should be past us by midnight. It may even be gone by morning."

Surprised, she craned her neck to look up at him. "Are you saying we can safely go back to Sand Dollar tomorrow morning?"

"Maybe. For sure, by afternoon. Like I said, plenty of time before the auction."

"I have to get busy!" Her progress to the front door was halted when Ben grabbed her hand.

"Whoa! Hold on. Where are you going? What's there to do?"

She chewed on her lip for a second. "I'm out of clean underwear—"

"Don't wear any on my account," he said with a grin.

She swatted his hands when he tried to pull her into his arms. "I am *not* going back to Sand Dollar without underwear."

"Okay. Fine." He held up his hands. "I see your point. I don't agree, but I understand. In fact, I'll even help you."

"I'm capable of washing my underwear. Thanks, anyway."

"Ah, there's where you're wrong." He bent to stare into her eyes. "Do you know how to operate a wringer washer? I can see by your face you do not." Grinning, he pulled her into the lobby. "Lucky for you, I was my grandmother's laundry helper."

"Is there enough electricity to run a washer?" Already heading for the stairs to get her clothes, she paused.

"Nope. There's enough to run the pump to pump water in and out. That's where I come in. I'm your agitator—"

"You can say that again," she teased.

"Hardy-har-har, Blondie. Better be nice. You need my muscles, not to mention my expertise."

"No offense, but how much expertise does it take to operate a washing machine?"

"Watch and learn, Grasshopper."

"That's a lot of suds." Reese eyed the rising foam. "Are you sure you don't have to measure the detergent?"

Ben grunted and continued operating the lever to move the agitator. "I've seen my grandmother do this a thousand times. She never measured." He increased his tempo.

"Maybe so, but she also had done it a lot, with doing laundry for the hotel."

"She didn't do the hotel laundry in this thing," he said through gritted teeth, muscles in his bare arms bulging. "There are about a half-dozen commercial-size automatic washers-and-dryers out back."

"Where?" She would have noticed a laundry facility. "And, more important, why the heck aren't we using it?"

"They're in the second outbuilding," he ground out. "And, if you recall, we don't have enough power to run them."

"But what about using the dryers?"

"Sorry, Blondie. We're going native. Have to hang them up to dry."

"Well, at least they'll be clean. I—oh! Look out!"

The old machine gave a ferocious-sounding belch. It spewed the rising wall of foam out in a geyser to coat the floor, as well as Ben and Reese, in a layer of slick soapsuds.

"Eew!" Reese slipped and slid, grabbing hold of the washer to prevent falling into the mess spreading over the floor.

That's when she noticed Ben coughing and gagging.

"Ben! Are you okay?" It was slow going, but she finally covered the three feet of treacherous floor to get to his side. "Ben?"

Since he continued to have problems, she thumped him hard on the back.

It knocked him off his feet, his arms windmilling, feet slipping in a desperate attempt to remain upright.

"Oh, no!" Grabbing to steady him was not her best idea.

They went down together in a sliding, oozing heap on the floor.

"Why the hell did you do that?" At least, she noted, Ben had stopped coughing.

"I was trying to help you!" She tried getting to her feet, only to fall again and rap her elbow sharply on the edge of the washer leg. "Ouch!"

"Help me? You were the one who knocked me down!"

"You're welcome, by the way." He was right, but it still hurt her feelings. She had been trying to help him. Why couldn't he see that? Stupid tears stung the backs of her eyelids.

He scooted closer and pulled her the rest of the way on the slick floor until they were nose to nose. "Thank you," he said in a low voice. "I'm sorry I yelled at you."

Swallowing, she looked up into his eyes. A giggle erupted. "You have a cute little foam hat."

With a wry grin, he scooped up two handfuls of foam and slopped them on her breasts, then fashioned the suds into pointed peaks. "There. Now you're not so skinny."

Reciprocating, she put a pile of foam on the zipper of his cargo shorts and bared her teeth in a smile. "My dream man."

"You don't need a dream man," he said, pulling her hand back until she'd rubbed away all of the foam. His hand forced hers to cup his arousal. "Not when you have the real thing."

His free hand brushed away the suds from her breast, stroking her until she bit back a moan.

"Now I'm too skinny again," she said in a husky voice.

"Naw." He pushed her shirt up and over her head, baring her breasts. "I'd say you're just about perfect." Bending, he touched the tip of his tongue to first one peaked nipple, then the other. "Although you do taste sort of soapy."

Lying back on the tile, she cupped her breasts, offering them to him. "Maybe you should clean me off."

She'd thought he'd rinse her breast, then continue their sex play.

Instead, he surprised her by laving her breasts with his tongue, then sucking her nipples until she was writhing on the hard tile, slipping on the slick surface, desperate for more.

Desperate for Ben.

"Ow!" Ben's head conked the tub of the washer, but he managed to strip the rest of his soggy clothes away and reached for her.

Her shriek echoed in the tiny back room when he pulled her shorts off, accidentally shooting her in the opposite direction.

"Stop clowning around, Blondie." He grabbed her ankle and dragged her back, sliding his soapy hands up and down her inner thigh along the way.

"And these," he said, hooking his finger on the thong between her legs, "are in the way." He lingered, his finger stroking and petting her until she was bucking her hips wildly, begging for more.

"Take them off," she finally managed to whisper.

"Your wish is my command." His smile was white in the dwindling light.

Thong dispensed with, he spread her legs and rested her calves on his tan shoulders. He reached between her legs to stroke her, his touch gentle. "So pretty and soft," he said appreciatively of her waxed area. "But I have to tell you, I'm a little disappointed. I had hoped to find out if you were a natural blonde. But this is good too." His voice was soft and hot against her folds.

His tongue was smooth, its warmth caressing her, relaxing her to open more fully to him.

Arching her back, she thrust her hips higher, greedy for his intimate kiss. His finger circled and tickled her opening, while he sucked and worried her nub with the edge of his teeth.

Soapsuds sloshed into her ears, drowning out the beat of her heart with the hissing sound of thousands of bubbles.

In an intimate cocoon, Reese allowed bliss to reign for the first time in her life. While Ben played and sucked her, she ran her slick restless hands up and down her torso, circling her breasts, pinching her slippery nipples.

Ben's probing tongue her sent her over the edge. Every muscle clenched, including her thighs, which held his head prisoner while she rode her personal wave of ecstasy.

Before she could catch her breath, Ben raised to his knees, arranging her limp legs around his hips and plunged into her.

She wanted it. She wanted him.

He obviously wanted her.

The soap-slicked tile floor had other plans.

37

Dorinda swatted Halston's hand away as the limo crunched on the gravel parking lot of the Sand Dollar Inn. Bad enough he'd groped and probed her all the way down on the plane.

Not that she was really complaining. In addition to being well hung and a gifted lover, Halston was as horny as they come. Quite possibly he was the first man she'd been with who loved sex as much as herself.

Together, they made a dynamite team, in or out of bed.

Halston regarded her with a lazy look as he reached to buzz their driver. "Take a walk, Javier. Come back for us in about fifteen minutes."

"Yes, sir," came the voice through the speakers. Immediately the sound of the driver's door opened and closed, followed by the unmistakable sound of footfalls on gravel.

"You seem on edge," Halston said, reaching under the skirt of her business suit. "Let me help you take some of the edge off." Their eyes met as he slid her thong down her legs. He tossed it aside. "Now pull up your skirt. Let me see how happy you are to see me."

She took orders from no one. Especially a man.

But she needed him. In business and in pleasure.

Together, they would be invincible.

He tickled her seam with the tip of his index finger as she hurried to wiggle up the tight-fitting skirt.

She bit back a groan, wanting to pause and spread her legs, luxuriating in his touch.

But she wanted to experience everything he was offering, and they only had fifteen minutes.

When her skirt was wadded around her bare hips, he smiled and petted her inner thighs until they parted.

"Relax. Let go of control and let me pleasure you." He winked. "It's the least I can do after you were so obliging, sucking me dry on the ride from the airport." He did an exaggerated shiver and shot her a smoldering look. "Just thinking about it makes me want to come all over you." He toyed with her labia, never breaking eye contact. "But that will have to wait. Right now," he said, kneeling between her legs, "I want to taste my sugar pussy."

"O.M.G." Bailey squinted down into the parking lot.

"Bailey," Travis said from behind her, "for some reason, I don't think your comment has anything to do with what I just did."

"Hmm?" On her knees, she looked back at her newfound lover. "Oh. Of course not! You heard me scream. You were great. Fabulous. The best."

"But . . . I have a feeling there is a *but* in there."

She pulled him tighter against her back and brought his hand around to kiss his fingers. Placing his hands on her breasts, she smiled when he immediately began fondling.

"Well, you're right." She motioned to the window. "Look down. Tell me if you see what I thought I saw."

Rising to get a better view, he pressed his already recovered erection against her back. "Wow!"

Bailey nodded. "*Wow* is right. Are you looking through the sunroof of the limo? What do you see?"

Travis chuckled, his penis rubbing in an interesting way. "I see some guy eating a skinny older chick. She seems to be getting off on it. Him too, if his pace is any indication. It's like he's trying to suck her brains out through her crotch."

"Hmm." She leaned back and rubbed against him. "I think you interpreted it better than I did, but that was my general opinion too." She giggled. "I can't believe they're going at it in the parking lot, in broad daylight."

"I wouldn't mind trying it—but only with you, of course." As if he were trying to prove it, he reached around and toyed with her nipples.

"Of course." She did a little shimmy, pressing her derriere into his arousal.

"Any idea who it is?" His voice sounded strained as he pressed into her.

Bailey smiled. She'd never had that particular effect on men. It was exhilarating.

"I know who it looks like, from up here," she replied, sinking back to the bed with him, "but I know it can't be her, thank goodness." Gripping his head, she met his hungry gaze. "Let's pretend we're in a limo."

Reese knocked on the locked bathroom door again. "Ben, open the door."

"No thanks, I've had enough humiliation for one night. Hell, I'm set for life!"

Sighing, she rested her head against the eight-panel door. "It could have happened to anyone."

"Maybe, but it happened to *me.*"

"Well, you did ingest a lot of soap."

"Reese, I threw up while we were making love."

No matter how hard she tried, she couldn't keep her laughter out of her voice. "I know." She slapped her hand over her mouth, but she couldn't contain her peals of laughter.

The door opened and Ben walked stiffly past where she was doubled over with laughter.

"I'm glad I amused you," he said in a dull voice. "Just shoot me now."

He flopped onto an upstairs bed, his arm thrown dramatically over his eyes. "As soon as I gather my strength, I'll go sleep in the lobby."

"Ben! Don't be ridiculous—"

"Right. I'll make up a bed in one of the other rooms. No point in going all the way downstairs. I'm probably too weak, anyway."

He was the picture of health, the white towel wrapped around his lean hips setting off his tanned body to perfection.

Was this really how they were going to spend their last night on the island?

Not if she could help it.

Hands shaking, she quietly stripped, then sat on the mattress close to his towel-clad hip. "Is this a private pity party or can anyone attend?"

He peeked out from under his arm. "What are you doing?"

"I'll give you three guesses, and the first two don't count." Smiling with more confidence than she felt, she walked her fingers up his leg and under the towel.

"Stop." He shoved her hand away and closed his eyes again.

"Ben," she implored, "it's our last night on the island." She moved until she was stretched out along his side, facing him. Taking his hand, she placed his palm on her breast, breathing a silent sigh of relief when he didn't immediately jerk it away.

"I'm sick." He flexed his hand, gently squeezing her breast, his thumb idly rubbing the tip of her nipple. "Who throws up during sex?"

"Anyone who ingested soap, I'd imagine." With stealth movements, she loosened the towel and brushed it aside. "Did you chew the antinausea tablet I gave you?" Her hand dipped to cup his testicles, her thumb brushing back and forth at the base of his recovering penis.

He nodded, eyes still shut, but she was pleased to notice he'd increased the activity of the hand caressing her breast. "Yeah. Thanks, by the way. Thanks, too, for loaning me your toothpaste."

"You're welcome." It was all she could do to keep her voice neutral when all she really wanted to do was beg him to make love to her. Or jump his bones. Or both. "I have something else that will make you feel better," she purred, moving higher and closer.

Turning, she guided her other breast to his mouth, teasing it open with her puckered nipple. Cajoling him, she jiggled her breast, encouraging him to take her into his mouth. When he finally began sucking, she almost swooned with pleasure.

Her hand began making longer and firmer strokes. Soon Ben's hips were rising from the mattress, seeking the counterpart of her movements.

To her disappointment, he didn't take things any further. His body was obviously interested. Now, how did she get his mind to follow?

Granted, her sexual expertise was limited. She'd never been the aggressor, hardly knew where to begin. But tonight would be their last night alone. For a while, at least. Maybe even forever.

Emboldened by that thought, she rose on her knees and gently tugged her nipple from Ben's mouth.

When he opened his eyes, she dragged her breasts across his open mouth, teasing him, daring him to take her.

Swallowing disappointment when he didn't make a move, she inched lower until she was up close and personal with his now-impressive erection.

Again, she dragged the tips of her beaded nipples across the bulbous tip, then sandwiched him by pushing her breasts tightly together.

Finally he made a move, bucking his hips off the mattress, his erection going in and out. The drag of his skin on hers made her squirm, aching for more.

Their breathing became ragged.

Lordy, she wanted so badly to climb on top of him and sink down until he was buried deep within her aching flesh, then ride him. Hard. All night long.

If this was going to be their last night together, she wanted to make it count.

Rubbing her aching folds against his leg, she all but whimpered her frustration. How desperate was she to be humping his leg?

Suddenly his fingers found their way between her legs. Up, up they went, until they were buried deep.

She went wild, bucking and thrusting, riding his hand. Too intent on seeking gratification to think about anything but reaching her climax.

Close. She was so close. When he removed his hand, she bit back a scream of frustration.

"Reese." Ben's voice seemed to be coming from far away, instead of almost next to her. "Reese. Open your eyes and look at me."

Forcing her eyes to open, she looked up at him. The look on his face went beyond lust, but she couldn't identify it.

He nodded, directing her gaze downward. "Look at us. Watch what we're doing."

Embarrassment flooded her when she saw the wetness—her wetness—covering his hand, wetting the sheets. He probably thought she was some kind of pervert. A desperate pervert, which was even worse.

He wouldn't allow her to pull away. Instead, she watched in horrified fascination while he continued to play with her slick folds, occasionally dipping into her, then rubbing and pulling on her distended clitoris.

The sight turned her on more than she would have imagined.

She wanted more.

She reached for him, but he stopped her.

Their gazes locked.

"Wait," he said, his breathing fast and shallow, "I have to know. Is this a pity fuck?"

Ordinarily, she'd have been mortified to have someone ask her such a thing, but now all she felt was overwhelming desire. A desire that would not be doused by fear or doubt. Or stupid questions.

"You could say that," she said with a smile as she climbed to straddle him. With slow, precise movements, she lowered herself until she'd taken him fully. "I plan to keep going until you beg me to take pity on you and let you get some sleep."

He gave a lazy thrust and smiled. "You can try, Blondie."

38

"No offense, but green beans aren't my idea of breakfast."

"We ate all the cured bacon. It was this or sauerkraut."

Reese smiled over her cup of hot chocolate, enjoying the sun shining through the window, warming her back.

Ben's heated gaze was doing a pretty good job of heating her front.

Having breakfast naked had been Ben's idea. At the time, she'd been all for it, since she was desperate to look at as much of him as she could, while she could.

Now it was slightly embarrassing.

"Maybe we should think about getting dressed," she began, pressing her legs together to keep from squirming on the oak chair.

Slowly he shook his head as he rose. "There's one more thing we need to do before we pack up."

She tried to focus on his face, she really did. But with something as impressive as his arousal heading straight for her, it was pretty much impossible.

"Oh?" Her voice squeaked.

He nodded and took their cups, placing them on the sideboard. Next he stacked the plates and set them on the counter. Returning to her, he bent and kissed her as he lifted her to the table.

His kiss tasted like chocolate and green beans.

Before she could mention that, he had her spread-eagle on the table. With the first swipe of his hot tongue, she was incapable of coherent speech.

While he nipped and sucked and licked her to oblivion, his hands moved constantly, stroking, tweaking, petting.

On sexual overload, she didn't feel her orgasm coming until it slammed into her, taking her breath. Her heart skipped a beat. Or two. Her blood roared in her ears, drowning out all other sounds.

So focused inwardly, she scarcely noticed when Ben picked up her limp body. At the bay window, he placed her hands to grip the center window frame, then gently pressed until she was bent over the window seat. Before she could draw a breath, he slid into her from behind.

"Don't. Forget. Me." He seemed to be saying with each thrust. *"Please. Don't. Leave. Me."*

Although she'd have sworn her last climax wrung her out, her eyes widened at the tiny spark low in her belly. It quickly spread to a flaming inferno, threatening to consume her, branding her.

Making her his.

Was that a man looking in at her? At them? A scream ripped from her throat as tiny nerve endings all over her body stung and quivered.

Ben increased his tempo, making her forget everything but the feel of him gliding in and out.

Within seconds, he followed her over the edge with a guttural groan.

He collapsed on her back, weighing her down. She welcomed the warm weight of him, wishing she could bottle the feeling to open and relive in the coming years.

After a while, Ben straightened and pulled out of her. Cooler air wafted around, chilling her.

Here she stood, legs spread wide, totally naked, bent over, flashing her assets. What, exactly, was the protocol?

She knew she should be embarrassed. Instead, she realized she wanted nothing more than to wiggle, to entice Ben to do it again. And again.

She'd never felt as alive as she did when they were having sex. Making love. Getting it on. Whatever you chose to call it. The thought of living the rest of her life without that feeling, that closeness, that feeling of utter completeness, was scary. And depressing. And flat-out sad.

"Okeydokey, Blondie, that should do it." Ben's slap stung her bottom. It said something about her recent sexual deprivation that it made her a little turned-on.

Straightened, she resisted the urge to rub the offended area. "Excuse me? Do what?"

"Take your mind off being seasick on our ride back to Sand Dollar." Grinning, he stepped into his now-dry, if stiff, cargo shorts, sans boxers.

"You really think sex would do that?" She snorted. "You hold yourself in mighty high esteem. While I appreciate your, um, effort, Ben, I have a patch for that."

He used a little more force than might have been necessary as he washed their dishes. "And we see how well that worked on the trip to the island."

Indignation immediately left her. Walking to him, she put her arms around his middle and gave a little hug. "I'm sorry." She sniffed. "I guess I'm just a little sensitive this morning. A lot has happened over the last few days." An image of piercing eyes staring at her while Ben was pounding into her flashed through her mind. "Ben! There was someone outside the kitchen window."

"What?" He dried his hands and threw the towel on the counter before turning to take her into his arms. "When?"

"Just now! When we were, you know." Her cheeks burned at the thought of what the mystery man had seen.

"Who the hell was it?"

"How should I know?"

He started for the front door, Reese at his heels. "Stay inside," he ordered, striding through the double front doors onto the porch.

He stopped abruptly, scanning the front lawn.

Reese barreled into his back. "Sorry."

With a sigh, he turned and gripped her arms to steady her. "Blondie, I told you to stay inside."

"Since when do you tell me what to do? For that matter, since when do I do it?"

"Good point." He turned, rubbing his neck and looked out into the trees. "Whoever it was, he seems to be gone. Do you remember what he looked like?"

"Ah, I was a little, um, preoccupied. Remember? It was pretty shocking to open my eyes and find another pair of eyes staring back, I'll tell you." She shuddered.

He gave her a quick hug. "Of course, it was, darlin'." He turned her toward the door and gave a little push. "Let's finish getting packed up. Do you want to hike to the boat or would you rather me get it and come around to get you?"

"I can walk with you." She shrugged. "It may be my last time to see the hotel or the island."

Damn Dorinda's hide. She didn't deserve to have the island, regardless of her intentions. Especially not the hotel.

Ben nodded as he began shoving folded clothes into his duffel bag. "Yeah. Or if you do, it will be remodeled and be a bed-

and-breakfast." He said the last words as though they left a bad taste in his mouth.

She could identify.

"It just burns me up," she said, slinging her stiff clothes into her bag, "to think about the oil testing. I have no proof, but I just know my boss is behind it. And it's not even her danged island yet!"

"But you're still going to bid on her behalf, aren't you?" Ben had stopped, his voice quiet.

"You said you don't want it. If she doesn't buy it, someone else will."

"I never said I didn't want it." He tossed his bag aside and strode to take her hands. "I need to tell you something."

He pulled her to sit on the sofa, now once again against the outer wall, then sat next to her, his hands tightly clutching hers.

"What? Were you lying before, about being married?" Her attempt at a joke fell flat in the silence.

"No." He licked his lips, his thumbs idly rubbing the backs of her hands. "Remember I told you my late grandmother owned this place?"

She nodded, her mind jumping around in an attempt to second-guess what he was about to say.

"She left it to me."

"Why don't you want to keep it? Why are you letting it go to auction?" She shook her head. "I don't understand."

"Of course, you don't, Blondie. You strike me as the type who always pays her bills and does the right thing."

"And you're not?" How could she have been totally wrong about the man she'd been so intimate with?

"Yes and no." He held up his hand. "Let me explain. I was a little, well, wild as a teenager. I played the rebel card for years, ignoring my family. Even, I'm ashamed to admit, my grandmother."

"Ben, we all make mistakes when we're young—"

His chuckle was dry. "Yeah, but I made it into an art form. After I graduated from college, Gram begged me to turn myself around and use my degree. She said she wasn't always going to be around to bail me out when I screwed up." He shrugged. "I guess I didn't believe her. Anyway, after all those years of school, I thought I deserved to party before settling down. Hell, I'd done my bit with helping Rick and Rita, I felt the world owed me. After I spent some time with Gram that summer, I set sail, determined to be the king of the bachelors."

"And were you?" Did it really matter? She'd thought about it most of the night. She already knew what she needed to do.

He looked away for a second. "For a while." Tears sparkled his eyes, making them appear aquamarine. "I didn't even hear about Gram's passing until it had been almost a year. Then it didn't seem like there was any point in coming back. I didn't know she'd left the island to me. Or that she'd neglected to pay the taxes. So, of course, I didn't pay them either. By the time Rick caught up with me, the place was already under a tax lien. Hell, I had no money. Not enough to pay the back taxes. That's when I started scrambling, doing every job that came along and socking money in the bank."

"Ah, that would be your taxi and limo service?" she asked with a sad smile.

He nodded. "And charter service, and handyman work. I even helped birth calves. Did you know that?"

Shaking her head, she wiped away a tear.

"It was pretty gross, but it paid decent."

"I've seen the tax records. You're seriously behind, big-time. But if you can come up with the back taxes, you can stop the auction. What about your friends? Is there anyone who could loan you the money?" Poor Ben. He'd lost so much. He didn't deserve to lose his inheritance.

"They have. But it wasn't enough. The whole town tried to help. They've had bake sales and car washes." He heaved a sigh and stood up. "None of it was enough. Don't cry. I wasn't telling you to make you feel sorry for me." He pulled her up into his arms. "Don't cry, sweetheart, it's going to be okay."

She sniffled and lifted her head. "You're right. Because I'm going to loan you the money."

"What? Are you crazy?"

"Probably, but that's beside the point."

"No way!" Running his hands through his hair, he stalked from one end of the lobby to the other and back. "I can't take your money," he said in a strangled voice.

"Sure you can."

"You said your boss didn't pay much. How could you have that amount of money on hand?"

"She doesn't. But I've worked for quite a while and have built up my 401(k). I can borrow from it. You can pay me back when you can."

"How—no, I can't. There's no guarantee I will ever get this place back up and running, much less turn enough profit to repay you. So, thanks, but no thanks."

"Ben Adams, how dare you tell me I can't give you money! It's my money, and if I want to invest it in you and your island and this hotel, I dang well am going to do it." She poked him in the chest with her index finger. "Got it?"

His chuckle sounded rusty as he rubbed the spot she'd poked. "Yes, ma'am."

"Good, as soon as I—oh! I have a signal!" Furiously, she began typing. "I'm transferring the money to my checking account right now. There! Done. It should hit my account by midnight tomorrow, at the latest, in plenty of time to be available before the auction."

"I have some money, Blondie, you don't have to loan me the entire amount."

"But you'll need some money for restorations. You did say you wanted to get this place back up and running, didn't you?"

"But—"

"This is going to be your business. If it helps, you can think of my money as a business loan." She stroked his face. "I believe in you, Ben. I know you can do it."

He swallowed. "Okay. I'll take it. But it's just a loan."

"Absolutely! It's coming from my retirement. I'm going to need it someday. But not now. Right now, you need it more."

"I'm paying you back with interest. Just as if I'd borrowed the money from a bank."

"Dang straight you will."

"And I intend to sign paperwork to that effect, or it's not a deal."

She nodded.

"And the only way I will accept your loan is if your name is on the deed with mine."

Wow. That took her by surprise.

"That's not necessary, Ben—"

"Yes. It is. Or no deal."

"Okay, but as soon as you pay me back, I'm signing my half back to you."

"Deal." He stuck out his hand and she reluctantly shook it.

During her restless night, she'd wondered if the reason she wanted to offer the money to Ben had anything to do with the feelings she had for him. It was too early to fall in love, but she'd definitely fallen in lust. And, after their somewhat rocky start, she'd genuinely come to like him.

It was a lot of money. But it was the right thing to do.

A hint of a smile curved her mouth.

Stopping the Dragon Lady in her tracks just made it that much sweeter.

39

"**W**here is that sniveling little nothing assistant of mine?" Dorinda grabbed Paige something-or-other as she walked through the lobby of the pitiful excuse for a hotel. "You're one of her few friends, aren't you? I thought I recognized you. Well, speak up! Where is she hiding out?"

"First of all, yes, I'm one of Reese's *many* friends. Secondly, I have no idea where she is at the moment, due to the recent tropical storm. That's the reason I'm here. Unlike you, I was worried about her. And thirdly," she said, her voice full of scorn, "take your fucking hands off of me before I break every bone in your skanky body." She leaned close and hissed, "I'm a doctor. I know where every one is located."

Dorinda gasped and dropped her hand. "Bitch," she said under her breath as she watched the younger woman walk toward the restaurant area.

"I heard that," Paige called back, but she didn't stop walking.

Dorinda finished signing in as Halston walked up. He knew

how she felt about public displays, so his proprietary hand on her ass was doubly offensive.

"Save it for the privacy of our room, lover," she said in a low voice she hoped was not a snarl. She needed Halston. Monetarily, at least until she recouped her losses and could get back on her fiscal feet. Physically . . . well, that was more complicated.

For the time being, she'd do whatever he wanted, whenever he wanted. And she'd try to draw the line at the wherever part. Although her recently donned thong was already dampening at the thought.

"All checked in?" No doubt about it, there was a definite gleam in Halston's eye.

It didn't take a rocket scientist to figure out what he had in mind.

"I finally contacted my team," he said, ushering her into the elevator. As soon as the doors slid closed, he wasted no time in rubbing suggestively against her. "I'm meeting them in the lobby in an hour. Thought maybe you could help me with something before then. Something to help me take the edge off." He ground and rubbed his hardness against her.

And, damn her weakness, she rubbed right back.

Too soon, the elevator dinged and the doors *whooshed* open.

Both breathing hard, they stumbled out and made their way to the room.

"Hurry," he said, grinding and thrusting his erection against her buttocks. His hand slid around to squeeze her breasts through her suit jacket.

It took two tries, but she finally managed to get a green light and the door clicked open.

"Spread 'em!" Halston's voice was guttural, thick with his arousal, by the time the door fully closed.

Shoving her skirt up to her waist, he bent her over the upholstered arm of a guest chair. Not bothering to divest her of what little panties she wore, he simply shoved past the barrier, entering her with a hard, somewhat intrusive thrust.

It took her breath.

Hands shaking, she fumbled with the buttons on her jacket, shrugged out of it, and tossed it aside, while Halston pounded into her from behind.

Her skin was on fire, every nerve ending on alert. Excited beyond rational thought, she could only feel. And clothing was an intrusion she didn't want.

Squirming against Halston's hips as they continued to pump, she peeled off her tank top. The bra was easier, its front closure giving way with the first touch of her fingers.

Finally she was free. Totally and gloriously naked. Except for her skirt around her waist, of course. But that couldn't be helped. Closing her eyes, she smiled and sighed, leaning lower and enjoying the abrasion of the upholstery on her erect nipples almost as much as she was enjoying the thorough fucking.

He reached beneath her and probed until he found her aching nub and proceeded to ratchet up her arousal.

Biting back a scream, she frantically rubbed against his hands, seeking a deeper release than the one she knew was about to break from the friction of his cock.

More was always better.

Reese clung, spread-eagle, her hands gripping the edge of the table, belowdecks, while Ben's boat rocked gently on the water. Ben, on the other hand, was rocking with much more force as he pounded into her welcoming body.

Every so often, he'd pause to lean over and lick or suck one of her nipples before resuming his sensual activity.

"Sweet God in heaven, Blondie, I love—I love to fuck you." His breathing picked up, as did the force of his thrusts. "Come for me again, baby, like you did earlier. I love the way your pussy sucks my cock."

Had anyone in her limited sexual experience ever talked to her like that, using such explicit terms, she was sure it would have been a turnoff.

Yet, surprisingly, it had the opposite effect on her when Ben did it.

Was it love?

Or was she just developing a more jaded sexual appetite?

Maybe both.

Using the last of her strength, she put her legs around his waist, hugging him as close as possible while her climax roared through her.

Ben's back stiffened. He yelled something, but the pounding of her blood in her ears drowned out his words.

He collapsed on top of her, breathing hard, their sweat mingling.

After a few moments, she began feeling his weight on her chest.

"Ben," she mumbled, tapping his shoulder with a limp hand, "move. We're going to break the table."

"Worth it," he said in her ear, not budging.

"Seriously," she said, shoving on his shoulders. "I can't breathe."

"Breathing is overrated." But he did raise to a push-up position above her, allowing her to draw air into her oxygen-deprived lungs. He bent to kiss the tip of her nose. "How's the nausea?"

Taking a deep breath, she realized Ben's preposterous theory on motion sickness had actually worked. "Gone," she said with a smile. "That's amazing!"

"My pleasure, ma'am." He pulled up his shorts and reached for his shirt. "Anything I can do to help, just holler. Anytime."

She glanced out the tiny window to hide her smile. All she saw was water. "Hey, we're not drifting out to sea, are we?"

"Does it matter?" He paused by the steps.

Did it matter? The thought of drifting around, making passionate love with Ben, held a definite appeal.

Then again, so did food. And they were running more than short of pretty much every supply.

"I like the idea," she finally said. "But first things first. We need to get back to Sand Dollar to pay the taxes before the auction." She smiled to let him know she wasn't averse to the idea. "But maybe, after that, we can stock up and go for at least a little trip. Heck, it's a pretty safe bet I'll be unemployed in the not-too-distant future."

"Are you going to be okay with that?"

"Sure. I guess. And there's always a chance she won't fire me. Maybe she won't even know I loaned you the money to stop her from bidding on the island." She shrugged. "I'd planned to look for another job when I got back home, anyway."

"Like I said before, you could always come work for me." He grinned and winked. "The pay isn't great, but the sex would be plentiful and often."

"I'll keep that in mind." She managed a weak smile as he climbed the rest of the way up to the deck.

That was one of her problems. Staying with Ben was occupying most of her thoughts.

40

Dorinda reclined on the flowered comforter, one leg propped high above her head, while Halston insisted on giving her a thorough sponge bath. Sponge optional.

Ordinarily, she'd enjoy the lavish attention, possibly even return the favor.

But now she was restless, a little tender from his rough sex so soon upon check-in. Not to mention preoccupied with her missing assistant and the upcoming auction at the courthouse.

She shouldn't have had to make the trip. Even Reese should have been more than competent to handle the sale.

Yet, here she was.

She glanced around the nauseatingly cheerful room. The screaming yellow paint was enough to give her a migraine.

A flicker of arousal caught her unaware.

Halston was rimming her opening with his fingertip.

She tried to back away from his temptation, but he held her hips to the mattress with one arm.

"Relax, sugar pussy." He blew on her wetness. "You're way too uptight. You used to love having me bathe you. And go down on you. And fuck you," he added in a whisper just before probing her with his talented tongue. "Feels good, doesn't it? Do you like it when I lick and suck you?" He proceeded to do just that, still holding her in a firm grasp, preventing her from doing anything but feel and react to his ministrations.

She released her grip on the brass headboard to pluck at her aching nipples. For not the first time, she wished for another man in bed with her and Halston. While Halston did what he did best, the other faceless male could pleasure her above the waist.

Maybe she'd start looking around, once she was back at the office. There were a few interns who might fit the bill.

Halston's sharp nip on her swollen nub brought her back to the present.

"I'd love to finish what we started, but it's going to have to wait awhile. I have to be in the lobby in ten minutes." He crawled toward the headboard, not stopping until his monster erection was right in her face. "Just enough time for you to take care of this for me." Reaching back, he spread her legs and resumed stroking her.

Moving her hips rhythmically, she pulled him into her mouth.

He groaned when she circled his shaft with her tongue. She wasn't without talents of her own.

Her hips moved faster.

Giving blow jobs was always exciting. But she especially liked to give them when she knew she was going to get off first. . . .

Then she would stop.

"What if someone sees us?" Bailey shielded her eyes and looked up and down the deserted beach as she hugged the beach blanket tightly to her chest.

"Risking getting caught is part of the fun." Travis hugged

her tightly from behind and once again ran his hand down the front of her walking shorts. His fingers immediately found her wet center, the part aching for his touch. "C'mon, let's make love on the beach with the warmth of the sun on our skin." He petted her wet folds. "You'll love it."

I think I love you, Bailey thought grimly. Why did she always do that? It was like she couldn't have sex until she fell in love. No wonder she'd had her heart broken more times than she could count.

When she and Travis had first hooked up, she truly thought he was a seaside romance, a frivolous fling to enjoy and be forgotten when she went back to her real life.

She certainly didn't feel very carefree and fun-loving now. Forget frivolous.

"C'mon," Travis urged, his mouth against her ear. "I know you love it as much as I do, when I'm inside you." He licked the shell of her ear, making her knees weak. "I want to look at your pussy and see your excitement sparkle in the sunshine," he whispered. "Please."

Turned-on, she licked her lips and looked back at him. "But . . . where?"

In response, he walked her several yards down the beach from the hotel, his arousal bumping her buttocks with each step, his fingers never leaving her needy femininity.

"What's this?" It appeared to have once been some kind of building, maybe a house. A crumbling brick wall faced the direction of the hotel. The wall curved, its opening facing the water.

The remains of at least one old fire pit made up the center of their little shelter.

"Sometimes people party here. Mostly kids." He took the blanket from her and spread it on the sand, parallel to the surf. After shucking his T-shirt, he quickly unzipped and stepped out of his shorts. He went commando.

Golden hair framed his jutting penis, its shining head bobbing in the sunlight.

Stepping close to her, he arched around her, gathering her in his arms, swaying them back and forth as he dragged his erection across the front of her shorts.

With one hand, he tilted her face up for his kiss. As soon as she opened for his tongue, he released her chin. His hand lightly skimmed her chest, only pausing momentarily to stroke her breast through the flimsy barrier of her halter.

Disappointment washed through her when his hand left her chest. She'd have loved for him to play with her nipples like he'd done the night before.

How needy could one girl be?

But Travis clearly had more adventurous things in mind.

Sun warmed her leg where he tugged up the loose-fitting leg of her walking shorts. It took a second for her to realize the smooth firmness sliding on her thigh was the head of his penis.

"Travis! What are you—"

"Shh," he said against her lips, quickly reclaiming them for another soul-deep kiss.

The leg of her shorts was now bunched tightly against her groin. Travis's erection stroked her dampness. Ever so slowly, he dragged it up and down the thin barrier of her panties.

Her muscles began vibrating. She locked her knees to remain upright, although the blanket was holding more appeal by the second.

"Feel how much I want you?" Travis's breath was hot against her lips. "I need you." He shoved her panty leg aside and stroked her excitement higher, his bulbous tip nudging against her weeping flesh, spreading her wetness. "You want me too, I can tell."

Quivering with need, she could only whisper, "Yes."

"Poor baby. You're shaking! You're as turned-on as I am. Let me help you."

In no time at all, Travis had her naked and spread out on the blanket as he knelt between her legs.

The sun blazed down, blinding her, making him a looming shadow.

Hot. It was so hot. A droplet of sweat trickled from beneath her breasts to track down her rib cage. Travis caught it with his tongue, licking his way back up until he could draw her nipple into his mouth.

Arching her back, wanting more, it was all she could do not to moan her frustration when his mouth left her breast. The gulf breeze now seemed cool as it blew across her, drying her nipple. Both nipples puckered at the sensation.

Travis made his way downward, trailing kisses on her abdomen, his tongue dipping briefly into her navel before continuing its journey.

Eyes closed, Bailey reveled in his touch as she basked in the heated caress of the sun.

When he reached his destination and closed his mouth over her clitoris, she smiled and sighed.

Sex on the beach.

She could so get used to this. . . .

Before she realized it, she'd come three times, in rapid-fire succession.

Languid and worn-out, she lay on the blanket and watched in bemused fascination as Travis rolled on a condom.

"Your nose is sunburned." Travis dropped his T-shirt over her face.

"But I can't see you with this over my face!" Before she could drag the shirt away, he stopped her.

"Leave it, Bailey. I don't want your gorgeous face getting any more sun. Besides, not watching will heighten your pleasure."

She relaxed. Now that he mentioned it, her nose did feel a little tender.

Travis's tongue took another leisurely journey, making her squirm on the rough-textured blanket while the sun baked her breasts.

Just as she was going to mention how hot her nipples were getting, his mouth sucked first one, then the other. He dragged his tongue around and around each nipple as he pushed into her receptive body.

Everything was forgotten as she focused on the joining of their bodies and met each enthusiastic thrust.

The thrusting was a little uncomfortable, but then again, she hadn't had sex like she'd enjoyed with Travis in a very long time. If ever.

It made sense she'd be a little tender . . . down there.

And Travis's hungry mouth on her breasts helped ease whatever discomfort she might be feeling.

Orgasm number four rushed up to slam into her, taking her breath. While she was still enjoying the aftershocks, Travis withdrew. Before she could protest, he was back, pumping energetically, his pubic bone bumping hers with each hard thrust.

His very hard thrusts. Painfully hard.

She tried to relax, to take herself to the point of climax again, but it was beginning to be really uncomfortable.

He bit down hard on her right nipple, the pain shooting through to her womb.

He must have heard her gasp, because he began licking and soothing her abused breast immediately.

But it still wasn't enough to relieve her discomfort.

Inhaling through her nose, she smelled Travis on the shirt covering her face and smiled.

This was Travis. Her Travis. He was just excited by making love with her on the beach. She took another deep breath and willed her body to relax and go with the flow. He wasn't doing anything they hadn't already done, many times. . . .

"What the fuck is going on here?" Paige's strident voice cut into Bailey's thoughts. "What are you doing to my friend?"

As Paige yelled, the T-shirt was jerked from Bailey's face.

Travis was naked, but he wasn't making love to her. He was kneeling next to her, his hand still cupping her wet breast.

But . . . if Travis was next to her, whose penis was still deep inside her, even though it was no longer moving in and out?

Her gaze whipped to the man between her spread legs. A man she'd never seen before in her life. Her gaze shot back to Travis's guilty face.

Breath wheezing in and out, she could only whisper, "Who, who . . . ?"

"That's my friend Rich," Travis said in a matter-of-fact way.

Rich nodded as he pulled out, his cheeks ruddy. "Trav said you were okay with it."

Numb, she could only stare.

Paige, however, had no problem with letting the men know exactly what she thought.

"What are you two, some kind of fucking idiots? Who the hell puts a bag over their date's head and then gangbangs her?"

"What are you doing?" Travis looked panicked, so Bailey swung her gaze to her friend, who was frantically punching the buttons on her phone.

"What the fuck do you think I'm doing, you cocksucker? I'm calling the police! You and your idiot friend just raped my friend!"

"Whoa!" Rich lunged for the phone, jerking it away from Paige, then holding it out of her reach. "Travis told me she was cool with doing both of us. It wasn't rape!"

"What?" Paige snarled, looking ready to pounce. "Are you trying to tell me it was consensual? You lying sack of shit!"

"Tell her," Travis said, nudging Bailey's bare hip.

Wide-eyed, she could only gape at him for a second. If she

tried to speak, she knew she'd start screaming and might never be able to stop.

"Tell her," he insisted. "Tell her you got off. A lot. And don't think about lying. You know you did." He pulled up his shorts and stood, looking down at her, his eyes cold and hard. "Tell her. You were really into it. Does it really matter who was fucking you? You came with both of us. Don't deny it."

Shaking, she could only stare as both men put on their clothes and left.

"Wait!" she called in a wobbly voice when Paige started to go after them. "Stop." She licked her lips and looked at her friend. "He's right."

Paige dropped to the sand, Bailey's clothes clutched in her hand. "Do you hear what you're saying, Bay?"

She nodded and began pulling on her clothes with Paige's help.

Paige continued to stare. "So you really were okay with fucking two guys? No offense, but that sounds nothing like the Bailey I know, the one who falls madly in love with every guy she sleeps with—"

"I thought I loved Travis," she said, wiping her eyes with the back of her hand.

"So, what are you telling me, you agreed to a threesome to prove your love?"

"No." She sniffled. "I thought Travis really wanted to make love to me on the beach. I was scared, but excited too, you know?"

"But why did you let them cover your face like you were some faceless, nameless fuck? I don't get it."

Bailey whirled. "It wasn't like that, Paige! It was just Travis and me. It was sexy and exciting. I thought maybe he loved me. And he told the truth, I had multiple orgasms."

"But you thought they were with him!" Paige gripped Bailey's shoulders and looked in her eyes. "Didn't you?"

She shrugged away and started walking back to the hotel. "I don't know."

Paige caught up with her. "What the hell do you mean, you don't know?"

Bailey stopped. "I knew it felt . . . different." She held up her hand to stop the next question. "And, no, not in a good way. But we'd been going at it hot and heavy ever since we met, so I thought maybe I was just tender."

"Intercourse without consent is still rape."

"But I did consent. And I did come. Multiple times. Rape would be very hard to prove, since it's doubtful there would be any physical evidence. I've been having so much sex of late, I'm sure there would be no tearing, nothing to prove I tried to prevent it. Can't you just let it go, Paige? Please? For me?"

"For you, yes. Not that I agree, but I see your point. But I'm still calling the police."

"Because . . . ?"

"The son of a bitch stole my brand-new phone!"

41

Dorinda threw some money on the granite and watched the eye candy tending bar. Would he be willing to go up to her room for a while? Who knew how long that tedious Halston would be gone, and she was getting bored. And restless. And horny.

"Everything all right?" The squeaky-clean–looking owner walked up, her perky-as-hell ponytail swinging. "How was your drink?"

"Fine. Thank you." Of course, it would have been better if the yummy bartender had served it naked. In private. And let her lick it from his hard body.

The woman beamed at her. "Jason is a great bartender, isn't he? His margaritas are top-notch. Draws a big crowd on the weekends. Of course, his wife misses having him home with her and the kids at night, I suppose." She shot Dorinda a pointed look. "But we sure do like having him around. Enjoy your stay." With another insincere smile and a perky nod of her head, she walked away.

Halston striding through the lobby snagged Dorinda's attention.

Any penis in a pinch. She tossed back the rest of her scotch and slid from the bar stool.

Maybe Halston could scratch her itch before dinner. And, if he played his cards right, for the rest of the night as well. Tomorrow was a wash. They would spend it in bed, finding new ways to fuck each other's brains out. Then, bright and early the next morning, Halston could show her what he'd learned before they had to leave for the courthouse.

The thought of her future acquisition made her wet. Sure, she wasn't really going to open a bed-and-breakfast, like she'd told that fool Reese, but anytime you made a lucrative business deal, it was a turn-on.

She stepped off the elevator and hurried to her room.

The prospect of getting rich from the mineral rights that came with the island was an added aphrodisiac.

Whoever said menopause killed sex drives was full of shit. If anything, perimenopause made her hornier than ever.

Her blouse was already unbuttoned when she opened the door. Wait until Halston got a glimpse of her new, naughty bustier. With its ultrasheer lace and half cups that bared her breasts, she'd practically come when she'd tried it on, just looking at herself.

She could hear him moving around in the bathroom. Hurrying, she shucked her clothing and was standing, posed, by the foot of the bed, in nothing but her stilettos and the bustier when he came out.

Halston stopped in his tracks. "I didn't hear you come in."

His hungry gaze licked her from head to toe and back, pausing at the juncture of her thighs just long enough to make her wetter.

Standing still, she let him enjoy the view. She might be skinny, but she knew she was in damn fine shape for a forty-two-year-old woman.

Judging by the front of Halston's slacks, he thought so too.

"How do you like?" For effect, she raised her foot to the bed, taunting him with a better look at what she knew he craved.

He swallowed and nodded, obviously stupefied by lust.

That was okay. She wasn't interested in what he had to say. She was more attracted to other activities he could perform with his mouth.

"Why do you have your shaving kit?" Her smile was lascivious, but she couldn't help it. "More flavored condoms?"

He nodded, grabbed a handful, then dropped the shaving kit to the chair.

Reese stretched and rolled to the sun-warmed deck. It felt wicked and decadent to make love with Ben in the middle of the afternoon, right on the deck, where anyone going by might see.

"Feeling better now?" Ben rolled to his side, casting a shadow over her as he toyed with her nipple.

"Ah-huh." She grinned at him and intimately cupped him. "But maybe we should try it again, just one more time, to be sure."

"I've created a monster," he teased, reaching for his shorts. "We really need to get back to Sand Dollar, though. I'm sure everyone is worried, and we want to get to the courthouse as soon as it opens tomorrow morning to file the papers."

Right. The tax office. How could she forget?

"Reese? Are you okay?" He touched her arm, steadying her as she pulled up her shorts.

She pulled her top over her head and straightened it. "Sure, why wouldn't I be?" To underscore her words, she flashed a bright smile.

"Look, if you've changed your mind, it's okay. I can find the money somewhere else."

"There is nowhere else. We both know that. It's not the money. Trust me."

"Then what is it?" Crossing his arms over his chest, he made it obvious he wasn't starting the engine again until she told him.

"It's stupid. I know it's stupid." She blinked back tears. "You'll think it's stupid too, if I tell you."

"Try me."

She sniffed. "It's just that, well, you're the best time I've ever had—"

"Really?" His grin shone white against his tan.

"Don't look so pleased, it's a very small group."

"Gee, thanks, Blondie. Way to make me feel special."

"You are! That's the problem." Her shoulders slumped. "We didn't get off to the best start, but now that we're, well, you know, it's really hard to think about going home."

"Then don't," he said mater-of-factly as he started the engine.

"I have to," she said, not remembering when she'd felt so glum. "I have responsibilities."

"Sometimes being irresponsible is more fun."

Suddenly irritated at his attitude, she snapped. "Yeah, and that's exactly how you got yourself into your present predicament!"

As soon as the words left her impulsive mouth, she knew she'd made a mistake.

The look on Ben's face told it all.

She'd scored a direct hit.

42

Weak, Dorinda could barely raise her eyelids when she heard Halston moving about in their darkened room.

"Halston?" She struggled to sit up, wincing at the unaccustomed tenderness between her legs. Their sex had been even wilder and more uninhibited than usual.

Not that she was complaining.

In response to her calling his name, he just grunted. She bit back a grin. She'd probably worn him out every bit as much as he had her.

"What time is it? Come back to bed." She patted the mattress.

"Can't sleep," he grumbled, opening drawers.

"I bet we can come up with something to tire you out and make you sleep." Just the thought had her tingling as moisture surged in anticipation.

He flipped on the bedside lamp, temporarily blinding her.

His suitcase, half packed, was open on the settee.

For the first time since they'd met, she didn't see any trace of attraction or sexual hunger in his gaze.

"Not interested." His tone of voice told her he was telling the truth.

A chill wafted over her. She drew the sheet over her nudity. "I don't understand."

"It's over. How much clearer can I make it, *sugar pussy*? You were a great fuck, but I'm done. Time for us both to move on."

"You can't walk out on me, on us."

"Watch me."

"But we're a team! Both in bed and out."

He scrubbed his face with his hand. "Yeah, about that, I'm selling my half."

"What! What the fuck is going on, Mr. Conrad?"

"Nothing. That's what I've been telling you." He finished packing and zipped his suitcase, the sound echoing its finality in the quiet room.

She swallowed back the stupid, weak tears that threatened. She'd be damned if she'd let him or anyone see her cry.

Another part, the rational part, of her brain scrambled through her assets, trying to come up with enough to buy him out.

Nothing. If he sold out, she'd end up losing everything.

The only hold she had on him was sexual.

And she wasn't above using it.

Summoning up the sexiest look she could, she crawled to the end of the bed, letting the sheet fall away. If she could get him back into bed, everything would be all right.

And, if she was wrong and it wasn't, he could show her one last good time.

"How about coming back to bed and doing whatever you want to me . . . one more time?"

"You pathetic cunt." He threw a pile of papers between her spread legs. "Take a look at the report on the island you were so hot to acquire for me. That'll dry up your juices in a hurry."

The words on the papers blurred together. Angry, she tossed them to the floor.

"Why don't you just tell me what they say?"

"Most of it's mumbo jumbo, geology talk. It's the back page that shriveled my dick. The one titled 'Recoverable Oil Report.' "

Leaning down, she shuffled through the papers until she found it. It had quite a bit of technical terms, but the gist of it was there was oil, a lot of oil, on the island.

"But it says there's oil. What's the problem? We can buy the island and—"

"Keep reading—and cover your tits."

"Too tempting?" She forced a smile and plucked at her nipples to taunt him. If she could just get him back in bed, she could talk him into anything.

"Not hardly. You have no idea how hard it was to suck those little titties with any enthusiasm. I don't want to be reminded." He gave an exaggerated shudder. "They disgust me."

Recoiling at the verbal slap, she pulled up the sheet. "What exactly is it you want me to read?" It took effort, but she kept her voice neutral and, she hoped, cold.

He stalked to the bed and smacked the paper with one pudgy finger. "The part where it says it wouldn't be cost-effective to pursue extraction."

"So you don't want me to bid on the island?"

"What is wrong with you? Maybe I really did fuck your brains out! I don't give a rat's ass if you buy the island or not. I'm out of the equation."

"Maybe I'll go ahead and buy it, anyway. Then just hold on to it until it becomes financially feasible to pursue production."

"Do whatever you want. But don't count on using my money. Like I said, I'm out of it." He picked up his suitcase.

"Wait! Where are you going?"

"Home."

"Can't you at least wait until morning?"

"Nope. The jet's fueled and ready to go."

"You're not taking my jet and leaving me. Find another way to get home." Her eyes narrowed. "Slithering comes to mind."

"The plane is half mine. I'm taking it."

"But"—her words faded when he slammed the door—"how am I going to get back to Houston?"

For several minutes, she sat in the darkness, scrubbing at the stupid tears continuing to leak from her traitorous eyes.

"Who the hell needs Halston Conrad, anyway? S-so what if it was the best sex I've ever had?" A sob escaped. "I'll find someone else, someone younger, better-looking, someone who's ten times—no! One hundred times better in bed."

Sliding to the floor, she crawled to the bathroom and turned on the shower.

Standing under the cold, stinging spray, she calmed down. She would go to the auction, as planned, and buy the island. If it took all their reserve, so be it. Conrad couldn't take back what already had been allocated.

Yes, that's exactly what she would do. Then she would just sit and wait until the time was right to extract the oil.

And then she would laugh all the way to the bank.

43

"You found your phone," Bailey observed in a dull voice when Paige joined her at the table in the restaurant.

Paige held it up before pocketing it. "Yeah. Somebody turned it in at the desk." She reached across the table and touched Bailey's arm. "Are you sure you're okay?"

"I'm fine. And if you offer to take me to the hospital or examine me again, I'm going to hit you." She sniffled and wiped her eyes on the cocktail napkin. "Let's just try to forget what happened and concentrate on finding Reese so we can all go home."

"I just tried calling her. It went straight to voice mail. Again." Paige picked up the menu. "I just talked to Rick, in the lobby, and he's getting worried too. The storm is over and no one has seen or heard from her or that guy who took her to the island. A group is going to go out looking for them, if they don't hear from them soon."

"Try her again. Rita said they're using the part-time chef tonight and he's really slow, so we have time. Call Reese again."

* * *

"I didn't mean it the way it sounded." Reese followed close at Ben's heels as he strode up the dock at the Sand Dollar marina after tying the boat.

He stopped at the end and she ran into his back. Automatically he reached out to steady her. "Will you stop following me?"

"Not until you listen to me!"

"I heard you. Now stop following me." He turned and picked up his pace.

Trotting next to him, she said, "I'm not following you if we're going to the same place. Slow down!" She grabbed his arm and held on. "Do you still want my money?" she asked when he stopped. Jerking on his arm, she pinched it for good measure. "Look at me when I'm talking to you! Answer me!"

"Ouch! You have a mean streak, woman. It's not attractive." He would have resumed walking, but she clung to his arm, digging in her heels. "Yes, I want the money." His eyes narrowed as he loomed over her. "Why? Did you change your mind? Am I too irresponsible?"

"See? I knew you'd take that the wrong way!"

"Far as I can tell, there's only one way to take it."

"Well, however you took it, it was wrong. Ben, we've been all through this. I totally understand why you did the things you did, even if you don't. And I'm okay with it."

"Gee, thanks, Blondie."

"You have a huge chip on your shoulder. Anyone ever tell you that? I—"

"Answer your phone."

"Huh?"

"Your phone. It's buzzing. It's almost as annoying as you are lately, so answer it."

After some rummaging around in her bag, she pulled out her phone.

"It's Paige," she told Ben, but when she looked up, she was alone.

44

"Reese! Oh, thank God! We were so worried." Paige smiled and nodded across the table to Bailey, whose eyes widened. "Are you all right? Where are you?"

"Standing behind you."

"What?" She whipped her head around to find Reese and an exceptionally hot, though scruffy-looking, guy standing right behind her chair.

With a shriek, she dropped her phone and launched herself into Reese's arms.

After a long hug, she stepped back, gripping her friend's upper arms.

"Do you have any idea how worried we were? You could have at least called!"

"Don't you think I tried? There was no signal out on the island."

"So, Rita and Rick were right. You were stranded out there during the storm?" Paige gave her a thorough visual exam. "You look okay. Fairly clean and well fed. So I gather you took supplies."

"Well," Reese said with a smile as she glanced at her companion, "between the two of us, and what was left in the old hotel, we did pretty well. Don't you agree, Ben? Oh! I'm sorry, Paige and Bailey, this is Ben Adams." Everyone nodded in greeting. "He's, um, my, ah, guide. I hired him to take me out to scope out the island before the auction." Her smile faded. "Crap. Now that I'm back, I guess I should try to contact the Dragon Lady."

"Oh!" Bailey spoke for the first time since they'd walked in. "Paige, let me tell her!" She grinned, showing the first amount of animation she'd exhibited since the beach assault. "The Dragon Lady is here."

Reese sank to a vacant chair. "Shut. Up." After rubbing her forehead and shaking her head, she looked up again. "Why? Did you talk to her?"

Paige patted Reese's hand. "Unfortunately, yes. I saw her when she checked in. Seems she came down because she hadn't heard from you."

"Oh, no! Don't try to tell me she was worried."

Paige snickered. "Hell no. Pissed off was more like it. I gathered she didn't trust you to get the job done, so she decided to do it herself."

"Have you seen her since?"

"No, thank the Lord. She had her latest plaything with her. They've been holed up in their room ever since then, doing who knows what kind of deviant things to each other." She shuddered. "Yuck! That's a mental image I could do without."

Reese laughed. "I agree. Trust me, that is not something you want to witness in person. I felt like I needed to wash my mind out with soap."

Both friends began nodding emphatically, urging Reese to turn and look.

Ben was walking toward the door.

"Ben! Wait!" Reese caught up to him in the lobby. "Where are you going?"

"Home. Unless you need me to do something else. Cook and clean for you? Maybe run your bath? Or did you have something more intimate in mind? I aim to please." His smile was frosty. "After all, I'm on your payroll. May as well get your money's worth, right?"

Blinking back tears, she could only stare at him. "If this is because of what I said back there, what was I supposed to say? *Hey, this is the guy I've been boinking for the last few days while everyone was worried about me?* Why are you being like this?"

Taking her elbow, he pulled her into an alcove by the front door.

"I'm just being myself, Blondie. It's who I am. I'll take your loan, but only because I need it, and there is no other option. But don't expect me to play your lapdog."

"You don't sound very grateful. I am bailing your sorry behind out, and instead you give me grief?"

"Sorry." He didn't sound it, but she let it go.

He glanced around the lobby and then lowered his voice. "The courthouse opens at eight in the morning. I'll be here by seven-thirty so we can be there when it opens and get the taxes taken care of before auction time. Be ready."

"I'll be ready and waiting in the restaurant. If you can make it by seven, I'll even buy you breakfast." There. If he wanted a free meal, he could put up with her company. Take it or leave it.

He grinned and her heart fluttered.

"I'm not easy, but I can be bought. Deal." His warm lips brushed her cheek as he passed her, heading for the door.

She resisted the urge to touch her cheek like some lovestruck idiot, but she couldn't turn and walk away before he was out of sight.

At the front door, he turned on his heel and strode back.

"I swore I wasn't going to do this." He ran a hand through his tangled hair, the light catching on the sun-bleached strands. "I know you probably want to catch up with your friends and all, but . . . if you want, you can come back and spend the night with me on the boat." He bent his knees and looked into her tear-filled eyes and smiled. "If, that is, you can refrain from puking in my bed. Or worse, on me."

She slipped her hand into his. "I'll try."

After a step, she stopped. "I should at least tell Paige and Bailey where I'm going. I mean, they came all the way to Sand Dollar because they were worried."

Instead of speaking, he pulled her into his arms and covered her mouth with a kiss she'd probably remember the rest of her life.

He broke the kiss, resting his forehead against hers. "Call them from the boat. I want one more night with you."

One more night. Only one. The thought brought a lump to her throat.

With a curt nod, she allowed him to lead her out.

"Bailey!" Paige transferred the ice bucket and wineglasses to the hand already holding a bottle of champagne and banged on the door with the hand holding the other bottle.

Bailey threw open the door. She was obviously not expecting visitors, since she already had on her pink pajamas with the fluffy white clouds printed all over them. Her hair was scraped back into a gelatinous mess, and a shiny green facial mask covered her whole face except her eyes.

"Hey," Paige said, hurrying into the room and setting down her burden, "you didn't say anything about a girls' night!"

"I assumed you had other plans. Why aren't you with Brett?" Her hands went to fists on her hips. "Paige, I'm not a charity case. I'm fine. Really. Go. Have fun."

Paige smiled. "I am. I have snack trays too. I just need to run back to my room and get them. I may be a few seconds, though, because I want to put my jammies on too."

"What about Brett?" Bailey called after her friend.

"I left him a voice mail," Paige called back. "He won't mind."

Maybe I will. She trudged into the adjoining bathroom and twisted the shower control. May as well hurry and wash out the conditioner before girls' night officially began.

She wondered if Reese would join them, but she decided with a hottie like Ben, it was unlikely they would hear from their friend before morning. If even then.

Just as she'd finished applying deep moisture cream to her face, Paige came back into the room.

"How'd you get in?" she asked, taking one of the two trays of food from her friend.

"Don't panic. I talked Rita into loaning me one of her passkeys. Remind me to return it before we leave, okay?"

"Paige. Stop. Listen to me, will you?"

Paige paused in the act of opening the first bottle.

"I'm fine. Really. What happened was just . . . unfortunate. I made a mistake, and before I realized it, well, it got out of hand. So stop babying me. Please. And if you want to spend tonight with Brett, that's fine with me." She winked and picked up some cheese. "But you have to leave the food here."

"Not a chance! I'm starving. And I am not checking up on you. Well, not totally." She poured the bubbly and handed Bailey a glass. "I really do want to relax and celebrate Reese's safe return. With you. I'm so busy at work these days, Thursday margarita nights are the only time I can even begin to relax. And only then if I'm not on call." At Bailey's raised eyebrow, she shrugged, the spaghetti strap of her purple pajamas sliding off one shoulder. "Okay, I might still be a little concerned about you. So sue me. I'm your friend, it's what friends do."

Bailey lifted her glass, mentally shutting down her pity party. "To friendship."

"I'll drink to that," Paige said, clinking glasses.

Bailey snorted. "You'll drink to anything."

Paige laughed. "True. Now, let's put a serious dent in the food! I'm starving! That new chef was pretty skimpy with the portions tonight."

Halfway through the second bottle of champagne, they were watching TV and giggling at a romantic comedy, when a loud knock rattled the door.

"Expecting anyone?" Paige eased from the bed and picked up the empty bottle.

Bailey shook her head. "Put that bottle down," she whispered. "You're liable to hurt someone if you hit them with it."

"I'm a doctor," Paige whispered back, edging toward the door. "If I hurt someone who didn't deserve it, I can fix them."

"Either you two aren't whispering very quietly or the door is too thin," Brett's muffled voice said. "I can hear everything you're saying. And, for the record, if you brain me with a bottle, Paige, I will not be amused."

Laughing at her friend's stunned look, Bailey opened the door. "Hi, Brett! Come on in!"

"Thanks." He walked right to Paige and handed her shoes and robe to her. "Put these on."

"How did you get into my room?" Paige's voice was a little slurred and very un-Paige-like.

Bailey noticed her friend did as she was told.

"You left the door open. I would have been concerned, but I could hear you two laughing all the way down the hall."

Paige gave a faint nod, then looked confused. "Why—why am I putting on my shoes and robe?"

"Because you're coming with me."

She snickered. "Usually several times, thank you very much." Slapping her leg, she dissolved into laughter.

"Are you s-sure you want to take her anywhere?" Funny, Bailey felt clear-headed, but was surprised to hear her speech was slurred as well.

"Oh, yeah. I don't have a choice." He leaned close and whispered, "I have some stuff I need to tell her before she leaves."

"Hey!" Paige walked unsteadily toward them. "What are you two wh-whispering about? I—oh! Put me down!"

In response, Brett patted her backside, where it rested on his shoulder. "Soon, party girl, soon."

"But I love you," she blurted out from her upside-down position.

"That's what I'm counting on."

45

Reese raised her head from Ben's slick chest and smiled down at him. "You certainly have a way with curing motion sickness."

He ran his hands up and down her sides, then patted her bare hip. "I aim to please, ma'am."

The boat undulated with the movement of the gulf. Ordinarily, the action would have made her violently ill. Instead, the slight movement rocked her hips against Ben's, creating a delicious friction that was already turning her on. Again.

"You should market it," she managed to say in a breathy voice. "You'd make a fortune."

His hands cupped her breasts, his thumbs idly rubbing the tips of her nipples. "My cure only works for you."

"Good," she said in a growl, grinding harder against him. She bent and nibbled his earlobe. "I think I feel another bout coming on. Let's do it again." Stretching, she almost lost their intimate connection in her effort to pull his mouth to her breast.

He sucked a few times, then released her, his hands bracketing her hips.

Gazes locked, he moved his hips, burying himself deep in her welcoming body.

"This has to be the last time, Blondie," he said through clenched teeth, increasing the pace of his thrusts. "We need to get some sleep."

"Maybe I don't want to sleep!" She panted the words, riding him hard.

Neatly flipping her on the hard mattress of his bunk, he continued pounding into her. "Maybe I do."

Raising her hips, she smiled and ground into him. "I could probably change your mind."

The only answer he made was guttural grunts and groans as the sound of their labored breathing echoed in the little cabin.

Reese found she could stave off nausea if she wedged against Ben's naked back.

Sleep eluded her as she lay in the dark, listening to his even breathing.

She'd told the truth—she didn't care if she slept tonight. In all probability, it was their last night together.

Heart heavy, she held him tighter and fought back the tears.

Desperate. That's what she was and there wasn't a dang thing she could do about it.

What had she expected Ben to do when she'd offered the money? Did she think he'd fall on his knees and profess his undying gratitude and love and beg her to stay?

Maybe.

She didn't really care about the gratitude, but the love part would be a welcome change.

Instead, though this relationship, if you could call it a *relationship,* had lasted longer than any she'd had recently, it was going to end too. And it was ending soon.

And there was nothing she could do about it.

So she'd listen to the night sounds of the ocean and hold him. Inhale his unique scent. Memorize his body and remember the sound of his breathing for the rest of her life.

Ben held himself still and did his damn best to keep his breathing even while Reese's hot little body branded his back for life.

Would she stay if he asked? Would she stay if he begged? *Probably not.*

He had nothing to offer.

Not even love.

Tonight, while they'd made love, it had been on the tip of his tongue to tell her he loved her. But he'd never told a woman that, and wasn't sure the words would come this time.

Wasn't 100 percent sure it was true, so what was the point?

But he did know one thing. He'd never spend the night in bed with another woman. And he'd never take another woman into his bed on the boat. Or at the hotel.

He just couldn't.

46

Reese shoved a pile of scrambled eggs around on her plate. Ben didn't seem to have much more of an appetite.

He set down his mug. "Ready? The courthouse will be open by the time we get there." Digging in his pocket, he threw some money on the table and stood, offering her his hand.

Of course, she was perfectly capable of getting up on her own. But she gladly gripped his hand and stood, pleased he didn't let go as they walked toward the exit.

The morning sun shone on the white columns of the courthouse, making it glow.

Paying the back taxes took less than five minutes. It may have been due to the early hour, but within another thirty minutes, Reese's name was on the deed to Serenity Island, right next to Ben's.

They may never be life partners, but at least they were business partners. For now, anyway.

Mrs. Hamilton, the court registrar, beamed at them. "Congratulations, Benjamin. Your grandmother would have been so proud."

"Thanks, Mrs. Hamilton, but I don't see what there is to be proud of. I should have paid those taxes years ago. I'm just glad I could do it before the auction took place." He leaned forward on the desk separating them. "It's canceled, right?"

"Absolutely. I've already typed up the cancelation and entered it." Now she leaned closer. "By the way, I meant your grandmother would be proud you've found a nice young lady and settled down."

"What? Oh, I, I—mean, we, we're not, that is to say we're—"

"Business partners," Reese supplied with a smile.

"Why didn't I receive my wake-up call?" Dorinda barreled into the lobby, sliding to a halt at the front desk. "And there was no bill under my door! I left word I'd be checking out this morning."

Rick smiled and slid the sheet of paper across the desk to her. "My apologies about the wake-up call, ma'am. Most people don't request them anymore. It must have been an oversight."

"No, it wasn't," Rita said, coming up behind her husband. "Your gentleman friend said you didn't want to be disturbed this morning, so he canceled it."

"What!" Dorinda's screech brought lobby conversations to a halt. "When did he tell you that?"

"When he checked out and paid your bill last night."

"He what?"

"Checked out and paid your bill." Rita tapped the paper with her index finger. "Here's your receipt. Thanks for staying with us."

Taking a deep breath, Dorinda stuffed the sheet of paper in her briefcase. "I need a cab."

"None available right now, ma'am. I can call one for you, but it might take nigh unto an hour. Jimmy Dean Trumball is the only cabdriver working today, and it's milking time. He'll be available after, though, if you can wait."

"No, I can't wait! I have to be at the courthouse in less than an hour!"

"Rick would be happy to take you, wouldn't you, sweetie?"

Rick glared at his wife but nodded. "Let me get my keys."

Rita answered the phone as they walked to the door. "Wait! There's a call for you."

Dorinda would like nothing better than to ignore the annoying innkeeper, but she trudged back and grabbed the phone.

"What?"

"This is Justin Keys, your pilot."

She frowned. Why would the pilot be calling? "Where are you?"

"Still fueled and waiting on the tarmac for your instruction, ma'am."

A sly smile curved her lips. "Oh, really? And what about Mr. Conrad? Have you spoken to him?"

After a pause, the pilot answered her in a low voice. "Yes, ma'am, extensively. I told him I had express orders, and those orders only come from you. It's just that, well, he's getting a little . . . perturbed. So, I said I'd call. Do I have your permission to take off, or should I wait for further instructions from you?"

It was all she could do to keep from laughing. It was really too delicious. She could only imagine how pissed off Halston was about now.

"I'm so sorry. . . . Justin, wasn't it?"

"That's right."

"I'm sorry I neglected to inform you of my change of plans, Justin." She waited while Rick opened the door to an old truck for her.

"Change?"

"Yes, keep the engine running. I'll be there within the hour, if all goes well. Regardless, I do have a request. I need you to do something for me."

"Sure thing."

"Kick Mr. Conrad off the plane." *He can slither his way back to Houston, after all.*

47

"When are you planning to leave?" Ben rubbed the back of Reese's hand as it rested on the table in the restaurant.

"I'm not sure. I thought I'd see when Paige and Bailey were leaving and see if I can get a seat on the same flight. Probably today sometime. Or maybe tomorrow."

A commotion preceded Dorinda's entrance. She tromped over to their table, nostrils flared. "What the hell is going on?"

"Dorinda! I thought you left." Reese clutched Ben's hand, warning him to stay and be quiet. She prayed he could read her silent plea.

"I just bet you did, you two-timing bitch!"

"Now, just a minute—" The warning was clear in Ben's voice.

Reese tugged on his hand. So much for having any sort of mental connection.

Dorinda wheeled on him. "And you! You must be her partner in crime. Ben Adams, I presume?" She switched her narrowed gaze back to Reese. "I have to hand it to you, when you spread your legs, you do it in style." She leaned down until she almost touched noses with Reese. "Tell me, how many times did you have to fuck him to get your name on the deed? I hope he was worth it, because *you're fired!*"

They sat in silence after she flounced out.

"Reese," Ben said, grasping her hands, "I'm sorry."

"It's not your fault. I'm a grown woman. I make my own decisions." She forced a laugh. "It's not like I wasn't planning to quit, anyway."

O.M.G.! I've been fired! I lost my job! Now what am I going to do? Don't panic, don't panic. You have some money in savings. She took a deep breath, willing the panic away. *Crap! Not enough!*

If she was lucky, she could make her rent for two more months. Maybe three—if she cut back, didn't go out, and ate a diet of Ramen noodles. Maybe.

She felt light-headed. Where was a paper bag when you needed one?

"Reese?" Ben's voice came from far away. "Are you okay? You're not going to pass out or throw up or anything, are you?"

Another deep breath.

"No. No, I'm okay." Her smile felt brittle. "I was just, um, thinking."

"So, I was wondering . . . are you still planning to go home right away?"

Give me a reason to stay. About now, any reason would do. No reasonable offers refused.

"Um, probably. Why wouldn't I?"

"No reason, I guess." Standing, he threw some money on the table and bent to brush a kiss on her cheek. "I'm going to miss you, Blondie. Bye, partner."

She was still sitting where Ben left her, when Bailey entered the restaurant.

"Morning!" Bailey slid into the chair Ben had vacated. "Did you eat already?" Squinting, she read the menu.

"Bailey, aren't you wearing your contacts?"

"Hmm? Oh, no, I lost one. And I left my glasses in my room. It's okay. I can see to read the menu." She held it close to her face. "Sort of."

"The special today is cinnamon French toast, with a side of bacon or sausage."

Bailey sighed and set the menu aside with a smile. "Thanks, I'll get that."

Rita came by with coffee and took the order.

"Paige still sleeping?" Reese poured creamer into the extremely strong coffee.

Bailey shrugged and smiled. "I have no idea."

"Uh-oh. Did she pick someone up last night?" She loved her friend, but she wished she would stop playing the field with such enthusiasm.

Bailey giggled and took a sip of coffee. "I'd say it was the other way around."

"Okay, tell me, I can see you're dying to, anyway. Spill it."

After Bailey finished filling her in, Reese leaned back in her chair and gave a low whistle. "Wow. That's got to be a record for Paige. This guy, Brett, has been the only person she's slept with the entire time y'all have been here?" Bailey nodded, her ponytail swinging. "That's amazing."

"You want amazing, you should have seen them last night. Paige and I were hanging out in my room when he came to get her."

"Uh-oh. Guys don't do that with Paige. Or if they do, they're history."

"That's what I always thought. But not only did he come to my room," she said in an urgent whisper, "he told her to put on her shoes, and she did! Then he picked her up and left, and I haven't seen or heard from her since."

"Do you think there's a problem? Should we go find her?" Maybe Ben would go with them.

Bailey shook her head. "Thanks," she said when the waitress set her plate in front of her. "I'll tell you the truth, Reese. I don't think Paige would appreciate seeing us." She took a bite of bacon and chewed thoughtfully. "She told him she loved him."

"What! Are you sure?"

Bailey nodded. "I heard it with my own ears."

"Wow," Reese said again, taking another sip of coffee. "I don't think I've ever heard Paige say the *L* word. Not to a guy, anyway."

After breakfast, Reese walked back to Bailey's room with her. "Have you made reservations? I thought I'd see if I can get on the same flight."

"Really?"

"Sure. Why do you look so surprised? There's no reason for me to stay. I foiled Dorinda's evil plot." Rocking back on her heels, she smiled and cracked her knuckles. "My work here is done."

"But you said she fired you." Bailey dragged her suitcase out of the closet and plopped it on the bed.

"All the more reason to go home. I need to look for a job!"

"True." Bailey tossed a plastic bag of cosmetics into her suitcase and reached for the clothes hanging in the closet. "I guess, if it were me, and I had someone like Ben drooling over me—"

"Yeah, well, first of all, Ben is not drooling over me. We had—well, we had some fun while we were stranded on the island. But that's over."

"Is it? I saw your face when he left the restaurant. You didn't look like it was over. Neither did he, for that matter." She tucked a pair of walking shoes into the end pocket of the suitcase. "And you did loan him money from your 401(k) to pay the taxes. That doesn't sound like a casual-interlude-type thing to me."

"For goodness' sake, Bay, it was just sex! Okay, it was hot sex, the best I've ever had. But that's all it was. For either of us." *Unfortunately.*

"If you say so."

"Whatever we had, it's done. What choice do I have but to move on?"

"You could stay, silly."

48

"Permission to come aboard!" Rick's jovial voice broke into Ben's dark thoughts.

He raised his head from the warmth of the deck and stared at his smiling friend. "Only if you brought beer."

Rick held up a twenty-four–pack and Ben nodded, slowly rolling to a sitting position.

Rick sat beside him, not speaking until they'd drunk half of their first beer. "How long you planning to hole up and drink yourself into a stupor?" At Ben's sharp glance, he held up his hands. "Rita just wanted me to ask."

They finished their beers and opened another round.

"She's still here, you know."

Ben chugged the rest of his beer and reached for another bottle. "Who?"

"Who? Don't bullshit me. You know good and damn well who. Reese, that's who."

Ben let loose a loud burp. "Last I heard, it was a free country. She can go or stay anywhere she wants."

"True. But, seems to me, as long as she's here in Sand Dollar, we don't see your sorry ass. Why do you think that is?"

"Dumb luck?"

Rick tossed his empty into the plastic barrel by the steps. "Shit, man, and here we thought you'd changed."

"Why? Just because I finally paid the taxes on the island?"

Rick sat for a minute, picking at the label on his bottle, then shrugged. "I dunno. You just seemed, well, different, since you hooked up with Reese."

"Was I such a piece of shit before?"

Rick got to his feet. "I didn't come down here to argue or take abuse. I told Rita this was a piss-poor idea."

Ben sat and finished his beer while he watched Rick stomp away.

At least, he'd left the beer.

"Don't mind if I do." Ben opened another bottle and took a long swig. "Ah. The breakfast of champions."

Without anyone to gripe, his statement wasn't nearly as much fun.

Though he'd never admit it, Rick had a point. Since Reese, Ben hadn't been around much.

"And," he said, crawling to the door and pulling up to stand, "if I don't want to land right smack-dab in the same place I was, I need to get my carcass in gear and get to the renovations so I can at least keep the taxes current."

Could he go back to Serenity House and be around all the places he and Reese had been, all the places where they'd made love?

Where he had his miserable heart broken.

Work. He had work to do, and work would help keep his mind off Reese and the *L* word.

"Okay, now it's my turn to worry," Reese said, sliding into the chair across from Bailey. "Have you heard from Paige yet?"

Bailey put down her menu. "I had a text this morning. She didn't say much, just that she was still at Brett's place and would talk to us soon."

"Good morning, ladies," Rita chirped as she walked to their table with a carafe of coffee in each hand. "Regular or unleaded?"

"Thanks," Bailey said after Rita poured.

"No problem." Rita shrugged and looked away, then back at Bailey. "I want you to know I had no idea what that stinker Travis pulled. When I found out, well, to say I didn't approve was putting it mildly."

She walked away to refill another cup of coffee.

"Travis? Who's Travis?" Reese stirred a generous amount of cream into her coffee. "What's going on?"

"Please. Not before we eat."

"That bad, huh?" Reese nodded to the waitress, who set her plate on the table.

"You have no idea."

Reese choked on her last bite of muffin as she listened in wide-eyed shock to Bailey's story.

"Didn't you even report him?" A sip of coffee helped dislodge the muffin.

"No. Paige wanted to, but they took her phone. By the time we got back to the hotel, I'd had time to think and I told her not to make the call." She dabbed at her eye with her napkin. "I was so embarrassed! I just wanted to put it all behind me and move on."

"But, Bailey, it was not consensual. That creep needs to be prosecuted!"

Bailey shook her head. "Reese, I seriously doubt that would have happened. I'm the outsider. And I didn't fight them. Heck, I enjoyed it . . . until I realized what was really happening. Bottom line is, I doubt Travis would be found guilty of anything more than misrepresentation. Meanwhile, I'd be dragged through the mud. Thanks, but no thanks."

"You say he's Rita's brother?"

Bailey nodded. "Yeah. I don't know how she heard about what happened, but as you saw, she was definitely not on his side. I don't know if she said anything to him, but he hasn't been around the hotel since that day."

"I'm so sorry I wasn't around for you."

Bailey chuckled. "Believe me, Paige more than made up for it."

A server refilled their coffee.

"So, what are you going to do, now that you're unemployed?"

"I know I need to find another job." Reese sighed. "But, right now, my heart just isn't in it."

"Will you be okay to hold off for a while, financially?"

"I don't know. I have some money saved." She chewed on her lip. "I just wish things had turned out differently, you know?"

"You mean you wish Dragon Lady hadn't fired you, and you had bid on the island for her, after all?"

"Lord, no! Not that different. No, I'd planned to quit, anyway, so getting fired wasn't really horrible." She sighed and looked out at the sunshine sparkling on the water.

Rita reappeared and dragged a chair up to the table. She sat and let loose a relieved-sounding sigh. "I need a break! My feet are killing me. I need to save my strength for tonight."

"What's going on tonight?" Reese took a last swallow of tepid coffee.

"A dance, right here. Didn't Ben tell you?"

"I haven't talked to Ben since the first day we were back."

Rita made a disgusted sound and shook her head. "Ben Adams is an even bigger fool than I thought." She sighed and met Reese's curious gaze. "Sand Dollar has been having fund-raisers, to help Ben. Car washes, bake sales, raffles. And dances. All proceeds go to his tax fund."

"But he paid the back taxes."

"Yeah, and we all know how. Well, Rick and I do, anyway." Rita shot her a meaningful look. "The dance was already planned, and everyone loves them. So, even though it's not a fund-raiser, we're continuing. You have to go."

"Oh, I don't—"

"Go, Reese," Bailey chimed in. "It'll be fun."

"Only if you go with me."

"Oh. I don't think—"

"Travis isn't invited," Rita said flatly. "And if he shows up, he will be turned away."

Bailey smiled. "In that case, I'd love to go."

49

"Here." Rita tossed a shirt on Ben's bed. "Wear that."

"I already told Rick I'm not going." He reached for another beer.

Rita slapped his hand away. "You absolutely are going! We're doing this for you, you ungrateful beach bum."

"Don't hold back, tell me what you really think," he grumbled.

"Believe me, you don't want to know my thoughts right now." She sat on the edge of the bed and patted his foot. "Ben, we all love you, you know that. But you have to get out of the self-destructive mode you've been in for the last few years. You've been given a second chance with Serenity Island, and what have you done? Nothing."

"I paid the damn taxes. Let me ease into this turning-over-a-new-leaf thing, will you?"

"No. You're out of time and we're running out of patience. Everyone has bent over backward for all the fund-raisers. The least you could do is show up."

"Fine. Now get out of here so I can get ready."

Standing, she smoothed her skirt. "Good. Rick will be back for you in an hour."

"Rita, I can see the damn hotel from my deck. It's not likely I'd get lost."

"With you, we're not taking any chances. Rick told me he's going to help you haul the supplies for the renovations tomorrow. You owe us. Be ready when he gets here."

"Do you see Paige?" Bailey scanned the crowded lobby full of people gyrating to the music. "She texted she'd be here."

Reese sipped her margarita and tried not to be obvious in her search for Ben. "If she said she's coming, she'll be here." She nudged her friend with her elbow. "Cute guy at two o'clock."

"Not interested."

"How do you know? You didn't even look!"

"Reese, I'm just not . . . ready, for lack of a better word."

She grabbed Bailey's elbow. "You said, you *swore* to me, you were okay."

"And I am! Really. I guess I just don't feel like I can trust my judgment right now, where men are concerned."

"I know the feeling." She watched Ben enter, all the other men in the room fading from view. The indirect lighting glowed from the streaks in his freshly combed, damp hair.

Next to him was a striking blond woman. They weren't touching, but they obviously knew each other.

Ben bent his head, then laughed at something the woman said. As he straightened, his gaze honed in on Reese.

He turned back to the woman, who laughed and rose on tiptoe to kiss his cheek.

Nausea gripped the pit of Reese's stomach.

She hadn't seen Ben in days. They had no claim, no commitment to each other. Why did she feel like crying?

"Look!" Oblivious, Bailey grabbed her arm. "There's Paige."

Reese followed her line of vision, watching as Paige spotted them and made her way through the crowd, a tall, *GQ*-type guy following her.

"Is that him?" she whispered to Bailey.

"Yeah, that's Brett. He's amazing. He runs a dairy farm outside of town. I don't think I've ever seen Paige happier."

Reese watched them approach. Leave it to Paige to find the diamond among a pile of coal.

And speaking of diamonds . . .

The light reflecting from the rock on her friend's left hand was enough to cause blindness.

"I'm engaged!" Paige shrieked above the music.

And I'm out of here.

Of course, she was happy for her friend, and plastered a smile on her face while she told her so.

After being introduced to Brett, who seemed genuinely smitten with Paige, Reese made her excuses and pushed through the crowd.

The silence in her room was overwhelming.

Collapsing in a chair, she held a tissue to her leaking eyes.

"Stop," she whispered, wiping her nose. "Crying is so nonproductive." Tears again blurred her vision.

She ignored the soft knock on her door. She didn't want to see anyone, didn't want to talk to anyone. Not now. Not yet.

"Reese?" Ben's voice was low. He knocked again.

She sat in the darkness until she was sure he'd gone.

"Probably went back to his bimbo date," she grumbled, dragging her suitcase to the bed.

It was past time to go home.

50

"I still don't understand what you're doing," Bailey said as she cut another piece of packing tape to seal a box.

"I told you, I have to get some of this stuff ready to go so I can move as soon as my notice runs out." Reese grunted and hefted the box to the top of the pile by her door.

"But you haven't found another place yet, have you?"

"You know I haven't."

"You could go back to Serenity Island, you know. You technically are a part owner." Bailey wiped her forehead with the edge of her T-shirt. "Let's take a break. Is your air on?"

"Yeah, but I have it set high to save money. Here, have a Coke."

Bailey cracked open the sweating bottle and took a long swallow. "It's July in the Deep South. You have to have air. It's uncivilized." She took another drink. "I wonder how Paige is adapting to country life. I bet it's cooler in Sand Dollar."

"So I've heard. I still can't believe Paige quit the hospital."

"Love makes you do uncharacteristic things, I guess."

"Tell me about it. I'm still trying to wrap my mind around

Paige being with only one man for the rest of her life. Is she still planning to open a clinic in Sand Dollar?"

"From what I understand, it was Brett's idea. I'm sure Paige could find a position for you in the new clinic, if you would consider moving to Sand Dollar."

"She already offered."

Bailey paused in taping another box. "She did? Then what are you waiting for? Think about it, Reese. You wouldn't be lonely—you'd already have a friend. You'd have a job. The cost of living is lower, so you'd probably be better off. Plus," she finished brightly, "you would be able to keep an eye on your investment."

"It isn't like it's a real investment. I just loaned Ben money to prevent the island from selling at auction. He's going to pay me back." She shrugged. "Besides, I don't want him to get the wrong idea. What if he thinks I'm chasing him?"

"Who knows? You'll never know if you don't go. Maybe he'll let you catch him."

Tears sprang to Reese's eyes—as they had been doing at an alarming rate since her return to Houston. "I don't think that's what he wants, Bay." She sniffled.

"Have you heard from him?"

Reese shook her head. "No. Don't you think that should tell me something?" She swiped at her eyes with the back of her hand. "It's obvious he got what he wanted from me, financially and sexually. If I show up, I'll just look pathetic. Worse, what if he thinks I'm trying to take over the hotel? It's his island, his hotel, his inheritance."

"Who says it has to be one way or the other?" Bailey sat down next to her, giving her a quick hug. "Paige could really use your help. Plus, we both know she's useless when it comes to planning a wedding."

"True," Reese agreed with a laugh.

*　*　*

"Ben!" Rick tapped on his shoulder.

Ben turned off the sander and removed his ear protection.

"I'm going to take off before the weather gets any worse." Rick pointed to the darkening sky. "Weather bureau is saying we could get another tropical storm. Is your boat secured?"

"Yeah. But I may still move it to the other side, if it looks like the storm is getting worse. Thanks for all your help."

"No problem. Oh, Rita told me to remind you she's expecting you for dinner."

"Not tonight. I don't want to get caught out in the storm, if it develops. I still have most of the supplies she brought out last week. I can fix a sandwich or something. I'd like to get the lobby floor done so I can get the sander returned tomorrow."

Rick nodded. "Understandable. I'll tell Rita. But I gotta tell you, she's worried about you. We all are. Don't be a stranger, you hear? See you."

Instead of turning the sander back on after Rick left, Ben walked to the window. The sky was already dark as midnight. Judging by the movement of the trees, he could tell the wind was kicking up.

For about the millionth time, he remembered another tropical storm.

His mouth quirked as he recalled Reese's butt as she hung over the side of his boat. And the look on her face as she bobbed around after falling overboard.

He looked around the lobby, now bare of furniture. In his mind, he saw the makeshift bed in front of the fire, Reese lying naked in his arms, smiling up at him.

Everywhere that he looked reminded him of her and what he'd lost.

It was nuts to be missing her so much when they'd spent such a brief amount of time together. And a lot of that was spent arguing. And loving.

He scrubbed his face with his hand. It was just fatigue and

hunger making him take a stroll down memory lane. Maybe he'd eat, then finish the sanding and call it a night.

He knew he was lying to himself. Nights were the worst. Even when he tried sleeping in one of the beds he hadn't shared with Reese, he didn't get much sleep.

The only solution he'd found was to work until he dropped from exhaustion. And, even then, sometimes sleep eluded him.

"Eek!" Paige ran across the lobby of the Sand Dollar Inn to hug Reese. "I can't believe you're finally here!"

"Me either."

Paige's smile dimmed. "Rough trip?"

"Actually, no." At her friend's disbelieving look, she continued. "I sipped on a Coke and chewed gum. The worst part was the ride out here from the airport."

"I heard that," Rick said with a smile as he entered the lobby with Reese's suitcases. "I'll just take your stuff on up to your room."

"You're not staying with us?" Paige gripped her hand. "We have plenty of room. Wait until you see Brett's house! I swear, it's like the plantation house from *Gone With the Wind*. Only nicer and with modern conveniences, of course."

"Of course." Reese gave her another hug. "I've missed you! Margarita nights just haven't been the same."

"Really? Mine have improved. Now they're naked margarita nights!" Her smile faltered. "Seriously, I'm kind of surprised you're still doing margarita nights. I know Bailey isn't a big drinker, and you're, um, well, kind of strapped for cash."

Reese grinned. "You're right. We make our own. Believe me, Bailey and a blender . . . not always a good combination."

As they laughed, Rita came hustling into the room. "Reese! Thank God you're back!"

"Um, thanks, Rita. I missed you too." She accepted Rita's hug. "But is there a particular reason you're glad to see me?"

Rita glanced around the lobby, then said in a low voice, "Ben."

Cold fear gripped Reese. "What about Ben? Is he okay?"

Rita shook her head. "We've all been so worried . . ." She wrung her hands. "He's been out on the island alone for weeks. And, the last time I saw him, when I went out to Serenity, he looked positively ghastly."

"Is he sick? Hurt?" Panic welled. "I have to go out there."

"There's a storm heading in," Paige told her, pointing to the dark sky on the off chance Reese hadn't noticed. "But if you can be ready soon, Brett can run you out there. He's already at the marina. But you have to hurry. He needs to get back before the storm hits."

"Of course." She turned to Rita. "Which room am I in? I'll just grab my suitcase and—"

"No!" Paige and Rita said in unison.

"Brett's waiting at the marina. I already called and told him you were on your way. Hurry!" Paige shoved her toward the door.

"But my suitcase—"

"Wait!" Rita ran to the check-in desk, then hurried back with a gift bag. "Here. There's a toothbrush and toiletries. That will hold you until we can get your suitcase out to you. Marina's that way." Rita shoved her out onto the porch and closed the door.

"You don't think she'll figure it out and come back, do you?" Rita peeked out the window.

"No, I saw her face when you told her how worried we all were about Ben." Paige gave her a high five. "Besides, I told Brett not to stop until she was on the island."

Reese was too concerned and worried to be sick on the rough ride to the island.

Brett was polite, if tight-lipped, during the trip. It made sense, she supposed, if he was worried about the impending storm.

The engine of his big cabin cruiser roared away by the time Reese had taken two steps on the old dock.

Ben's boat was not at the dock. Had he left or taken it to the protected side of the island?

As she climbed the path, relief flooded her when she saw lights shining from the windows of the old hotel.

Even in the dimness, it was evident the hotel had received a major overhaul. The shutters were all freshly painted and intact. The siding sported a new coat of paint as well. The old porch looked well scrubbed and boasted several new posts.

The sound of some kind of motor echoed from the interior.

Reese paused with her hand on the doorknob. What if Ben was fine? What if he didn't want to see her?

Worse, what if he wasn't alone?

Pictures of the blonde kissing his cheek flashed through her mind.

No point in waiting. If he wasn't alone, and/or didn't want her, she'd know soon enough.

It wasn't like she could leave. At least, not right now. If the worst-case scenario happened, there were plenty of rooms for her to hole up in and wait out the storm.

A definite breeze caught Ben's attention.

Through his dusty goggles and the haze of sawdust, he saw her. Was she really standing there, or was it just wishful thinking?

When he realized she was speaking, he motioned for her to wait while he turned off the sander. He removed his ear protection and goggles.

"What are you doing here?" Great, not exactly a warm welcome. "I mean, I thought you went back to Houston."

"I did. But I decided I'd like to try small-town life. And when

Paige called and offered me a job in her new clinic, I figured what the heck." She walked into the room, looking around. "You've done a lot since I've been gone. The outside looks great, by the way."

"Thanks. It's been a lot of work, but not as hard as I expected."

She drew her finger along the sawdust coating the railing. "Need some help?"

"I probably wouldn't turn it down. But I thought you said you were going to work with Paige."

"She doesn't have the clinic up and running yet, so it could be a while. Plus, I think she's planning to wait to open until after their honeymoon."

"How'd you get out here?" He took a step closer and tried to control his breathing.

"Brett brought me. But he had to take off again right away because of the storm."

He looked at the trees bowing in the wind. "Yeah, it looks like we're in for another one."

"Do you have food? As I recall, we ate most of it last time."

He grinned, feeling the pressure in his chest ease. "Is your stomach empty after the boat ride?"

"Yes, but not because of what you think. I was in such a hurry, I didn't have time to eat lunch."

"Want something? I know how cranky you get when you're hungry."

"Not right now." She stepped closer, lifting her arm to run her hand along his jaw, making him wish he'd shaved. "I missed you," she said in a choked whisper.

"You haven't acted like it. Tell me, Reese, why did you come back?"

"I told you, I decided I needed a change."

"Where are you planning to live?"

"Well, for the time being, I thought I'd stay here." She hurried on. "I mean, I'm part owner, right? I have a right to stay here. And, if the renovations are done before Paige needs me at the clinic, I thought I'd stay on as a sort of resident manager. I can work for room and board until the hotel is up and running. Then, once you start making a profit, my salary can be whatever you can afford toward a no-interest repayment to my 401(k)." She paused. "Ben?"

"I'm just wondering what you plan to do after you're paid back." He stepped closer and began unbuttoning her blouse.

"Um, I haven't thought beyond repaying my 401(k)." Her breath caught when he dipped his finger into the cup of her bra.

"Probably wise," he said, pushing her blouse from her shoulders. "It could take years," he said, trailing tiny kisses along her jaw.

Lips against his, she whispered, "I can wait."